HIS DISCIPLES DECEIVE

BOOK THREE OF THE TERRY REID SERIES

PATRICK D FERRIS

CONTENTS

Also by Patrick D. Ferris: vii
Acknowledgments   ix
Foreword   xi

1. Who's Flying?   1
2. Attu   8
3. Dreamland   12
4. Spike   20
5. Friendly Jail Cell   25
6. Home Sweet Home   29
7. Carwash Rules   36
8. Secret Password   47
9. Sleeping with the Enemy   56
10. Dental Plan   65
11. Guess who's Coming to Dinner   73
12. Dinner Aftermath   81
13. Deadly Preparations   90
14. Hindered Escape   97
15. Sneaking Away   108
16. Freedom at Last   117
17. Debrief   127
18. Sleeping with One Eye Open   134
19. Alive and Scarred   145
20. Troubled Waters   154
21. Mole   163
22. Friendly Dictators   173
23. Trapped in a Submarine   180
24. Good to be the Pretend President   189
25. Acting Presidential   196
26. Chess   206
27. Tete-a-Tete with the CIA   216
28. Lonely Vigil   227

29. Cavalry Has Arrived   235
30. Invitation of No Return   243
31. Media Crush   250

Afterword   255
Also by Patrick D Ferris   257
About the Author   259

Print ISBN 978-1-9990920-1-6

ALSO BY PATRICK D. FERRIS:

Larry and Giselle Series:

A Gypsy Romance

A Gypsy Engagement

A Gypsy Haunting

Terry Reid Mystery Series:

His Disciples Watch

His Disciples Sleep

His Disciples Deceive

Short Story Collection:

Fragmented Thoughts Random Directions

ACKNOWLEDGMENTS

Thank you all for your kind support. The best compliment you can offer a writer is to read their books.

His Disciples Deceive is the next book in the Terry Reid Mystery series. His Disciples Watch is #1 and His Disciples Sleep #2. Yes, there is a fourth one in the works.

Thank you to Ronnie Pelletier, Robert Sapp, and Glenn Palmer, who were a huge help with suggestions and ideas on how to make this wild tale into a readable, interesting story.

Thank you, Natasha Pasincky, for tips on flying a Cessna.

Kristin Bryant designed this cover.

Ronnie Pelletier got the unenviable task of editing this which she did superbly despite an injury.

And thank you "Writers of the Peace", our superb local writer's group. I learn from you every time we meet. You are patient and wise.

Thank you, Patricia, my understanding and adored wife, for being the sounding board for yet another of my wild imaginings. You honour me with your kindness and patience.

Patrick D. Ferris

FOREWORD

Once again, Pat Ferris is up to no good while creating Book Three of the Terry Reid Mystery Series, **His Disciples Deceive**.

How does he do this? How does he lasso the crazy stuff happening around the world, create heroes we fall in love with, baddies we love to hate, and fictionalize it all in such a satisfying, tongue-in-cheek way?

This book does double duty, moving the chess pieces forward in Terry's efforts to save the day, while taking us back to witness how a young and starry-eyed Terry Reid evolved into the woman we all know her to be—irascible, clever, funny, and deadly. I love this book! Terry's experiences in the Montreal underworld are worth the price of admission all by themselves. Add in President Page's coming adventures and you'll be chortling in your chair and raising a cheer.

Sometimes a rogue player is exactly who we need.

When I read a Pat Ferris book, I always feel like there's hope for us all yet.

R.R. Roberts

April, 2019

*"1 Kings 14.9: You have done more evil
than all who lived before you.
You have made for yourself other gods,
idols made of metal;
you have aroused my anger."*

1

WHO'S FLYING?

Violent shaking brought Terry to her senses. Vaguely, she became aware of her head snapping back and forth, shoulders hitting the back of her seat and the wall.

So groggy... So sleepy...

There was a terrible taste in her mouth. Dry.

Prying open her eyes, she dimly registered she'd drooled onto a small window. She forced herself to focus on the window itself—plexiglass—then *through* the plexiglass. Pawing the drool off her mouth she recognized a rattling airplane wing, complete with dents and bullet holes. She broke into a clammy sweat as the plane shook and rattled.

She needed to take stock of her situation...

Her head slammed against the wall, bringing her to her senses once again.

Oh yeah. Window. Tiny, beat-up plane...

Must wake up. She lurched forward, sitting up straight, forcing her eyes to open wide, desperate to focus. She blinked hard to read the little sign on the seat back in front of her. It was written in Pashtun!

In a panic she yanked at her arm and found she was anchored, attached to something foreign. There was a clutch of metal handcuffs clamped to her wrist. Something—*someone*— nearby twitched as she jerked on the cuffs to no avail. They were attached to a green army sleeve which was in turn attached to an unconscious soldier.

Sluggishly she lolled her head to see who the stranger was. Seemed familiar. With her free hand she slapped at her cheeks. Waking up a little, her companion's identity clicked into place. "Trev? Trevor! Wake up! We've been drugged!"

Trevor's head continued to bounce as he mumbled, his eyes fluttering open and closed. "Where... are we?"

Sitting up straighter now, her body alive with alarm, she shook Trevor weakly. "Come on. Snap out of it!"

"What... the..." Trevor struggled to an upright position, his confused gaze landing on her face, then darting around the interior of the plane before squinting out the window. "What's going on? We're in... We're flying? Are those... mountains?" He blinked with shocked recognition at the terrain spread below them. "This can't be! Is this... Af... Afghanistan?

"Yes!" She glanced around the interior of the plane, recognizing it as an old Cessna, cast off from other nation's ambitions, not unlike her own present situation. In horror, she saw the pilot seats featured friendly safety messages in both Pashtun and English on the head rests but *no pilots*. This old Cessna was now a self-flying drone, apparently over remote Afghanistan with no human pilots aboard. *A.I.? Remotely flown from somewhere? No pilot to go down with the 'ship'?*

This venerable and simple Cessna aircraft had probably endured many bad human pilots in its lifetime, the final insult being the crudely added drone controls— hopefully properly done—but unlikely. Wires hung down from under the instrument panel, probably installed by the worst contractor with the best bribes.

The drugs were finally wearing off.

Now she saw the plane was crammed with equipment in the

aisle, the other seats, and the overhead bins all around them. For what?

She spotted a black-eyed remote camera peering down on her from the cockpit area, unblinking. She was unable to give it the finger as her free hand was cuffed. Best not piss off whoever was remotely controlling this plane, anyway.

Terry scanned the countryside laid out before them, straining for any sight of familiar landmarks. Trevor was right. This *was* Afghanistan. She'd spent years in Afghanistan and knew the landscape intimately.

Peering down she saw a smoking projectile race upwards from the ground like a giant tracer, exploding through the end of their raggedy wing. Nothing important was lost, apparently. What was once an elegant rounded wing now featured an alarmingly blackened hole. Could it keep going with a hole in the wing? She'd find out soon enough. Might be dead, too. She regretted not leaving goodbye notes for Dean and Jess. Damn.

"We're gonna die!" screamed Trevor, wild-eyed and wide awake beside her, having heard and felt the wing being hit.

"Seatbelt, buddy! Lean to the seat in front of you!" Trev was never a good flyer. The plane wobbled back and forth as the autopilot fought to keep control. Despite her efforts to remain calm—it never helped freaking out in situations like these—it *was* creepy to see the yoke jerking around, as if possessed by deranged ghosts.

Another projectile was coming their way, this one narrowly missing them. Something good for our side.

She made an exaggerated pointed motion toward a poppy field on the base of a mountain and shouted into the all-seeing camera eye. "Land there! There!!" She repeated it in Pashtun, just in case. Hopefully whoever was watching them in the camera would hear and see her. "Land there!! Right—east! Two-o'clock!"

As if understanding, the unseen drone-pilot wrangled the plane's yoke, the throttle magically moving to slow down the tired engine which was beginning to smoke a little, but, the plane *was* headed where Terry pointed, for good or bad.

Terry breathed a sighing, "Fuck!" in Pashtun, the universal curse for all languages.

The crippled plane's audio speaker began to play a cheerful but garbled automated message, "We are landing. Seatbelts on, seats in the upright positions and thank you for flying Forward Air." This was first announced in Pashtun then repeated it in Russian. After two repeats the recording stuck on the last sentence, announced in Russian, "...spasibo za polet vpered Air." "...spasibo za polet vpered Air." "...spasibo za polet vpered Air."

Terry crouched low in her seat seeking protection for the coming crash landing, dodging the wild swings of Trevor's un-cuffed arm. "'...spasibo za polet vpered Air." The little plane teetered left and right, somewhat lining up with the field of poppies dead ahead. "...spasibo za polet vpered Air." She shoved Trevor's head down behind his seat for his own—and her own—sake. *I'd rather be handcuffed to a living person than dragging around a corpse... or dismembered arm.*

Hopefully they wouldn't end in an explosion of aluminum and body parts.

"...spasibo za polet vpered Air." The plane wobbled in the air on this terrible final approach to the suspicious poppy field. *Will there be land mines?*

Just feet from the field, the plane teetered left, hooking its wing into the soft dirt of the poppy field, spinning into a violent cartwheel. Terry hung on. This was the worst midway ride, ever.

Boxes and freight bounced around her like a load of ping-pong balls while ancient dirt filled the cockpit, in her eyes, her mouth. She hugged the back of the seat for dear life, not easy with the little plane's wild spins.

As if sensing her fears the plane abruptly flipped over on its back and slid into a very old stone building on the edge of the field.

"... spasibo za polet vpered Air," was the last sound she heard.

———

THE RUSSIAN COLONEL watched the computer screen as the little Cessna plane cart wheeled a few times, then flipped over on its back in a cloud of dirt. "слово ебать!"

The Colonel glowered down at the sweating enlisted man operating what looked like a video game controller. After the plane stopped sliding the operator fell back in his chair, raised his hands in mock surrender and peeled off a litany of excuses.

The colonel waited for his excuses to end. "Call the American patrol and tell them where to find their Major—*if* she's still alive."

"American patrol, sir?"

The Colonel scowled. "Yes, *THE* American patrol! We want to greet Major Reid with people she's accustomed to working with. You have your contact, correct?"

"Yes, Sir!"

———

THE ONLY NOISE disturbing the silence after the crash was the sizzling and crackling of the overheated broken plane engine. Terry and Trev were piled in a heap in the plane, covered with boxes and pieces of cargo. They sweated, breathed and bled.

Locals were already arriving at the scene, anticipating stripping all usable weapons and cargo. It could be a prosperous day for them all. The chieftain directed an old woman to leave water for the two injured occupants as a sort of exchange. As she moved the injured female to pour water between her cracked and bleeding lips the old woman heard her mumble, "So sorry... Jess... Dean," over and over in Pashtun. She fed the unconscious woman, then her companion the water, a sacrifice to the dying. They would not last long in this unforgiving desert.

———

It was four hours before the three member American patrol found the damaged plane, frying in the heat. Tom stood guard as Gerald and Ross, their medic, rummaged hurriedly through the wreckage hoping for signs of life.

They'd been sent to meet a plane, not scour a wreck looking for survivors.

They found two heartbeats—miracles were what they were—and pulled them from the crumpled metal out onto the hot sand then onto make shift stretchers. The handcuffs puzzled them but they managed to break the chain connecting the two with big rocks. At great effort the patrol carried and dragged them into the hills, out of sight. The relative coolness of a cave was chosen as a haven for the time being.

They cleaned up both victims as best they could, using precious water to reveal the extent of their injuries. The lieutenant woke up while his face was being swabbed clean. Trevor looked over to see two US men guarding the cave entrance, one watching the nearby area and the other scanning further with binoculars. Must be Special Forces. He nodded at them, then dragged himself over to his companion lying on a nearby stretcher. She wasn't moving and was barely breathing.

"Terry! Terry! Do you hear me!" he called hoarsely.

"Easy Lieutenant. She's still out cold. That was a bad bash on the head," an army medic cautioned, pressing him back onto the cot. "She's out for a while. Here, you need to lay back down, too. That crash beat you up badly. I'm Ross. Let me look at those stitches."

Irritated, Trevor allowed Ross to look him over. "So we're holed up in this cave until Terry comes to and she may be the only one who knows what's going on. This is crazy."

"You're lucky to be alive after that plane crash. It was ready to catch fire."

"Yeah, thanks. That was a close call. You torched it, afterwards?"

"Yes. Hopefully you'll be presumed dead and incinerated, buying some time until Reid wakes up. Hopefully word of survivors won't spread—it's not like the locals have Face Book out here."

Trevor called to the two guards perched at the cave entrance, nearby. "Either of you pick handcuff locks?"

Tom grinned, "Are you kidding? I'm from Detroit. We have to pick a lock just to get born!" He pulled a few small bent tools from his sweat soaked pocket and went to work, attempting to open the cuff. "We were in a hurry so we busted the chain first, cuffs later," he confessed.

After a half an hour Trevor was tired of holding his arm out. "How's it going, there, Sport? Thought you were a pro at this shit?"

"This is old CIA hardware. Tough stuff."

"Sooner would be better," Trev murmured.

2

ATTU

On a bleak rocky Alaskan coastline, the prison guard looked up into the skies from his post on the Attu, the last desolate island in the panhandle, between the North American continent, Japan and Russia.

This was the definition of the middle of nowhere. Temporary buildings were stacked three stories high, surrounded by rusty razor wire. The only inhabitants were guards like himself and two thousand "Disciple" prisoners. It was summer but you wouldn't know it by the constant barrage of snow and squalls hammering the place. After glancing longingly back at the sad compound perched on the moss-covered rock behind him, he clutched his rifle, shivered and turned away. It'll be two more hours before he would wrap his icy hands around a mug of the swill they were passing off as coffee.

Squinting, in the distance he saw one—no two... no *four* black whales appear on the surface in a puff of splashing water. They all sat strangely in formation. Submarines?

Big ones.

Russian?

Who should he call about this? This was definitely *not* in the handbook.

A series of flames appeared out of each submarine, in rapid succession, forty tons of high explosive on twenty missiles headed his way, giving him only seconds to realize his time on this earth was over. Each missile came down as part of a set pattern eradicating everything in its section. Attu was left a lifeless, smoking hunk of black rock.

The island now looked like an extinct volcano.

———

BILL PAGE WATCHED the missiles vaporize Attu from the safety of a small Korean trawler bobbing ten miles away. It had been a well-executed escape. He was comforted to know he still had friends willing to risk their lives for him. Now they were utterly gone.

He knew there were more Disciples where they came from.

Bill Page was used to being pampered and soothed, even in prison. He was rich, with a far-reaching influence over people's souls. Parishioners looked up to him as if he was the son of God, which he never discouraged. He knew he was placed on this earth to make it in his own dominating image. His reign as king was so very close. He had only to reach out to grasp his rightful crown.

Being locked up on the lonely island of Attu was as far away as the current US president could send him other than Mars—a forbidden weathered rock on the Aleutian chain. Even the hardy Japanese army had found it unbearable during their brief stint in WW2, their hasty retreat evidenced by the abandoned gun emplacements and rusted out vehicles that still littered the desolate island.

Attu was the perfect isolated place for political prisoners. Even the most dedicated, hardy reporter wouldn't consider coming here to see where America locked up the secret society that very nearly took over the country, the militant arm of the Revisionists—The Disciples.

Page was cruel, fastidious, overbearing and vain. Even in prison, his clothing was hand washed, ironed and cleaned twice a day by his dedicated valets. He had three showers a day to wash the disgusting prison smell off his body. The thought of lice terrified him; body odour disgusted him. The mere thought of either drove him for yet another shower.

His people ensured Attu officials were sufficiently paid and influenced so Page was housed in a huge, plush room complete with a carpet, computer and the unusual provision of heated rooms. Other, grateful prisoners volunteered and took turns being his personal butler. An honour. He was a prince who would be king, someday. On Attu, Page was Napoleon on Elba but even Napoleon had to escape.

Page surrounded himself with fawning, deferring Disciples, all trying to curry favour. Every Sunday they'd flock to hear him preach a stirring sermon of fire, brimstone and world dominance. He could stir up emotion and anger with a few sentences.

Guards nervously watched the prison population and listened for signs of upheaval or riot from Page's restless fanatics. After a few bloody riots, the head guard had discovered he could bring order immediately by shooting the nearest Disciple and ordering the unfortunate body to be tossed over the guard rail and into the icy water of the bay.

Splash! Bleed, freeze or drown. Shows over, back to your cells!

On Friday, Page's prisoner-butler passed a piece of paper to him as he sat at his computer writing this Sunday's sermon. On it was written, *Sunday eleven a.m. Be ready. Go about your business.*

The message puzzled Page. He normally gave his sermon at ten a.m. and wrapped it up about eleven fifteen. Eleven o'clock seemed like an odd time for... escape?

Go about your business? Was this a hoax? He decided to take a wait and see attitude.

He looked forward to Sundays. And this Sunday began like any other, with the revered Doctor of Divinity, William R. Page, dressed in his holy robes, regally stepping up to his usual crude prison pulpit which oversaw all the cells and other prisoners.

The assembled Disciples all removed their prison caps and fell to their knees. At ten a.m. he began to speak. "God told me to make Revisionism great... the time has come... fear not Disciples... yadda yadda..." It all ended at eleven fifteen, with silence descending upon the prison at the last of Page's sermon. The guards watched carefully, fingers twitching on triggers, expecting trouble.

Page watched the reaction of the guards as he heard screaming starting at the cell block furthest away from where he stood. Projectiles were thrown by prisoners and guards discharged the usual warning shots harmlessly into the air.

This is what they had been waiting for—the predictable post sermon unrest.

The head guard stood near Page. Already weary of the post-sermon riot routine, he pointed his rifle at the nearest prisoner and shot him in the head.

Bang!

The prisoner dropped dead, almost bleeding on Page's feet.

To Page's surprise, the guard stepped into him and bashed him in the face with his rifle butt. Down, stunned, Page was barely aware of four guards picking him up, racing him to the rail and throwing him down into the deep icy bay and certain death.

It would have been a quick end for Page if a small rowboat had not been there waiting.

Four Korean men reached over and hauled the gasping, floundering Bill Page into their boat. Its motor started and they roared out of the bay as if they were being chased by the devil himself, headed for a rusty fish boat on the horizon.

3

DREAMLAND

TERRY WAS OBLIVIOUS TO THE REAL WORLD, FLOATING IN A dream-like state. She opened her eyes, looked out onto a familiar, wet, Vancouver alley. She saw her deceased sister, Gloria, lying in the rain, long dead.

History.

Ah...I'm dreaming.

An apparition of Gloria rose up from her chalky body, transparent, a wisp of former humanity, dripping wet. It regarded Terry, wondering, almost smiling. Too familiar.

"Uh... Gloria. Am I seeing you because I'm dead?"

The ghost of Gloria replied, "I don't think so. You were knocked out in the plane crash. Decent concussion, though. It'll be a while before you wake up."

"Can you let Jess know I'm alright?"

"Not yet. She doesn't know you're here. Big secret. Let's not tell her you're okay until we know for sure. You had a serious knock on the head."

"Sounds ominous."

"Rest your mind Terry. Let it go where it wants, long ago. Do you remember?"

Terry's eyes drifted closed against the rain and alley and the crash. Confusion. Blackness... long forgotten memories. Her mind wandered through time seeking truth. Eventually she settled on a time when she was so much younger, at the start of the life she had chosen. When she was tough, but still young and naive.

———

SHE DREAMED she was in Army training, years ago, back in 2019. Camo life, living in camps, marching, shooting at things, following orders, bayonet charging, giving orders and practice kills. An invincible twenty-two years old.

Parachutes were her favourite—jumping out of a perfectly good airplane and landing safely.

That fateful survival course... It started an early morning at the Armed Forces airstrip, a nice day. It was to be three weeks in northern Canada, contact with another living soul strictly forbidden. Hide for three weeks. Live on tree bark and ditch water; don't get eaten by bears and cougars.

Instructors went through her pockets to make sure she had nothing to help with survival. She had a little knife and a few matches hidden in her mouth. *Fuck 'em'* she thought. A few things to make her survival life a little easier to manage. As if reading her thoughts, an instructor stomped on her toes. Terry opened her mouth and yelled. The instructor grabbed her jaw with one hand and roughly dug out the tiny container she had hidden away with the other.

Hopefully she'd washed her hands recently, Terry thought, gritting her teeth.

The instructor smiled. "Heard it in there when you were talking. We've all tried it." She dropped the little package onto a nearby table. "You are now good to go. Here's a 'chicken phone'. Push this green button every three days to signal you aren't dead. Use the red button if a moose tries to bang you or something."

Terry had been superbly trained but was short on real-world action time. Her instructors saw she *could* kill but was hesitant. She needed "battle experience".

Inside the aircraft, Terry suited up with her parachute—she was the only one on this drop from the bright yellow transport plane. It flew her over a remote part of the country, down low. To make her stint more difficult the jump master made sure this cocky soldier was forced to land in the middle of the big, cold lake.

"Go!" he yelled with a smirk.

Surprised at a mid-lake jump, Terry tumbled awkwardly from the rear of the plane, near the minimum dropping distance. Her static line opened her chute immediately, deployed, straps biting hard into her legs and shoulders. No need for the emergency chute.

Parachute open, she attempted to steer from the big lake but there wasn't enough time and distance. Resigned, she hit the cold lake water so hard it knocked the wind out of her, wet parachute covering her like a bug in a giant net. Gasping, stunned, it took her a few moments to get oriented to where *up* was.

Pausing, she made herself relax, allowing her body to float to the surface. Not panicking, she caught her breath by breathing through the wet chute material, then worked on how to get out from under it. Good reflexes and training.

Her instructor's final words had been, "Drag the chute to the shore and leave it. Keeping it for shelter is cheating, plus we're on a tight budget—we'll come for it."

She swam awkwardly, both thanking and cursing her floatation vest. She was drenched, tired and shatteringly cold when she dragged herself and parachute up on the rocky shore. Gasping, she flopped down and rolled onto her back, staring up into the blue sky. Huh. The yellow drop plane was still drifting above her—had been watching her the whole time. Now it flew lower still, waggling its wings cheekily.

She gave it the finger while smiling at the pilot. "Thanks for your concern, assholes!"

Her eyes followed the plane's departure until it became a tiny speck in the ocean of sky and finally vanished.

All alone.

It was a warm day, so she dumped water from her boots, wrung out her socks, camo suit and waited for them all to dry somewhat. Blistered feet this early in the march would not be good. An hour later, footwear and suit somewhat drier, she dressed and started walking, sticking to a deer trail that went around the lake. Looking at the sun, she strode off towards her destination at the base, westerly, about a hundred and twenty miles away.

It was a nice, warm day. The bugs were enjoying an unanticipated feast which she largely ignored. No bug dope. Fuck. Her stomach growled which she ignored as well. Her butt itched terribly after a pee break in the bush. Some nasty plant? That was hard to ignore. One hour of hiking done with five hundred and three hours to go.

Terry noticed smoke over to the left. Looked to be a tame campfire or the like. This area was supposed to be remote, army only—no snoopers allowed. Might be worth a look. She left the trail, moving quietly through the bush to come up behind the source of the smoke.

As she neared, much to her surprise, she spied an older woman in police uniform laying on one of two chaise lounge chairs, mug of something in hand, beside an enticing little camp fire.

Is that coffee I smell? No way!

This is just cruel.

"Terry! Come on over," the older woman called over her shoulder, somehow knowing Terry was behind her in the bushes.

Is that Shirley Mac?

"Don't be shy. Come on over!"

"Shirley?"

"Yes—and I have coffee. I won't tell anyone. I even brought you a chair. We need to talk."

"You're kidding me." Terry shook her head as she emerged from the woods and approached. Soon they were both lounging on the chairs, looking over the serene beauty of the lake. "Smoky campfire, Shirley," Terry chided absently. "I could see it for miles."

Shirley Mac snorted. "I was fishing for snoopers and I found myself one."

"So, what's up, Shirley?" asked Terry warily, sipping the delicious, unexpected coffee. "I heard you were doing special projects for the RCMP?"

"I am, and I'm on a talent search."

Terry looked at her quizzically. "You see some talent around here, do ya?"

"Possibly." The Inspector sat back and seemed to be considering her next words carefully. "How would you feel about skipping this silly survival thing, getting a warm shower and eating a real dinner instead of eating grubs and peeing in stinging nettles?"

"Might be nice. What's the catch?"

"You'll have to be 'dead'."

Terry's eyebrows shot up. She snorted, "Me dead? Is that all?"

"That's it. We have a position for an informant—deep cover. We need a nobody, an unknown such as yourself."

"I'm not sure I like to think of myself as a nobody, thanks."

"Let me reword that...unencumbered; unattached. You don't have a hubby, six kids and a mortgage."

"That's true. I *am* unattached."

"We'll arrange for you to go missing and be presumed dead during this survival course. After some specialized training you'll appear in Montreal as part of the drug trade. You'll need to fit in fast, move up and try not to get exposed, killed or worse. You'll memorize names, dates, times and places. Live in the fast lane. One of the God Father's minions."

"What happened to the last informant...the one I assume I'm replacing?"

"Beth. Ah... a running shoe washed up on the banks of the St.

Lawrence River. We think it has Beth's foot in it. Nothing else washed up."

Terry's eyebrows shot up again, and this time they stayed there.

"We'd rather *not* find your foot. Let's plan on getting all of you back," conceded Shirley Mac.

Grasping the reality, Terry surmised, "I'll have to be at the top of my game, is what you're saying?"

"Don't screw up."

"Are the Army, RCMP and everyone in on this new job position?"

"Only a selected few... need to know basis. Less is best."

Terry thought for a full minute. "Let me see... live like an animal, pee in the bush and eat dirt, or live the high life in the Montreal drug trade but possibly be chopped up into little bits. You sure know how to make a girl an offer she can't refuse."

"You'll do it?"

Terry was hard as nails, her attitude stern and ever watching. Intimidating. She was proud of her image and achievements but knew it meant isolation. A "rock" doesn't attract affection or soul mates. She was perfect informant material. No cracks in her armour just yet. "Why not? All I've been doing is training for three years. Time to cut bait and do something with it."

"Perfect. I brought some clothes for you to change in to. Hand over your army duds and let's arrange for your sudden demise. What death do you feel like? Becoming bear poop?" asked Shirley.

Terry looked around, considering. "Drowning is better. I could have lost my footing in the river that runs from this deep lake. The river's full of log jams. It'll all freeze up in six weeks. They'll be forced to give up the search. We should leave a few bits of clothing for a trail."

"I like it."

"If Terry Reid is dead, who will I become?"

"We'll make someone up. We'll dye your hair, bit of a nose job, maybe boobs. Drug pedlars like 'em busty."

"No boob job and my nose is just fine, thanks. Nothing permanent."

"Okay. Change of eye color? Some tattoos? They'll only stay on for a year then fade. Latest tech."

"Sure, as long as it doesn't hurt."

"Done deal... Tammy Anderson."

"Tammy?"

"Yeah. Your undercover name." Shirley sat up with a satisfied expression. "Alright, Terry, let's arrange for your death before it gets dark, then take off. From now on, you answer to Tammy only. Your life depends on it."

———

News of Terry's "missing in action" and "presumed dead" situation was of little interest to anyone. There was no dad to call, her mom was long passed and any contact with her older sister Gloria was a vague and ominous "last seen in Vancouver downtown eastside". She was, indeed, unattached.

Tammy trained intensely to look and act like a drug courier. Police experts showed her how to strut, talk and look. She got a black dye job on her hair. Three sketchy tattoo artists splashed typical, garish examples of street art on her, taking care to make them look worn. Experts showed her the habits she needed to exhibit. She also learned how to watch and observe. They videoed her performance, which she would then study, looking for "tells" before repeating her performance, again and again, until she had it down to perfection.

"These tats will fade away in a couple of years or so, presuming you survive this assignment."

Now *there's* a sentence that sticks in your mind.

Her trainers gave her a few defensive tools of the trade. The sneaker shoelaces had wires in them to strangle. Tammy couldn't help wondering if the shoe containing Beth's foot still had its wire shoelaces when it washed up on the beach.

Tammy's red spike shoes had actual spikes in the heels. Lethal and chic. A small camera and tape recorder passed as cosmetic items. Panic button on a key fob with tiny lock picks. Two very small switch blade knives. Her bra was a working eavesdropping "wire". Not a bad fit, either.

They gave her a vape pipe complete with two extra batteries and a foil wrapper with a hidden switch connecting them together if an explosion was needed.

"Don't blow them in your pocket," said Spike, the female weapons tech advised her wryly. "Sometimes these blow even when you don't want them to. And here's a gun. You're 'army', so I take it you can use one."

Some kind of handgun was an expectation in her new "trade". She carefully inspected it. "Small revolver... serials filed off... keep the brass after the shoot. Close range. Tidy and handy."

4

SPIKE

Weapon's Tech Spike watched Tammy fondle the little pistol, obviously eager to use it. To Spike, all new undercover cops were the same—over-trained and under-experienced. They put too much emphasis on cool gadgets and not enough on the most dangerous weapon of all; a sharp, calculating mind. Only the smart ones survived this lethal game of chess.

"Anything... bigger?" Tammy asked, breaking Spike's train of thought.

"Bigger gun? Like a shotgun?"

"No. A bit longer range with more penetrating power, but still small."

Yup—all the same.

Spike slid open a nearby drawer and pulled out an exotic handgun. "Is a .22LR and silencer big enough for you?" she asked wryly.

".22? Isn't that... small?"

"It's an LR! The CIA liked it enough they made Gary Powers carry one." Seeing no change in her expression of concentration, Spike wondered if she even knew who Gary Powers was. Youth was wasted on the young. She said gruffly, "Here are a few different loads for it, one for short range and another with high penetrating power. Like I said, it comes with a silencer—and a holster. You'll need a good back story if you're caught with it, though. Hide it well."

"Cool. I'll bring it back when I'm done."

"You do that." *Kids!*

Spike instantly regretted her resentment. Hopefully this one would come back.

———

THE WEEKS of undercover training were difficult. Tammy lost weight, muscle and sleep, becoming thin, tired, sallow—with blood-shot eyes and blotchy skin. Tammy took pride in being healthy and strong but this was awful. She felt tired and mildly ill all the time, even mildly depressed.

Her instructors understood her dilemma. "It's part of your tempo-rary persona. Think of it as your uniform... your armour."

Tammy learned the look and walk of the defeated. It was all part of the training.

She hated make-up but they showed her how to splash it on. Change your look, your health, younger and older. Be someone else if needed for penetration, investigation or escape.

They made her walk around while carefully assessing her.

"Own the look or you'll be dead," they told her. "We want more of you to come back than a foot in a shoe."

"No marching around like you're still in the army. This isn't an inspection! *Slouch!* Look downcast, for God's sake!

"Be wary."

During lunchbreaks one of the instructors would sit with her in the middle of Toronto, the training base, sharing a bench, and together they would watch people from all walks of life drift past—from the rich to the homeless. Everyone stepped and looked out into the world differently. Tammy found it fascinating.

They showed her tips and ways to work social media to leave

subtle messages with fake profiles or find out who might be doing the same. They showed her how to seed untraceable emergency profiles.

Criminals and terrorists hung out in social media just like everyone else, the modern street in Dodge City where anything goes, and nobody cares. Buy a bomb, hit man, weapon or human being of any age, no strings attached. Free-range crime, suited for every level.

Tammy's social media instructor shook her head. "These companies have algorithms to learn a user's toothpaste or toilet paper preference, yet don't have one for the guy putting out a hit on his wife. Crazy. Too busy making billions."

Tammy looked at her. "Where's social media going to end? It's a cesspool."

Her instructor grinned. "Haven't you heard? That new American President Jackson is going to ban all internet activity, and social media in particular. Rumour has it he's afraid the 'bots and Ruskies' that elected him could boot him out. No more 'net in the near future in America."

"The sword goes back in the stone?"

The instructor laughed. "Yes, something like that. Going to wait for a new shining knight to come along."

"Good thing we're in Canada, then."

Tammy dragged herself home after what seemed like years of work. *What the fuck have I got myself in to?*

After tossing and turning in bed Tammy got up, dug around the internet to find out everything she could about the drug cartels. She always did research on a night like this.

The Montreal cartels were evil, organized and secret. Few arrests with zero convictions. She gave up and browsed across a few information feeds instead, coming across news of her own bogus demise:

Toronto Globe and Mail newspaper: "Army Special Forces member vanishes during survival exercise in remote lake country. Despite an exhaustive search, no body was found. A spokesman for the army said they suspect Private Theresa Reid may have drowned in one of the area's large, fast flowing rivers. The search is winding down after three weeks."

"Gave up on me after only three weeks of looking! Thanks for not busting your asses," she snorted.

As she explored old news stories she came across 'Operation O'Tremens'. It was about an informant who stayed and made it to the top of organized crime. There was another story of a police informant who managed to get near the top of the Klu Klux Klan and was a black man.

Ballsy and bold was the ticket, apparently. These guys made it to the top and didn't die. Quit while they were on top. Smart. "Wow."

Enough 'net time wasting. Time for bed. Today's training had been physically and mentally draining. When she looked in the bedroom mirror, she had to admit she looked and moved perilously close to someone on drugs, living on the edge... a lot like her sister Gloria. What little she remembered of her, anyway.

A low-level criminal's bio for Tammy Anderson was invented, backdated, and strategically placed. Tammy's life was built up on social media platforms. Her seedy work resume was conjured up along with a small-time crime history. *Drug mule—large quantities from source to street supplier or anywhere else. Caught twice. Didn't talk.*

While Tammy was being trained in her informant role, Montreal police launched a quiet crack-down, arresting any and all drug couriers of the Guardia gang they could find. This would position the new Tammy as a highly sought-after commodity. Then they placed their precious highly trained experienced drug courier where she would be appreciated and noticed.

Tammy entered the courier business by being thrown in a police drunk tank. She immediately slipped in a puddle of puke and fell sideways, skidding across the floor after the guard slammed the door on her back.

Gross! Three female occupants snickered as she slowly got up, splattered with vomit and whatever else was on the floor of this disgusting jail cell. She resisted her initial urge to crack some heads. *Patience! Don't blow your cover after one day.*

"Sorry, kid," said a fourth occupant, this woman appearing to be the oldest inmate, and who was clearly pale and ill. This was a surprise.

Tammy said nothing, looking for a sink or a water tap.

"Don't even try the shitter," warned another woman. "It hasn't flushed for days."

"Dandy."

5

FRIENDLY JAIL CELL

TAMMY FELT DISGUSTED, AFRAID TO LOOK AT HER HANDS OR HER clothes. What the hell? I'm sitting in a drunk tank, standing in god knows what with four crackheads, drunks or ho's—or all the above. "Blend in" they said. "It'll be fun" they said.

She sat on the least disgusting half of the narrow cot, leaning her head into the back wall and tried to get some rest. Her first day as a deep informant for organized crime and here she was, trapped in a cell.

She dozed, worried her new biography and life wouldn't hold under scrutiny from the crime bosses she may come to work for. Her handlers had said this was about a six-week job, depending if you were blown or not. Names, dates and incidents. Big fish.

"Tammy Anderson!"

She stiffened.

"Yes, Anderson! You!" called the irritated jailer, pointing at her. It took her a few seconds to register she was on stage for real this time —this was no dress rehearsal.

Groggily, she stood up, took stock of her surroundings so she kept her story straight and lurched towards the guard. *Will I end up as a foot in a shoe? Last chance to run.*

"Ya made bail, Anderson." The guard pointed to a well-dressed man standing in the entrance of the jail cell hall.

"Nice." Tammy walked toward him, openly assessing him as she sashayed towards him.

He looked like a tame crime lawyer, three-piece suit, slicked down hair. Shifty, though from his appearance, apparently crime paid well. Not sure what to do, she stopped and eyed him suspiciously, letting him speak first.

"Tammy Anderson?"

"Yeah."

"The name's Lewis." He made no effort to shake her hand. In fact, he didn't seem to want to touch her. "A benefactor paid your bail." He then used his arm in a sweeping motion for her to walk ahead of him. Tammy turned and walked as requested, glad to be out. She'd received his message loud and clear. *No speaking in the police station.*

After handing back her scant belongings, the police gave the pair a wide berth in the hallway. They all looked at the lawyer, disgusted but resigned to his kind. No doubt Lewis the shyster regularly sprung scum loose to go back on the street...perps the police might have spent months investigating or even had a partner take a bullet from one of Lewis's pals.

Bastard!

Tammy wondered how many of those officers would enjoy taking a shot at this man if they thought nobody would find out who did it. One less untouchable scumbag off the street. Lewis smiled at them, likely knowing he'd out-earned them all last year and would again next year, with impunity.

She turned away, having had enough of Lewis's smug expression and strutted ahead, concentrating on her new walk, feeling her skin crawl imagining the creepy lawyer's eyes ogling her back, butt, her straggly, clumpy hair, dirty clothes, poorly done tattoos, skinny arms and legs with mottled skin and a sad, defeated posture. Unhealthy drug user. Perfect. This was her first test. Would she pass?

They stopped outside the police station. Tammy looked at the nearest sign announcing, "Montreal Police Station #23."

"Go home. Stay sober. Someone will call you," the shifty lawyer said and walked away.

Home? She hadn't been to her new "home" as of yet. *I wonder what this place will be like? The Ville-Marie Hotel?*

It was a twenty-block walk for Tammy. She didn't mind—it gave her time to clear her thoughts. She enjoyed the exercise, and frankly, the fresh air, in consideration of what was currently ground into her clothes and hair. It was a very nice morning despite the bad night. The sun shone and birds in the few sparse trees sang, ignoring the sketchy neighborhood.

A tiny space in a bad rooming house had been rented for her and furnished in her name. Referrals to this place had been carefully rehearsed as they had been specially created as part of her background. The room would have an old burner cell phone, complete with cracked screen, set up with a suitable text and call history, hidden recording functions and GPS tracking.

There would also be a creaky old laptop, battered and third hand but inside it had been juiced up so it ran very well with all the latest cloak and dagger programs. The laptop came with a program to pick up any nearby bugs tracking her, intentionally or unintentionally.

All hidden.

Soon she came to the old Ville-Marie Hotel. The Ville-Marie was just a big pale blue box, three stories high. It was long past its prime with barred windows, dirty glass and peeling paint. It housed a bar at street level with two stories of sketchy rooms above. An old run-down rooming house.

It sat on a shabby street featuring a few homeless people, one with a shopping cart filled with precious belongings. Tammy made eye contact and nodded hello to each and every one. See who's watching.

As she entered the Ville-Marie she politely sidestepped a hooker in the doorway. Looking in she saw half the lights were burnt out or pulsing on and off erratically. Eerie. The front desk was to the right. A piece of plywood nailed to the sill served as the reception table. A chubby worn woman had her back to her, hunched in a battered swivel chair, putting papers in crude mail slots.

"Hey. Got my key?" Tammy called to her, trying to sound tough. She had no idea what her room number was.

The front desk woman turned to her. She was balding, missing teeth and wore cheap glasses with thick lenses. "What?"

Tammy was momentarily surprised. It was Shirley Mac in disguise. Well done.

They pretended to be strangers. Shirley said, "Key to room 201?" she winked.

"Yes, that's it."

Shirley handed her a key along with a piece of paper, adding for show, "You owe rent. Pay up or we'll kick your scrawny ass out."

"You'll get your money when I do," Tammy replied, turning away abruptly and climbing the stairs. The mood was set for whomever was interested enough to listen in.

The worn-out carpet hung loose on the steps, almost tripping her in the dark stairwell. She emerged into the second-floor hallway, seeking room 201. What's that smell? Urine?

6

HOME SWEET HOME

Glancing back and forth, she explored both ends of the hallway, observing the exits that worked and weren't covered over or blocked. Next, she found the door to the roof and went out to investigate. Cigarette butts, needles and condoms lay around. She wasn't the only one who came up here. Smoke, shoot up or sex. Maybe all three.

Neighboring buildings were almost close enough to jump over to them. Good to know. A bit far, yes, but a jump was always shorter when someone was chasing after you with a gun. She went back down the stairs, looking for her room.

She almost laughed when she found room 201 was the only one that had no actual number posted on the door. Many layers of paint revealed the number '201' had recently been pried off leaving a shadow.

The door had an eye hole. Handy.

Tammy took a minute to look all around the door edges for trip wires and bugs, looking closely for bits of hair stuck on the door. It was the oldest, cheapest trick in the book to see if there was an intruder waiting or someone had been there. For a full five minutes she stood in the doorway and listened. Suspicious sounds?

Satisfied, she peeked under the door for shadows, then stood and unlocked it. She pushed it and waited for it to bump the wall, full open. Nobody behind the door. Tammy stepped in and just looked around the room.

It was a bachelor suite, or so they called it. A bed was on the left and a minimal kitchen area on the right. A tiny simple fridge was closest. She had a window that opened onto a fire escape but judging by the thick layers of paint, it had not been opened for a very long time. It looked down on the parking lot, below.

Her room had a lived-in look. A double bed mattress was laying on the floor with sheets piled, used, nearby. There was a suitcase opened, full of clothes. There was a rough, ancient chrome kitchen table with three chairs. The sink was full of dirty dishes. Nice. Just like her own apartment, back home.

She opened the fridge and saw nothing but a takeout bowl of long decayed salad. The little freezer had a miniature iceberg of something she couldn't identify. Were those possibly blue popsicles?

She found the hidden phone and laptop.

The small bathroom seemed okay. The toilet flushed and the taps in the sink ran. No toilet paper! There was a filthy and elderly toilet plunger nearby but she decided it was something she would not touch ever, in her life. Appalling!

The rusty bathtub had hot water if she left the tap running for a while, going from black to rust colored, then clear-ish. The medicine cabinet was filthy and had a few empty prescription bottles. Oxycontin and methadone. The person's name on the bottles was 'Tammy Anderson'. Nice touch. The nearby vanity drawer was well stocked with cheap make-up, special shoes and a personal kit.

It took a while, but she did locate the hidden stash of weapons, frozen in that popsicle box in the freezer. She took a few minutes to insert the wire shoelaces in her sneakers. Thawed, she quickly slipped the knives and gun under her blouse. Damn cold!

She remembered the note the front desk gave her. It read: Rent: $99 plus utilities per month. No drugs. No police.

Handwritten underneath: *Money at your door.*

Tammy ripped the note into small pieces and flushed it, plugging the toilet. She had to use the disgusting plunger. *Fuck!*

After she washed her hands—twice—she looked around the room to see if everything was in order.

Time to eat and get a nap, maybe? *Will I catch something from this mattress?* Skip the nap.

Her phone lit up with a text message from Lewis, the shitty lawyer.

"Go to Bubbles Bikini Car wash. Dress for it. Ask for Ric."

She narrowed her eyes. How'd he get her number? Oh yeah. He was "her lawyer" now. From her intake sheet at the copshop.

Dress for it? Tammy rummaged through her suitcase of clothes on the floor and located some short shorts, a low-cut blouse and the deadly spike heels. She needed to look the part. The reality of her situation was hitting home.

She washed off whatever she'd brought home with her from the cell and dutifully put her make-up on, trying to utilize her new skills. Part of the new uniform these days.

As Tammy finished, her stomach growled persistently. Need to eat. Food money? Then she remembered *"money at your door"*. Door? She considered the doors she had. Unlikely to be an outside one. She ran her fingers along the bathroom door, top and sides. Nothing. She went over to the little wardrobe folding door and felt all around. Aha! A hollowed out door edge. She felt a roll of bills squeezed into a slot on the top. Twenty-tens.

Feeling prepared, Tammy locked up her place, taking note of the feeble doorknob lock and where a much sturdier one could be installed. The door and jamb were intact but the actual lock was long gone, no doubt removed and sold for drug money.

Tammy was off towards the car wash. She grabbed a sandwich from a Q Mart, ignoring the judgmental expression on the clerk's face, and ran for the bus stop, barely getting on. She crammed down the sandwich on the stinky, lurching transit bus, while sitting next to an old lady who spoke to an imaginary cat the whole time. Named "Pebbles", apparently. Best get used to it.

The bus dropped her off next to Bubbles Car Wash. Grubby location in a bad part of town. As she got closer to the car wash, she wondered why so many very nice, expensive cars were coming through, each complete with a creepy looking driver. The drivers' gazes were riveted to the girl in a bikini scrubbing their car. Distraction.

I don't care what anyone says, I'm not washing cars in a bikini!

The girls bounced around in tight Bubbles green uniform bikinis, busily wiping off foam and rubbing the cars with great effort, bums and boobs jiggling. Nearby, a seedy looking tall man with red curly hair, looking about the age of thirty barked orders and pointed. "Ya missed a spot! There!"

He also wore a Bubbles work shirt, though his was soiled and had 'Ric' stitched onto the front pocket. When he turned around impatiently, motioning one of the girls to hurry back and wipe at a missed fender, Tammy saw the back of his shop shirt featured a caricature of a standing bathing beauty. *Oh my God...*

———

RIC CASEY HAD WORKED at the car wash for about five years. He'd been a pimp until Bob decided to give him a more respectable profession. All Ric had to do was run the car wash as Bob directed, and Ric was free to rent the girls out on the side. Flexible and lucrative. Bob seemed to be good to work for, though Ric wisely kept any complaints to himself.

The guy who had had the job before Ric complained a lot— before they found him in the river with a steel spike in his head. The only reason the police found him was when "bloat and float" overcame the concrete blocks tied to his ankles. Ric was sure to paste on a smile when Bob was around, like today.

Ric glanced at his watch, waiting for the new recruit to get here. Late. He saw a hard-looking girl headed his way. Might be her. "Tammy? Over here!" he barked.

He looked Tammy over as she strutted toward him. This one was no prize, that was for sure. She was clumsy in heels, plain with a lot of makeup, was way too tall and had small tits. No bikini for her. Must be a new mule. Something about her strut, her demeanor, didn't sit right with him, but he couldn't say why. He wasn't about to complain to Bob about it.

Ric pointed at Tammy. "Car wash office! Ask for Bob."

She followed his orders, struggled with the spike heels while trying to maintain her strut. She managed to get through the entrance without incident, and found the door labeled "office" or more strictly speaking, "OFF E". Behind its closed door she heard a conversation in progress. A room full of killers.

Knock? Why not?

She timidly tapped on the door. The conversation inside ceased and the door swung open. Two men sat, one facing her from behind a beat up desk and the other with his chair to the right of the door.

"What?" called the man behind the desk.

"I'm Tammy."

"Come in."

The two men looked at each other and waved her inside. It was a tiny office with barely room for the three of them. The man seated at the door slid his hand up between her legs as she squeezed by.

Ignore it or break some fingers? Maybe later.

The man behind the desk stood, reached over the computer and offered his hand to shake. "I'm Bob. Welcome aboard, Tammy. My friend with *no* manners here is 'Zoo'." He grimaced at his colleague, who just smiled, keeping his hand exactly where it was.

She bit her tongue and shook Bob's hand, saying nothing. What a looker Bob was. The proverbial tall, dark and handsome. Gorgeous. Seemed well mannered. Such warm eye contact.

"Follow me, Tammy, and I'll show you what you'll do for us." Bob nodded to Zoo, who stood and vanished, taking his disgusting hand with him. Tammy followed Bob to the wash entrance and saw a car coming out of the completion door, getting the final rub down by a short bikini clad girl in her late teens. She opened the doors of the expensive sports car, wiping the sills and insides with a dry clean cloth. The car sparkled in the sun. The car's owner watched her every move, lecherously, unblinking. Ric busily worked near the passenger seat.

Bob said, "Tammy, watch Ric with the clipboard. What do you see?"

Tammy saw the driver spellbound by the bikini girl while Ric inspected the car, then smoothly reached into his pocket, pulled out a sandwich sized bag and stowed it under the seat.

"Ric is putting a stash of coke under the car seat and the driver doesn't seem to notice."

Bob nodded. "The driver knows, alright. That's Sam. He transfers the stuff around for us. Cops never know how we move our product. Who cares about a sleazy carwash, right?"

"Smooth," Tammy said.

"Ric's the manager and runs this place, he's not here to just hand out stuff. The last girl left our employ and you'll be her replacement."

Beth? The foot in the shoe?

Bob looked her over, but not in a creepy way. "You'll hate those shoes so wear something comfy. It's a long day standing around and the wet pavement's slippery. Keep the short shorts. You look lovely in them. I see they have a pocket which is good. Let me get you a shop shirt. All you do is stand there, write down the inspection list so it looks like a legit car wash activity and slip in the stash before the cars leave. Got it?"

"Write on the form and slip the stash from the bag."

"Gotcha."

"The main stash is in the employee change room in the locker marked, 'Beth'."

Tammy fought a shudder.

"Don't carry too much at once. Nothing goes missing or our... 'quality assurance team'... will be talking to you—understand?"

Tammy swallowed with difficulty. Probably, breaking fingers and toes, first offence. She forced herself to mutter, "Yup."

"The reason you're here is our girls seem to have either been arrested or retired. You have a good resume but see that camera over there? We'll be watching. You get two hundred a day to do this. Good pay for a shit job."

"When's pay day?" Tammy asked in a show of interest in the cash and no alarm at the job's duties.

"Cash, on Fridays from Ric. He's efficient but don't piss him off. He's a mean one."

"Yup."

"Let's get you dressed up and working. Call me if you have questions. Here's my card." She looked at his tasteful silver card that simply said: *"Make your troubles disappear. 458-522-9632."*

7

CARWASH RULES

Tammy replied, "Nice," while she inwardly gasped.

Bob winked, "I don't give many of those cards away so treasure it."

Killer joke? Tammy laughed as best she could.

In half an hour Tammy was stationed by the emerging washed cars, checked her inspection list, dropping the coke off inside, and warding off the frisky hands of the drivers. It was hot and humid, and she was in a sweat. She wondered if her sister Gloria ever had to do this.

Such a sad story with an unknown end.

She knew Gloria had had a child at some point. Gloria's last visit with her and mom, all of ten years ago now, had been awful. Her mother was upset with Gloria, her situation, drug use and the fact she was so obviously pregnant. Needless to say, it was a short, awkward visit. Terry never saw Gloria again. Their mother cried for days.

Before her mom's death she remembered seeing the returned birthday and Christmas cards. Her mom even had some so-called private detective look for Gloria. Likely, he took Mom's money and drank it away.

Terry had planned to search out Gloria when she was done school, but other priorities took over and all was forgotten. That was then, and this is now. Head in the game—*Tammy*.

Her first day at the wash was a long one but she didn't mind. She handed out thirty-two stashes, making note of who drove what type of car. The day was done at six. She put her shirt and clipboard in her locker, slipped past Ric's sneering grope and headed to her apartment.

On the way she went into a pawn shop to pick up a cheap little TV set and a heavy-duty lock that would fit her door. She also stopped for some food, soap, toilet paper and a Times from a tiny corner store, as well.

At the doorway of her apartment she looked carefully, all around, to see if there was anything suspicious. There was none.

Once inside, she plugged in the TV and turned it on. Nothing great but it had sound and not a bad picture of a nearby American cable channel. The picture was grainy but the real asset was the whistling sound it produced so well, perfect to drown a listening bug if there was one in the room.

She expertly installed the new heavy lock into the door and noted the jamb had metal strips guarding it. It was now as good as it was, ten years ago, before the old lock was removed and sold for a pitiful few dollars.

She made a point of looking through the peephole in the door, noticing the stains and holes in the wall opposite. Surveying the battlefield, so to speak.

What a dump! Tammy turned away and surveyed the room, looking for a place to start. Dishes were a good place. She scrubbed them up, leaving them on the miniscule counter top on a somewhat clean dishcloth while her little pawn shop TV hummed with high-light news from across the border.

Times were a'changin' in America. The kinder, gentler days were finished, if such times had ever existed. They were being replaced through a suspicious series of elections pushed by a harsh and aggressive administration. It was a throw-back to the nineteen fifties, white males, hand-in-hand with the church, firmly in charge. The world would be made in America's new image.

"This is Harry Fast of Detroit KMO News. Breaking, we have Sandy Thompson from Washington, DC.

"Good evening Harry. At the Whitehouse today US President James Jackson was on the defensive after a fire at an immigrant children internment camp in Texas. No lives were lost, but the fire destroyed all parental records of displaced immigrant border kids, the so called Huacho Children.

"Sandy: Where did the term 'Huacho' come from?"

"Harry: Huacho is the Argentine word for orphan. As you know the children who were removed from their parents were from Mexico and further south, some as far as Central and South America. This term has been around for the past month. President Jackson is not happy with the new label, preferring to call them what they are, illegal immigrant children of criminals.

"Sandy, is there a plan to return these remaining children to their parents? Is this latest fire hampering efforts?

"Officials told us off the record they didn't know where most of the remaining children were from, even before this fire. As you know, many have been re-united with their families over the past year but not all of them were documented. Some have deceased parents or parents who cannot return for them. It's a terrible situation.

"Here comes the bizarre twist to this story, Harry. President Jackson then took a complete u-turn at the conference, skipped over further questions to announce a brand new Mars space program in which astronauts will fly to the red planet to claim it for America. Here's what he said; "This Mars Program is very exciting and shows NASA is open for business! We are looking for young, exciting people who wish to become astronauts to go to Mars. This offer has been extended to any DACA and immigrant young adults who wish to become astronauts!"

His usual crowd of rabid followers cheered.

Tammy turned to look at the little TV in shock.

"S-Sandy, did I just hear this correctly...the President is going to shoot DACA kids and some of these older, lost immigrant adolescents into space, to travel to Mars with the idea he'll come back for them at some later date?

The reporter seemed to shrug her shoulders and raised her eyebrows in response, as if she couldn't quite believe what she was reporting herself. "Ah, yes, Harry. He claims the American taxpayers will train them to be astronauts and go into space, a huge honour. He claims it as good passage out of the detention centers."

"So. They're being deported to Mars?

"Essentially, that's what this looks like. Back to you, Harry."

"That's... that's unbelievable. Ah... Thank you, Sandy. The anchor man looked stunned, unable to move forward. He glanced to his right, seemed to shake himself free of the unusual story, straightened his shoulders and faced the camera, full on. He said, "And finally, look at the newest panda bears at the zoo! Aren't they cute?"

Tammy turned the TV down, shaking her head. Hopefully this is just the usual bullshit talk.

Only in America. From illegal immigrant to astronaut in one easy step? Were they insane? Deported all the way to Mars. Harsh.

Tammy found working the car wash an interesting look at how the drug trade worked. She diligently filled out the carwash form listing the wash functions that had been done, slipped the stash in the correct car and took note of the licence number.

She'd been there a week and the other girls were beginning to talk to her a little. Tammy learned they were vulnerable, preyed upon and often drug users themselves, caught up in the nightmare of pay to play, at any price. Pity. Ric knew how to pick them and keep them, with a kiss or a fist. He was such a scum bag.

It was just after one o'clock and Tammy had just finished with a black Ford Mustang with dark tinted windows, dropping in the drug package before it drove away. A moment later Bob followed the mustang driving in a mini-van. Rolling down the passenger side window, he shouted out at her, "Hop in Tammy! Tell Ric you're leaving for an hour."

Hopefully I'm coming back.

Tammy climbed in with Bob—*the killer*—then powered her window down. "Ric! I'm with Bob!" she shouted as they sped away, her heart in her throat. She fought to appear calm. Was Bob buying her act, or did he know she was a plant? The image of Beth's shoe rose again, the ghostly image that seemed to chase her every day.

Bob steered, braked and accelerated erratically through the traffic. He managed to say, "You weren't supposed to drop a package in that mustang."

"Uh-oh."

"He hasn't paid his bill for a while," said Bob grimly.

"I'm sorry Bob. I didn't know..."

"It's okay. Ric's fault. He should have told you but he fucked up. Let's go get that package. I need you to spot him for me, then we'll follow."

Tammy searched the vehicles around them, the passing businesses, the adjoining laneways, the—. She blurted, "There! He just came out of the gas station."

"Slide down. No point in him seeing you. Just watch."

They followed the mustang in a heavy silence that seemed to press down on Tammy's chest, making it hard to breathe. How fast could she get to the blade inside her shoe?

"Lots of Mustangs like that here. Is that the one?" he asked, glancing around quickly and changing lanes.

"Yes. His plate said 'STUD1A'."

Bob snorted, "Jake is such a Gomer. Let's see if he goes somewhere quiet."

She gripped the door handle, ready to jump and run if necessary. This could still be Bob taking her to a quiet place to get rid of her.

Tammy watched as Bob expertly stayed far enough back to remain out of sight and still retain contact. After twenty minutes the mustang turned into a small community park and pulled up, it's motor idling, as if waiting for someone. Bob put the nose of the van about a length away from the mustang.

"Wait here."

Tammy watched as Bob opened the van door, strolling over to Jake's car as casually as if he wanted to gossip about hockey. No hurry. Big smile. Jake's window was rolling down. She could hear the two murmuring but couldn't make out what they were saying. She wasn't sure what would happen.

It was a movement in her side mirror that caught her attention. A suspicious figure darted out from the bushes and raced toward her van. Reaching the rear of the van the man stopped, using it as a shield. He seemed to watch Bob and Jake talk with a great deal of interest. Too much interest. She watched him slide along the side of the van, his body coiled to attack. Attack who? Still Bob stood talking with Jake, unaware. *Ambush.*

The man bolted. She timed it perfectly, popping open her door as the runner ran past, catching his face with the corner. *Wham!*

Hopefully he isn't one of "our" guys, she thought. Too late—she was committed now. She stepped outside and kicked the stunned man in the head for good measure.

Bob glanced at Tammy, recognizing the ambush immediately. He roughly jerked Jake out of the Mustang and jabbed the startled man's face into a nearby flower bed. He did a quick weapons search, then, keeping a knee in the middle of Jake's back, yanking his arm in a direction it wasn't meant to bend. The dirt muffled most of the scream and all of Jake's tears.

While stretching his mangled arm, Bob lectured Jake as if they were talking about the weather. "Jake. You took our property and didn't pay your bill. Not a huge deal but your friend over there tried to jump me. That's just plain disrespectful. Punishment today will be this broken arm but next time it'll be a kneecap, understand?"

Bob stood up, slipping Jake's stash and roll of cash into his pocket. Crying, Jake craned his head and looked up from the dirt and nodded his head in a series of frightened jerks.

"Ten G's by tomorrow—eight o'clock sharp at the wash and come alone. You don't want to be late."

The man in the dirt nodded again, vigorously.

Bob brushed dirt off his knees as casually as if he just pulled a dandelion out of his front lawn. He hustled over to Tammy, who had taken in the whole scene in wonder. He gazed down at the unconscious man at Tammy's feet and grinned. "Good cover. Hop in." He nudged one of the fallen man's arms under a van tire.

Tammy was still shaking as she got in and clumsily tried to close the van door. It took two tries. Bob got in the driver's seat, started the van and put it in reverse. The van bounced hard over the stricken man's arm. Clump.

"Oops!" He made a funny face while shifting forward and backwards, going over the man's arm another couple more times before pulling away. Clump, clump.

He did a proper shoulder check, signaled and drove away as courteously as any civic-minded senior citizen. "Safety first!" Grinning like a man who won the lottery, Bob asked, "Lunch, Tammy? On me."

"...s-sure?"

"The White Spot's my favourite," Bob said as if he was showing a visitor around town. "Thanks for riding shotgun, Tammy. Zoo's at his Grandmother's funeral so I needed a spotter." He winked.

Granny's funeral? *Someone's* funeral more likely.

Tammy said nothing as they drove to the restaurant, watching Bob through her eyelashes surreptitiously.

Bob was hyper alert, his eyes bright, constantly watched all around him, in the mirrors, at nearby buildings, at people on the sidewalks. He turned left abruptly, entering into a back alley. Tammy swallowed her gasp of fright. Was it here that he meant to kill her?

Coming to a stop he rolled his window down. She checked that her door was unlocked, her body poised to leap. Bob was looking at a medium sized building being put up, now merely a hole in the ground with steel rebar everywhere. There would be concrete poured in the next few days.

"I love to see a new cement project happening. A sign of progress. History covered up for another fifty years." He nodded to her as he put the van it in gear and continuing to the next street and parking at the White Spot.

So, once again a reprieve. Bob did not suspect her, was not going to kill her. Yet.

She wondered at Bob's construction fascination. Pouring concrete over his victims, maybe? Was this his way of giving her a warning? *Oh my God.* She felt weak with fear.

Bob led her to the White Spot entrance, holding the door open for her. He asked the older man at the door for his "usual table". Tammy assumed this meant something far in the back where he could rip someone's leg off with discretion.

Lunch with Bob would be a strange experience.

———

Bob Carzoni had had his eye on Tammy ever since she arrived at the car wash. She seemed more confident than the other girls, less consumed by drugs or didn't show it yet. She was young enough to still have a nice tight body before the ravages of drug use would take its toll.

He saw she was having difficulty keeping the menu steady. "You alright?"

Tammy looked over at him. "S-sorry. It... it was a bit of a surprise, that's all."

"You did well. If you hadn't caught that guy with the van door it might have been curtains for me and maybe you too."

"Fuck, I didn't think about that," she said, quickly covering her mouth after swearing.

Bob laughed, breaking the tension. "It's all good. That's why I'm at my quiet table."

Tammy took a deep breath which seemed to settle her down.

"I'd suggest the burger-fries combo and a shake. Best diner in the city."

"Sure, I'm in."

Bob graciously gave the order for both of them to a nervous server.

"So, Tammy, where did you come from?"

She made an effort to smile. "Timmins, originally. A small, boring town."

"Seeking fame and fortune?"

"I started out that way. I can sing and act but not as well as everyone else in Montreal, apparently. There's no going back, now." A look of consternation crossed her face.

Bob continued, "That's true. It's hard to go back home. When we leave, we make ourselves into a different person—for strangers, for better or worse. We can't bring that persona home."

That made her smile. "We build our new disguise and can't bear to take it off."

She's sharp, he thought. Not many would understand.

The food came along, and conversation ceased for a while.

"Coffee?" the server asked when Bob and Tammy finished.

"Sure, we have time," he said, deferring to Tammy, who nodded her agreement readily. "Ric will be okay with it."

They were back at the car wash at about two. Bob cornered Ric while Tammy went to the washroom.

"Ric! I told you the stash wasn't to go to Jake."

"That bitch Tammy screwed up, not me," Ric white-faced and scared.

Bob gave him a look of disgust. Ric was such a sniveling whiner. "No Ric, *you* fucked up. I got the stash back but you'd better listen when I give you instructions. Got it?"

Ric didn't dare protest as Bob stalked away, furious. *That's fuck up #1, Ric.*

———

Ric felt furious and helpless. He barged into the women's locker room, spotting Tammy coming from a toilet stall. He kicked her hard in the abdomen. She collapsed from the blow but made no move to retaliate.

"That's for putting a stash in the wrong car," he shouted.

"I didn't know," Tammy gasped, rolling on the floor retching and coughing, playing it up. *That's all ya got, asshole?*

He kicked her once more. "Around here it's always your fault! You'll be dead if you tell Bob about this. Understand?"

She nodded.

He stomped away, slamming the door. Ric always liked to feel in control.

Ric knew Jake would be visiting him about today's lost stash. That's what happened when you worked both sides. He was also on Jake's payroll and Jake was supposed to get every stash, regardless of what Bob said. Getting paid twice was good so long as Ric didn't get caught.

———

After the beating from Ric, Tammy slowly got to her feet, noticing the other girls avoided her in the locker room. She didn't dare retaliate if she wanted to keep this informer role. Maybe later.

The other girls knew how Ric operated. Cruel and nasty, even if it wasn't your fault. The other bikini car wash girls had been sporting cuts and bruises and now Tammy knew who dealt them. Bastard.

———

Zoo waited for Bob in the miniscule wash office, seated in his usual chair across from him. The faithful lieutenant. He looked around the office, waiting, muscular arms folded over his big belly, almost as wide as he was short. This place was a shit hole. With all the cash Bob was hauling in, you'd think he'd put a few bucks into this operation.

"Hey Zoo," said Bob as he slid by and sat down in his usual chair.

Zoo just nodded. Not much of a talker.

Bob looked at his phone screen and computer for messages, then up at Zoo. "I had to chase down Jake, today."

Zoo blinked in surprised, "By yourself? How?"

"Chased in the little van—took the new girl, Tammy with me. She could identify the car."

Zoo laughed, "Chasing Jake's Mustang in a minivan with a car wash girl as protection. Funny."

Bob looked a bit embarrassed but managed to grin back shyly. "Couldn't be helped. Ric didn't stop the stash to Jake, like I told him. I caught Jake in Gables Park. Some guy tried to jump me while I talked to him, but the wash girl got him with the van door as he tried to run by."

Zoo was impressed. "A set up?"

"I wasn't sure. I broke a couple of arms and gave them a pep talk."

"You think Ric was in on it?"

Bob sat back in his chair. "Likely."

"Want me to squeeze Ric and Jake a bit more?" asked Zoo helpfully.

"I don't have any replacement for Ric and Jake owes us a fair pile of money just now. No, let this slide for a few days."

Zoo smiled in a menacing way, "Too bad. I see a new concrete job, over by the White Spot."

"I saw it—looked cozy. Room for two."

8

SECRET PASSWORD

Tammy was supposed to check in with her police handler once a week or so. Great efforts were made to do this on the sly. Initially she didn't know who the person would be or what they looked like. She was to put a cryptic message in a particular type of soda can and leave it in the trash in front of various locations around the city.

A messenger watched for the pop can. Someone unknown to her, passing as a homeless bottle collector would retrieve the can and the coded contents inside. Little rocks meant the meeting times—one rock meant ten o'clock, two rocks meant eleven. A balled-up piece of foil in the can meant no meeting this week. Three cigarette butts in the can meant help me which would trigger the deployment of a SWAT team within minutes. No mercy.

Her arranged meeting place was the nearest park bench east, west, south or north of the drop-off trash bin, depending on the day of the week. Cloak and dagger.

Tammy was nervous about this first meeting. She made every effort to ensure she was not followed or watched and arrived "clean"—spy talk for not followed. Her ensemble for the meeting was a combination she never wore and would be unfamiliar to anyone in her new world. Every bit of clothing she had was carefully inspected for tracker bugs. She made sure her Jane Bond equipment and gun were handy before she went to the Wiki-Mart for a bubbly can of Fanta orange.

She put one rock in the empty Fanta can, "meet at ten", and it went into the stinky trash bin at eight o'clock in the morning. Then she headed for the meeting bench taking a careful roundabout route, arriving at the bench at ten. She found it already occupied by a scruffy old man with a walker.

He was shabbily dressed but clean. One toe stuck out of his worn-out shoe because his sock was missing. About seventy years old.

Was this her contact?

Eyeing her up, the old man said, "Working, honey?"

"Fuck you," Tammy said, looking around, warily.

The old man laughed at her. "How's that for the secret password? I got the Fanta can."

Tammy looked around before sitting down on the far end of the bench. She said nothing.

The man continued, "I'm Alfred, your contact. This area is being watched by my people right now. You won't see them."

Tammy felt safe enough to speak. "Are you a messenger?"

"No. I'm your handler; supervisor so to speak."

"What do you know about this informer stuff? You're an old man."

Alfred smiled, "I know enough. I was hanging with biker gangs before you were born. I was sneaking around Afghanistan for five years as an intel officer in the army. Listening to me could save you from Beth's fate."

"The one in the shoe?" Tammy knew very well that Beth was shoe girl but was compelled to ask just the same.

Alfred dropped his head slightly. "She got unlucky, killed, weighted by concrete blocks and dropped in the river. Food for the fishes...except her shoe."

Tammy said nothing, looking grim.

"How's it going so far?"

Tammy found her voice. "I'm not dead yet. Their lawyer bailed me out of jail. I found my sweet little apartment you set up."

"Sorry it's a dump."

"I get that. Not long after one of the gang messengers came to me, gave me a burner phone and told me to move a half a kilo of coke to an airport locker. He was testing me out."

"Went well?" Alfred asked, surprised.

"Yes. Passed right through."

"Did you call in a prior so security would let you get through with the package?"

"No. Just snuck on by, easy peasy," said Tammy slyly. "Airport security are unionized Mall-cops. Not even paid these days. I could have smuggled a Zamboni through. They couldn't find their asses with both hands and a pencil."

"Be careful, smart ass. Met Bob, yet?"

She nodded, looking around absently. "A week ago."

"Was his buddy Zoo around, too?"

"Yes. Bob only calls on Zoo when they have something big happening."

"I think Zoo likes his job too much. Bob is more of a detached pro."

"I heard Zoo likes to hear them scream. Bob says that's good marketing to their competitors," said Tammy, grimly.

"Stories of screaming keeps everyone in line." Alfred raised his eye brows and asked, "Anything for me?"

"Can you copy a phone chip?" asked Tammy. "Pictures and contacts."

"Yes, hand it here." She did as he asked. He quietly put the chip in a napkin he had in his pocket, pretended to blow his nose then casually dropped it on the ground. In minutes a woman with a stroller and a dog on a leash came by. The dog happily picked up the hanky without stopping.

"We'll have your chip back in a few minutes," Alfred whispered.

The mom, stroller and dog were back in five minutes, dropping the hanky. Alfred smoothly got it and slipped it under Tammy's arm.

"What's Ric's background?" Tammy asked, slipping the chip into a leg of her shorts.

Alfred took a breath. "Ric is a very bad man. Pimp, cruel beater. Long track record with few convictions."

"Yeah, he likes to kick. Does Ric have friends with money?"

"Yes. He never talks and they always come to bail him out. Sadistic but reliable."

"I'll bet he'd talk under the right circumstances," Tammy said.

Alfred took note of the look in her eyes. "Don't do anything to blow this investigation!" He looked around before adding some advice. "Better to plan well in advance if you find someone who... needs to go, if you know what I mean. They need to be part of the chess game."

She nodded, then stood up abruptly and strolled away.

"Alfred" fed pigeons for a while then looked carefully around him and left the park as well, moving slowly on his walker.

Tammy took the bus, transferring a couple of times to confuse any possible followers, then made a trip to a thrift shop near her shabby apartment. The thrift store was a treasure of worn clothing for all ages from all fashion imaginings. She knew what she wanted. Soon she was back home, her TV blaring while she transformed into someone else.

"This is Harry Fast of Detroit KMO News. We have Sandy Thompson with a development from Washington. Sandy?

"Hello Harry. Breaking news today is from President Jackson who spoke at a rally in Atlanta.

"As you know the Department of Education merged with the Department of Labour. Education as we know it is essentially dismantled. The president said this minutes ago, 'Today we get rid of the expensive and unsafe public-school system, replacing it with home schooling for basic education. Parents know what's best for their kids and we save 700 billion dollars a year, which is the same amount the Pentagon gets to protect America. What would you rather have; the best defence in the world protecting us or a bunch of overpaid government teachers? America can't be great again without a great military!"

The raucous crowd cheered and chanted "Ar-Mee! Na-Vee!!"

"There you have it, Harry. Home schooling it is."

"Sandy, when will this new school program be in effect?"

"They'll be phasing it in starting fall of 2020."

"Does this mean all schools?"

"This doesn't affect private schools, or a few public schools kept open for the unresolved immigrant children."

"The ones that don't go to Mars?"

"...Uh...yes, that seems to be the current thinking." A fleeting look of confusion flitted across the reporter's face.

"Thank you, Sandy. And now a story about a lonely bird nest on an aircraft carrier set to sail on Friday."

Tammy spent an hour in front of the mirror carefully putting on make-up to look poor and elderly. She then mixed and matched her thrift store cache of old clothes until she looked just right. At last she slid a thin pillow on her shoulders to get a bit of an elderly hunch, grabbed her "best grandma" bag, red cloche hat, thick eye glasses and earplugs that looked like hearing aids. She had one last look in the mirror, happy with what she saw. On the way out she picked up the sturdy metal cane made to look like cheap bamboo except it was heavy and nasty, featuring a hidden spiked base for ice and snow.

She headed out the door, carefully locking it behind her. Tammy slowly sidestepped down the steps and hobbled convincingly out into the street. Be helpless and slow.

The neighborhood was rough and sad. Store fronts that managed to stay open did what they could to keep alive. Their windows were covered with rusty, bent bars to keep out the "smash and grabs" while clerks watched nervously to see who walked through the door.

Barry Henry stood on the same sidewalk as Tammy, leaning on

the wall of the closed-up peep shop. He had been down on his luck for over a decade and looked it. This drug habit wasn't going to finance itself, so he watched for suckers. Lucky for him Ric allowed him to roll a few old ladies each week to keep him in drug money. "Keeps the locals on their toes," he claimed. He was pleased to be one of Ric's urchins.

He glanced over the busy roadway, seventy-two feet wide, six lanes, traffic buzzing, beeping with roaring engines belching smoke, shifting gears, cursing. Cars, busses, cabs, and trucks made the area look prosperous, which it was not. Nobody stopped. Passing through on the way to work, aggressive and angry, texting. An endless freeway as relentless as army ants with inferred status from Mercedes or Cadillac and the like.

Occasionally, an unlucky ambulance or fire truck tried a surgical pass, sirens screaming, locked in crawling traffic, police cars marooned but this asphalt conveyer never stopped. There'd be hell to pay if it did. The flow of traffic trumped life and limb.

Barry warily watched Beemers, Caddies and Benz's with expensive shining wheels, music thumping. Exquisite leather seats jabbed with holes from gun barrels stabbing out from pockets. Passenger heads with crooked hats swiveling in all directions like bobble heads, staring out for cops and other gangs. They were on patrol.

Barry liked having a steady stream of "pigeons" shuffling down his sidewalk, on the edge of the freeway of death. Cheap, narrow, littered with trash, gum and pee, poorly maintained threads of concrete barely eight feet wide in places. An ant trail for those who couldn't afford a vehicle. Marginalized people on the edge of a prosperous road with speeding traffic only a few feet away. City priorities.

These narrow sidewalks were Barry's feeding zone. There might be fifty people on the walk, if you really counted them, including the invisible ones. There were a few relatively well-dressed young people, four hookers and a busker playing a stolen bent trumpet badly. A dozen people were leaning on walls or laying on the concrete, stoned or sleeping. A few elderly people struggled along, nervously dodging beggars while being impatiently passed by younger, more mobile people. Barry knew who to watch for.

It was getting close to the start of Bingo at the hall, that time when old ladies herded onto the bus with their pockets and purses filled with squirreled away cash hidden from drinking husbands. Easy pickin's. Snatch a purse and give them a shove. Don't even have to run because there's no cavalry coming.

Barry spied a stooped elderly woman coming towards him, really leaning on the cane. The bus was coming around the corner and time was tight. Perfect.

He stepped in front of her, shoving her backwards with his left hand, grabbing her bag with his right. He turned away, taking a quick peek into her purse for cash. It took a few seconds for him realize she hadn't fallen yet. Too late.

Bam! Barry was shocked by a stinging blow to the side of his head. He angrily turned and staggered toward the lady in time for her to strike him on the other side of his head... harder still. Panicking, he was scrambling backward and away to escape when the third strike smacked him. He didn't feel the fourth strike as he'd lost consciousness; his body added to the others, lying passed out on the grimy sidewalk.

The old lady smirked as she scooped up her purse.

Tammy kept going, not wanting to miss the bus, the loser cruiser, happy she bought the cane at the thrift shop. One jerk down. How many more would she meet?

She made it through the doors of the worn bingo hall, past the fat bored security man, just as the caller was getting ready, sitting in his cage. Old linoleum, dingy wallpaper, dim fluorescent lights, mildew, all stinking of cigarette smoke. Choosing a table near a bunch of other elderly ladies she sat down, quickly getting her dauber markers out, phony picture of her "grandson" and signalled for the coffee cart to come over. As she sat, she called the bingo paper girl for a set. Tammy paid her, then first glued them together in a big square, then made sure her daubers were in good working order.

Sipping her crappy coffee, she relaxed, giving full attention to the bingo caller as he read out the rules, making note of the game schedule.

"Early Bird! Under the 'I, nine'!" There was dead silence as the other old ladies all searched for nines on all their papers. Sounds of daubers tapping on tables filled the hall. As soon as they found their nines, they all started gossiping and talking. Tammy listened to what some said while ignoring others.

"Under the B, four!" Brightly colored daubers tapped the table tops in silence. Then the ladies spoke. One shouted in a thick English accent, "My word, them busses are so slow. I barely made it."

"Under the G, five." Silence except for the sound of daubers bumping on papers. The lady seated next to the English lady spoke again, "I think those bus drivers are afraid to come down here. The crime is dreadful."

"Under the O, zero." Daubers tapped in sudden silence. "Where's the police down 'ere? Back in England they'd have 'ad cops walking the beat, grabbing them 'oods."

"Under the N, nine!" Daubers thumping in silence. "Cops here are afraid to go on foot. They just drive around hidin' in their cars. Can't see or 'ear."

Tammy played and listened to the local gossip for four hours. It was fun to get out of her world. A few hours of invisibility in her present life of deception.

Finally, the last game was done. There was a stampede as the elderly denizens of the bingo hall stood, put their daubers and good luck charms in their bags and started shuffling away. The cleanup crew frantically shoved used bingo cards into garbage bags and carried them through a back door, presumably to a dumpster in the back alley. As she got her cane, she spotted someone talking to the bingo caller.

Ric! She thought about his boot print on her belly. Bastard.

He stood menacingly close to the caller who then waved the cashier over. They talked, then the bingo caller unhappily pushed a handful of cash over to Ric. He grinned, shoving the wad into his front pocket.

Protection money. Probably the usual story, "shame if someone robbed and beat up the elderly women" or "shame if the hall burned down" and such evil. Must be his sideline while pimping his girls. Scumbag.

Tammy won two hundred twenty bucks tonight. Lucky. She almost hoped Ric would come after her. Her knife in his windpipe would be what he deserved. Sadly, it would harm the investigation.

She made her way home in the dark, making sure nobody saw her enter room 201. Taking make up off took a while but she knew it was worth it. Street gossip was full of news.

9

SLEEPING WITH THE ENEMY

TAMMY WORKED THE CAR WASH FOR ALMOST A MONTH UNDER Ric's watchful eyes. Girls came and went, usually because Ric fired them or they just vanished. Rumour had it he had a hand in those as well. Transient lost people on the fringes and nobody cared. Wisely he left Tammy alone because she had become Bob's girl. Bothering Tammy would be hazardous to Ric's health.

They became in item. She had to admit she enjoyed Bob's company. He was charming, good looking, polite and worldly. His slight Italian accent and attentive brown eyes were panty removers.

He was willing and quite a catch, bringing her flowers and champagne. The safest place in a gang is the captain's bed, she thought. Keep the enemy close and all that. Skin to skin.

She started spending a few nights over with Bob. His apartment was expensive and tasteful. The bed was huge.

Pillow talk with Bob was strangely exhilarating. He spoke of his trade-skills, always trying to impress her with a clever execution or way to get a customer to talk. It scared her how his lurid stories thrilled her, and he could see it in her eyes. He spared no details to impress her.

Bob felt something about Tammy. She seemed like a long-lost kindred spirit, not like the scared, vacuous girls he usually screwed. She was confident and capable but green in the dark arts.

Tammy benefited from Bob's experience, listened and learned the tricks of the dark world of killers. After pillow talk came wild, willing sex.

Satisfying and completely weird.

———

Zoo SAT with Bob as they drove across town. The only thing they usually spoke of was a basic plan. Zoo hated small talk. He was unhappy with Bob's latest dalliance. "Another wash girl? This never ends well."

Bob took a breath. He respected what Zoo said because he was usually right. "I like Tammy. She's cute, nice and doesn't take drugs. She listens to me, Zoo."

Zoo said nothing more. He'd said what had to be said and left it at that. This girl, like all the rest, would be around for six weeks, three months tops. Then either Bob or Zoo made them disappear. They knew too much. Next.

As if sensing Zoo's annoyance Bob changed the subject. "How are your mom and dad doing?"

Surprised, Zoo said, "Pretty good."

"Still working?"

"They are but not the long hours they used to do. The City Zoo hired a few more people which helped a lot. Fixed the place up, too. Bigger elephant pen and glassed monkey house. Very nice."

That was a huge conversation from Zoo. Bob smiled at him. Most people looked at his odd size and huge ears and assumed that was why he was called Zoo. Not at all. He grew up in a zoo and that was why he had the nickname. So obvious.

Bob turned left and pulled into the alley, near the back of a store. Zoo pointed at the manhole cover in the middle of the narrow alleyway. Bob nodded while Zoo opened the passenger side door and slid out a five-foot-long steel bar. He used it to jimmy the big old rusty steel manhole cover off and pushed it to one side. It made a loud grating sound that should have traveled for blocks. Zoo wasn't worried.

Bob popped open the trunk, revealing a body with arms and legs duct taped together. The victim's mouth was taped as well but his eyes bulged wide open, trying to struggle... to scream. Still alive.

Together Bob and Zoo carried him over to the hole so he could hear the sewer water boiling below in the hole. Zoo carefully taped a concrete block to his feet.

"So long Jake. That was your last double-cross," Bob announced with finality.

They slid the squirming, wriggling silver worm down the hole, hearing a satisfying *splork* as it sunk in the thick flowing sewage. Headed to the river.

"You'd better not clog my toilet!" said Zoo with a laugh, grinding and sliding the cover back over the hole.

Bob shook his head and grinned.

Zoo was the master of the funny one-liner.

———

TAMMY LAID on her bed in her little apartment, wide awake. Bob was away on some assignment. A killer conference? Mafia inner sanctum like the Godfather? Best bullet ballistics in hits? She would ask him tomorrow night. Or not.

She got up and went to work her regular shift at the car wash, stopping for coffee at eleven. It was raining, on and off, so car washing was slow. Only cars getting drug shipments came for a wash. Wasn't this obvious to the police?

The other girls shivered in their bikinis. Ric would never let them cover up even if it was cold, regardless. He was such an asshole.

Bob walked into the room. "Tammy. Got something for you. Follow me."

Layoff notice and a bullet? No, she knew his manner and looks by now. He was very logical.

After kissing him, she followed him to the rear of the big car wash building. All by itself sat a two-year-old Chev pick up. Bob had a group diligently waxing the exterior while another was detailing the floor and seats.

"All yours," he said. "Project vehicle."

She made a big deal of being thrilled with the gift. Personally, she always thought a vehicle as a means to get around and nothing more, but Bob just gifted her with this one. Huge deal. The detailing meant evidence of various crimes and past owners was being erased. Might have been a mass murder truck. It had history.

Bob was pleased she liked it. "We've had some body work and painting done to it."

No kidding—covered the bullet holes, maybe?

The truck was a simple short cab, off-white pickup. Nothing special. So bland you'd forget what it looked like as it drove by.

"We had the box sealed up so it's easy to wash out."

For bodies and blood. Here's where she should be horrified. Just another day undercover in Montreal. She played it up, squealed and jumped with joy once more for good measure. "Can I try it?" She hated the phony jump and squeal.

"Sure. You can start right now."

"Cool!"

Bob handed her a business card. "Go to Reds Rental shop at this address. Zoo has something to pick up. Ask for Brendan and he'll slide it in the back. Zoo should be there, too. Help him out with this delivery."

Gulp. She pasted a wide eager grin on her face. "Sure." She kissed him again. She took the directions and went over to the truck. Everyone was done cleaning it, so she started it up and pulled away. Big engine. Stick shift. Fast.

She broke into a sweat as she drove. The truck was fun to drive with the engine roaring, changing gears and swooping around the corners. She arrived at Red's Rental main gate all too soon. Stopping, she asked the gate guard for Brendan. He pointed and waved her over to a parking spot.

Tammy parked and shut the engine off, waiting. She listened to the hot engine making clicking noises as the headers cooled off. It gave her time to think and worry.

This new, phony life was consuming her. Being an informant meant she slipped further into this evil world of crime. The gray area was getting murky and darker. Was there a line between good and bad or was it merely defined by the best lawyer money could buy? After risking her life she'd soon find out if her police bosses really did have her back or would throw her to the wolves. She'd best watch her own.

Brendan finally appeared, waving her over to the big rental shop loading dock. She backed up to it carefully and hopped out. Zoo was already standing there like a sentinel, watching a long and narrow wooden box with concern.

A coffin for her or was someone else already in there?

She went on the dock, helping him lift the mysterious box into the back of the pickup.

Zoo tied it down, then got in the passenger side and told her to drive. "Right here" and "Left there" and "In this back alley behind that small house."

Isolated.

Tammy shuddered as she got out and helped him put the heavy box in the little wooden shed.

"Thanks," he said, before opening the top of the box and gasping at the contents. Tammy wasn't sure if she should run or shoot or both. She wished she'd had a pee before she left.

"Wow," said Zoo looking in the box, clearly thrilled, oblivious to her subtle panic, "He gave me the better edge trimmer than we agreed on. Mom's lawn's gonna look real nice."

Did he set me up to scare the shit out of me?

"Nice," he repeated. "I'll come back and assemble it later," he said.

———

It was bingo night and Tammy busied herself with her senior's makeup. She was getting efficient at it after her third session. The 'intel' from the hall had been helpful in picking up the names of local messengers for local shitty hoods. Some had already been picked up and interrogated by police and that information was added to her file.

As she carefully inserted the phony hearing aid piece her little TV blared the day's news:

"This is Harry Fast of KMO news, Detroit. We have breaking news from Washington. Sandy?"

"Yes Harry, the White House communications director announced FOX News, Turner Broadcasting and PBS have all been purchased or taken over by Homeland Security to be our official news source. Here's the Communications Director: 'Today the White-house acquired Fox News, PBS and all their affiliates, national and worldwide. This radio, TV and multimedia service will be called 'Fax News' to provide official news directly from the White House to American homes without journalistic tampering and fake news endemic to the 24-hour news cycle. Fax News, not fake news!'"

"Oh my gosh Sandy. So, America has its own state news service like BBC, Xinhua in China, Canadian Press and TASS in Russia!"

"Similar to those Harry. There was a catch, unmentioned in the press release. It says and I quote, 'Fax News will accept no monies for any advertising, national and international, so their views can't be bent by advertiser's money, in order to provide fair and ethical news to viewers. This applies to all other media news services, inside and outside of the US."

"...um ...so...there will be no paid advertising allowed for news outlets, Sandy?"

"That is correct, Harry. This becomes effective in 2020."

"I'm shocked. So we may all be out of a job by 2020. (laughs) Glad I'm retiring. Thank you, Sandy."

"And here's a story about a boy scout troop in St. Louis who built a trail so baby weasels can safely cross a busy roadway."

The bus ride to the bingo hall was uneventful. She staked out her usual spot at a table near a group of chatty regulars. Everyone was hard of hearing so whispers came out as shouts of this week's neighborhood happenings. Good information.

They all smoked like chimneys. Tammy found it disgusting but never complained. Many elderly people around her coughed and gasped between puffs while unloading their invaluable take on the local gossip.

Silence proclaimed itself over the room when the caller said, 'Under the G – six!"

She'd just won two hundred and fifty bucks! Tammy made her way to the front and got her cash, then hustled back to her chair ready for another game.

The nearby elderly English lady gossiped, "Me rent's goin' up. Blimey! Where am I gonna go at my age?"

The other lady groused, "Mine too. My landlord said he has expenses to cover. That rough fellow makes the rounds and shakes them down for money. Scoundrel!"

"I wish me eldest lad was still alive. He'd catch him and break 'is fingers. Shhh...there the scoundrel is, right now. Look down," she whispered, including Tammy in her warning. " 'e's an evil lad."

Sure enough a rough looking man had arrived, pestering the bingo caller for protection money. He even collared a nearby elderly bingo winner and took some money from her winnings, giving her a rude shove in the process.

Tammy's blood begun to boil. He was none other than Ric!

She angrily kept up with the last game, not knowing quite what to do about Ric. He'd repeatedly crossed the line in her moral code, yet nothing would ever happen to him if she reported him to her handlers. They considered him small fry—too low on the food chain.

The games were over and it was time to go home. Tammy slowly made her way to the line-up for the crowded washroom, listening all the while. After she'd got through the stinking toilets, she ambled past the front bingo caller's chair where the managers all stood talking. She took it all in. It was time to leave for home, such as it was.

Stepping out, she looked carefully ahead, groping her way along the wall near the sidewalk. "As dark as the inside of a cow", as her mom used to say. Very few streetlights worked in this neighborhood. Reaching the corner of the building, she made an abrupt right into the alley, and under cover of the shadows, nimbly ran around to the rear of the sad bingo hall. She hid behind a couple of old plywood signs, watching the rear bingo hall entrance door open and close as workers brought out bags of garbage from the evening games. The dim overhead light turned on and off as the door opened and closed, lighting up their destination, a rancid dumpster shared with a Chinese food restaurant. As they threw in the trash she stood, close by, in the darkness.

She wasn't sure why she was there. You never know who you'll see or meet. There might be a bundle of accounting receipts that could be of interest. Bingo and gambling joints were notorious for being money laundering fronts. After a while she realized she had to pee. That second coffee...

To her surprise, the lights blinked on again and Ric appeared in the doorway, patting a bulge of cash he'd taken from the bingo game caller and the old lady. Grinning, he paused to light a cigarette before stepping forward. The door closed behind him and the light winked out, leaving him in darkness. He strutted away like a rooster.

A cane swept out of the dark, hitting his face like a home run batter's swing. There were a few more insurance blows, after that. Sweet dreams scumbag.

Ric would come to, finding himself sleeping with the trash, rotten food and rats in the dumpster. His money bulge would be gone along with most of his teeth. Asshole.

At home, Tammy had mixed feelings about battering Ric, as she removed the last of her make-up and got ready for bed. Part of her felt guilty about meting out justice on her own but she knew Ric was above the law and nothing would ever happen to him. Picking on the elderly lady in the bingo hall was the last red line he'd crossed. Unforgivable. One asshole tuned up and it felt disturbingly good.

Maybe Tammy was a vicious alter ego she'd get attached to.

10

DENTAL PLAN

Next morning the women's locker room at the Bubbles Car Wash was buzzing. Tammy said nothing as she changed from the red heels to loafer shoes with the killer laces. The other girls from the early morning shift whispered with excitement.

"Watch out for Ric, today. He's pissed!" said Mindy.

"Why?" asked Fay.

"Did you see his mouth?" said Mindy.

"No. Why?"

"A big gang jumped him last night, back of the Bingo hall. Busted a bunch of his teeth and a couple of fingers." Mindy made a mock sad face. "He woke up in the dumpster. Lucky they didn't slit his throat."

"Or unlucky for us," said Fay gloomily.

"Ric said he fought off two or three of them but got overwhelmed. He was so brave," snorted Mindy, rolling her eyes.

Tammy smiled to herself. Ric would never find out.

She was getting used to meeting with her handler, Alfred, using the pop can signal. They made sure meeting places were rotated. Clues with her phone chip and notes were passed to him. She wasn't a foot in a shoe washed up on a beach so it was all good. At least so far.

Today Tammy saw Alfred was nervous. He fidgeted on the bench as they spoke and she passed him information.

"What's up, Al? Everything going alright?"

He considered, then spoke, "It's all going smoothly."

"Is that a bad thing?"

"Sometimes."

"...not following you," said Tammy, puzzled.

"Smooth sailing makes me nervous because nobody asks the hard questions about what's going on or why are we doing this. Sometimes smooth means a lot of people know what's going on... too many people."

"You're not a fan of spreading information?"

"I only tell a minimum, enough to serve a purpose. Barest, need to know. I learned that in Intel. Everything you say and do can provide pieces for a puzzle. Someone puts it together and you get killed. Or someone else does."

"Is information manageable?" asked Tammy, a bit spooked.

"Yes, if you manage to say as little as possible to people who keep their mouths shut."

"Even if the bosses demand it?"

"Especially if the bosses demand it! Higher ups don't know what the stakes are down here. They sleep safely in their beds every night. The less those assholes know the better."

Tammy said nothing. She was glad to be on her way.

———

BOB SURPRISED her by taking her to a nice restaurant, skipping the basic diners they usually frequented. He wore a nice suit and tie while she wore a cheap, short cocktail dress with the killer red high heels. Classic sketchy couple.

The owner knew him, taking them to a corner booth with a wink and a nod. The place was dark with red carpets on the floor and matching red velour upholstery on the seats. The place had recently been renovated.

"Wine?" he asked, clearly wanting to make a good impression.

"Of course." Tammy dreaded drinking and saying too much. Alcohol makes for tales which make for dead men and women and sneakers wash up on beaches.

The waiter opened the bubbly with a flourish and filled both their glasses. Bob offered a toast. "Be brave," he proclaimed with a smile, clinking her glass.

Be brave?

They ordered. Bob had a steak and spaghetti while she had the Moussaka. She'd have ordered spaghetti too but she usually sprayed sauce all over her dress. Maybe on Bob's white shirt, too, and he *was* a killer.

They sat in happy silence, making small talk until Bob's phone rang.

He looked at the screen. "Excuse me." His eye brows went up. "Sorry, I have to take this."

He walked away and she didn't see him again for an hour.

———

Zoo PICKED up Bob at the door of the restaurant, with Bob jumping in as soon as Zoo's ugly blue sedan stopped.

"Sorry Bob. I didn't know what else to do."

"It's okay. Let's visit them and send a message. Leave one to run so he'll tell his friends. This won't take long and I'll be back before Tammy finishes dinner."

Zoo speeded off, confidently covering about six blocks, then turning right into an alley, slamming on his brakes behind the deserted warehouse. Wordlessly, they both donned disposable gloves. Bob pulled out his revolver. Keeps the brass. Zoo pulled a bat from behind his seat. He loved this part of his job.

It was a desolate part of the industrial park. High fences and poor lighting. No snoopers to look down from any apartments.

Zoo watched as Bob quietly walked up to the fence and carefully looked over it, held up three fingers, then two fingers with a cut motion across his throat, then one finger and pointed to Zoo's bat.

Zoo nodded.

They tip-toed to an open gate, surveyed and stepped through. They surprised three men pushing high-end cars into a grey shipping container. The one on the left guided a car in while the other two pushed it carefully inside.

"What are you doing?" asked Bob, as if he didn't know, his calm voice punching through the night air like a bullet.

The men stopped, turned menacingly towards them, all tattooed up, full-patch bikers and made a show of it. They faced Bob and Zoo. "What's it to ya?" one asked, fearlessly. His arrogance vanished when he spotted Bob's gun pointed at him.

Bob spoke in a neighborly manner while holding his pistol. "You guys! We've talked about this. Keep to yourselves and stay in your area and we'll get along just fine—yet here you are stealing cars from our district. Tsk-tsk."

"Who are you to tell us what to do, assholes," demanded the leader.

Bob frowned and shook his head, obviously perplexed. "You must be new. Am I right?"

The guy stood with his mouth gaping before he snapped it shut.

"Yeah—the new guy," Bob concluded. "Shall I say I'm a spokesman from an adjacent business and we don't like your attitude?" Bob's gun popped up, shooting the two who stood just inside the container. The surviving man stood outside, quaking in his boots. Bob gestured his gun at the man. "That makes you the messenger so take this back to your gang. Stay away. Zoo has something you can show your buddies."

Zoo strolled forward, his bat flashing out, striking the man's shoulder, then his left knee in quick succession. The biker collapsed in a writhing heap. Zoo grunted, "Show and tell."

"No! No! Enough!" the man whined. "We'll stay away."

"Has our message appealed to your sense of caution?" asked Bob, reasonably.

"Yes. I'll tell them!"

"Zoo, let's let this man escape tonight. A bit of mercy might smooth over this ugly situation. Some diplomacy." Bob winked and asked the writhing man, "Got a phone so you can call someone for help?"

The man reached into his pocket with his only useable arm, pulling out a cell phone while Zoo idly watched, struggling to hold the phone up enough to push a call button. Zoo's bat immediately smashed his phone and the hand holding it.

Zoo added, "We have excellent medical in Canada."

"Maybe run along, before we change our minds?" said Bob.

The man struggled away, grunting and crying. They heard a vehicle start up and drive away, steering uncertainly.

Zoo and Bob pushed dead arms and legs into the shipping container with the cars and closed the big doors. Zoo used the specially marked lock the bikers had so thoughtfully left behind. All the longshoremen knew it was death to touch this lock. It meant move this container and say nothing.

Bob looked down, and texted, *Container pick up, ASAP. Old Fine Foods W/H, east side.*

"Their usual container guys?" asked Zoo.

"Yes. Same one we all use." Bob looked up, "My dinner's getting cold so let's be on our way."

Zoo and Bob said nothing as they drove. They moved to the right lane on the Jacques Cartier Bridge where Bob tossed the gun and

Zoo's bat into the river. Disposable gloves were dropped on the rough rusty bridge decking and would be pulverized.

Zoo was unconcerned about anyone finding out their evenings business. Nobody watched or would admit it if they did. It would be called an internal struggle between low-lives. Nobody talks. No need to be concerned—unless it's an informer, of course.

———

TAMMY HAD LONG since finished dinner and was idly looking at her phone over coffee. She wasn't sure if she was supposed to stay or go but Bob was very old school and she didn't have anywhere else to go. Sit and wait.

If she had only brought her pick up. So far, she had only used it a few times and really didn't know much about it. Was it bugged? She should check it with her laptop, sometime.

Bland white, simple looking and powerful. Solid and banal at the same time. It was very nicely detailed for her so there wasn't a speck of dust, hair, drop of blood or errant shard of spleen. Zoo's old meat wagon.

She'd noticed the truck's open box had been thoroughly cleaned down to the metal and painted over to a smooth gloss. No wood or cracks to harbour blood or bone.

Sitting here Tammy thought about this life of an informer. It was exciting, the food was good, and she was barely accountable to anyone. It had crossed her mind she could 'go across' to the dark side and live with Bob happily-ever-after, permanently. Would her supervisors hunt her down or always wonder what her game was and leave her alone? Deep cover or gone rogue?

What a peculiar life she led.

Finally, she spotted Bob coming out of the restaurant bathroom. Needed to wash his hands, apparently. He came up to her with a big smile and kissed her. The waiter brought out his order, placing it in front of him.

"Sorry I'm late. You didn't have to wait, you know."

"I don't mind. Go ahead and eat."

She sat quietly while Bob ate, occasionally pausing to gulp from his wine glass. He was finished in record time. Tammy romantically dabbed his lips with her napkin. "Tasty?"

"Good! I was hungry."

"Busy night?" she asked, trying to keep as bland a tone as possible.

"Yes." He paused, as if considering taking her into his confidence. "We had an issue to deal with. Competition was trying to muscle into our territory. It's never ending."

"A new crowd or always the same?" She asked vaguely. Let him talk.

"Bikers. Normally we usually come to some agreement with anyone new and everyone gets along."

"These bikers don't work that way?" she asked.

"No. Bikers think they own the fucking world. If they aren't fighting amongst themselves, they're bothering us. They assimilate like 'the Borg'."

What's a Borg? "Is this a new thing?" she asked.

"Not really. We knew they were coming. It surprised us how they did it. They took over the area by acquiring rival gangs."

"Buying other companies like Wal-Mart?"

"Yes. They even have their own structure, complete with supervisors, policy and procedures. If the supervisors are bumped off, they just get more."

"The heads grow back?" she asked.

"They sure do. They'll be growing a couple right now. Buggers."

Tammy watched as Bob described this altercation with no more emotion than he would have dealt with a rabbit infestation in his backyard. Chilling.

"A couple? You mean you... *shot* two?" She widened her eyes with worry for him. "Won't the cops trace the bodies? Or do you and

Zoo always outsmart them?" She wondered if she'd stepped across the girlfriend-boyfriend line.

Bob smiled smugly, looking around the empty part of the restaurant. "The trick is disposable gloves, use a stolen gun once and toss it and never leave a body. No corpse, DNA or bullet—no case. That biker will never talk—unless he's an informer—which is unlikely. Informers get special treatment."

She put her arm around him and laid her head on his shoulder with a sigh of contentment. "You're so smart, Bob." *I'm such a phony.*

Bob perked up, looking at her nervously. "What do you have happening next Tuesday evening?"

Bob nervous?

"Nothing on the schedule," she said with a sweet smile. "Why?" *Missing bingo and I'm on a win streak? Fuck!*

"I'm inviting you home for dinner with my family. What do you say? Pick you up at five?"

Holy moly! "Oh, that would be lovely!" She hugged him.

"And dress like a school teacher," he said sternly, looking her over.

"Sure." School teacher?

"Ma and Papa think all my girlfriends are school teachers."

"Ah."

11

GUESS WHO'S COMING TO DINNER

Bob nervously watched the dinner date approaching. He hated these but his Papa always insisted, regardless if he had a steady or not. His mom didn't care, and his sister Eva always made a scene about something. In any case, the girls he brought were horrified at how dinner went, with few willing to speak to him afterwards. Just as well.

Bob had hoped his parents would like the girls he brought home but so far they hated them all. Too this or too that. What if she found out what "the family" was really all about?

His folks worried his girls were crackheads looking for cash or plants by the mob competitors or even informers. The girls knew too much—something would have to be done so don't get too attached.

Zoo was right when he said Bob's steady dalliances never ended well... for the girlfriends.

———

Tammy was nervous about dinner with Bob's family. It was one thing to skulk around, pretending she was someone she wasn't in the car wash or the bingo hall but quite another to show up at her boyfriend's family home and maintain her informer role going under intense family scrutiny.

She dressed as conservatively and normally as she could. Minimal make up, sensible shoes, no cleavage. She even dug out a pair of glasses to wear. Tammy did need them on occasion to read fine print, so it wasn't actually a lie. It struck her as funny that she would be a bogus person, an informant, worried about a little lie with the glasses. The least of her issues.

What had Bob told his family about her?

She carefully locked her door, made a subtle mark on it and passed the front desk. The desk clerk, a.k.a. Shirley Mac, pointed a finger at her and winked. Tammy paused and turned to Shirley Mac and said, "Meeting Bob's family."

Shirley's smile turned to concern.

"He's picking me up at the 'Sally Ann' down the block."

"Careful."

"Yup." Tammy left and arrived in front of the tired looking Salvation Army building. Two hookers in front gave her the evil eye. Territory. Luckily Bob arrived just after five, pulling up in a big Ford sedan. *Big trunk. I wonder if someone's in there.*

She slid in beside him and they drove off.

"Very nice suit, Bob. You're so handsome," she gushed.

"You look very nice, too. Very... school teacher-ish. I like it."

"Thank you."

"Something about my family you should know. Papa ran our business for years until his heart wouldn't take it, then I took over. He has a bit of a temper."

The head mafia guy with a bad temper. Not good.

"Ma's a sweetie, though. She's as old fashioned as it gets."

"Sounds nice."

"My sister Eva is a drama queen. She's always going to move away but never does. A conversation piece."

"How old is she?"

"Twenty-eight. She's a social worker. Eva loves her job but my parents keep telling her to get a man and have a bunch of kids."

"Maybe she's not ready for a family," said Tammy, immediately regretting it. Bob said nothing more.

Conversations with Bob were always the same. Better to speak of murder methods than family.

Bob parked the car in front of the high double steel gate. It had a big remote latching mechanism. He looked around before pulling out his phone and dialing a number and speaking to someone. "Yes. It's Bob with a date. *Bob Carzoni!* They're my parents, you moron! Yes. Fine. We'll wait."

Bob put his phone away and smiled at her. "Security people are such dick heads. We have a few minutes."

Tammy felt awkward, sitting in silence. She put her arm around him, and they sat and waited. After eleven minutes they heard the gate buzz and a little LED light glowed, their signal to pull it open.

"Looks like those assholes got around to us."

They went out and through the gate. It was an old home with a high, black steel fence, gothic style with tall nasty spikes in the tops. The yard was worn with brown grass and dead flowers everywhere. She noticed the subtle vidcam around the corners, watching. They looked outwards *and* inwards. Was someone watching to prevent intrusion or prevent escape?

The walk through the dead crunchy grass to the front door reminded Tammy of the Haunted Mansion in Disneyland. The area was grim and dark. The plants and trees were ambitiously planted at some point, only to grow in and look forgotten. Either the gardener had lost interest, or they'd lost their gardener.

The front door of the house looked severe and needed a coat of paint. For a brief moment it reminded her of the heavy, specially built doors her police instructors spoke of in cop school. Tough to batter down in a hurry. Got a tank?

A bright porch light came on, intensely shining on them as they stood. Bob rang the doorbell and they waited. Irritating. She saw the door eye hole darken as someone peered out at them.

"Open the fucking door!" Bob called impatiently.

She was surprised at how irritable Bob was getting. He murders and beats people with hardly a comment and here he was almost in a rage.

The door finally creaked open, slowly. An old face surveyed them suspiciously. Bob barged past him with Tammy scurrying close behind.

A big old man stood in the dark hallway, gun in a shoulder holster. He must have been eighty. For a few seconds she thought he was Bob's dad but in fact the old man was the butler-bodyguard. She imagined him as an elderly version of Bob in his declining years. After dumping their coats on him, Bob took her hand and towed her through the hall, heading for a room with lights on, which proved to be a living room area. An elderly couple stood up stiffly as Bob approached. They reluctantly hugged Bob, cold and formal, as if embarrassed. Tammy was ignored.

His mom was short, swarthy and stout, sporting a huge black eye. The long blue dress she wore was tired and old, making her look frumpy. Her hair looked like a jet-black mop plopped down onto her head like a mushroom cap. She didn't smile at seeing Bob or Tammy. Grim.

His papa looked like a taller version of Zoo. He was almost six-foot-tall with wide shoulders and a huge belly. His hair was almost a clone of Bob's mother's mop hairdo.

Got them on a two-for-one sale?

Papa had a fearsome, unsmiling face. His hands were huge and hairy, like an ogre.

Bob glanced in the corner of the room at a young woman, barely acknowledging her.

Was this his sister Eva?

"Ma, Papa; I'd like you to meet my...Tammy."

Just Tammy? Not my girlfriend? My date?

"Hello," she said weakly and awkwardly as they simply shifted their gazes to her in silence. What could she say? *Hi, I'm a cop pretending to be a drug mule while informing on your son who's a serial killer. Nice to meet y'all.*

The father eventually mumbled a greeting while the mother and sister said nothing.

Eva, the sister, leaned forward with her head lowered. She made no effort to smile. Tammy thought she looked older than her years with a tired face and graying hair. No mop top. Little effort had gone into her hair or make up. Her clothing was bland.

After introductions, a large dog leaped up from his bed in the corner and clumped to her, wagging his tail. She thought he was a Great Dane of some kind. Huge, drooling, bimbo hound. First thing he did was shove his nose under her dress and snort and she had to gently push him away. Everyone watched dumbly, silently.

The only one here showing any interest in their guest was the dog.

Bob's dad finally grunted, "Domino! Go back to bed."

The dog didn't move until Eva sullenly got up from her chair, grabbed the dog's collar and dragged it over to its bed in the corner.

"Sit," said Pa.

Tammy sat in a single chair while Bob sat over by his mother on a couch. They sat in silence, awkwardly listening to the big dog lick himself with noisy slurps.

Bob sat, hands together beside his mom, glancing back and forth between his dad and his mom's huge black eye. Finally, he blurted out, "How'd you get the black eye, ma?"

Tammy heard her say something in Italian to Bob along the lines of 'fell' or 'tripped and fell.'

Bob shook his head, stood and angrily pointed his finger at his dad. "You did this!"

The dad jumped out of his chair and yelled at Bob in Italian.

Soon they were both waving their arms and pointing dramatically. The mom and Eva ignored them as the argument got more animated. Tammy understood some of what they were saying, and it sounded like an old discussion about domestic abuse. Beating up mom.

Eva sighed, stood up and walked over to Tammy. "Let me show the rest of the house."

When they got out of earshot, Eva added, "This argument will go on for about half an hour, then Papa will need his blood pressure meds. Follow me."

Eva shuffled along as if life had wrung her dry. They went down the hall, turning left into what looked like a billiard room. Eva droned, "This house was originally built by my grandfather Giorgio Carzoni. Yes, he was the original Don of the Organization in Montreal. Powerful and rich. This mansion cost him ten million dollars. Nothing but the best materials and workmanship. A week before he was scheduled to move in, someone blew his car up. Ka-boom!"

Tammy jumped a little.

"Papa got the house and moved in right afterwards." Eva looked at her strangely. "There was some rumour that Papa blew up Grandpa to get his house and the organization. It didn't stick."

Tammy was shocked.

"This billiard table is called a Luxury Billboard which costs about the same as a decent Ferrari. Gold leaf and ivory, everything. Papa decides who plays. We never touch it. We're afraid to."

"Never?" asked Tammy.

Eva walked over to the back corner and pointed her finger at a black hole. "Papa and one of his buddies were playing and one of them lost their temper."

"Lost the game?"

"Yes. and lost 200g's, then shot a hole in his fancy table. Papa left the hole as a trophy."

"Ah."

"Follow me to the conservatory."

They walked around to the back of the gigantic house. Eva

looked into her eyes, "Bob is taken with you, Tammy. He said you are quite bright and not a coke head."

Tammy was careful to be non-committal with her reply. "Ah... Bob and I get along very well."

Eva and Tammy arrived at a large, glassed-in conservatory. It was well lighted. Despite the opulent setting all the plants were brown and dead.

Tammy glanced around. "Quite a room. This must have been lovely three months ago. What happened?"

Eva shook her head, ignoring her question, murmuring, "Did you notice the senior citizen we have at the door? He's seventy-nine but works cheap. Our previous bodyguard poisoned the water supply because Papa didn't give him a raise."

"Your last guy poisoned your water supply? Seems drastic. Was he after more than a raise?"

Eva sighed. "We'll never know."

Likely Bob and Zoo took the errant bodyguard for a little ride to a funeral.

Their next stop was the library. They could barely hear Bob and his dad arguing from here. Eva put her arm around Tammy's head and drew close to her ear, whispering, "My family is so violent. Nothing is sacred. Do you understand?"

Tammy nodded.

Eva continued in a desperate whisper, "No you don't. All Bob's girlfriends disappear or are dead." She let go of Tammy's head and resumed her touring voice. "This is my grandfather's library. It contains the top one hundred classic books of all time though he's never read even one. Papa smokes his cigars in this room and sips brandy."

Tammy tried to digest the secret Eva told her.

Bob and Papa's arguing died down. Eva led Tammy back to the dining room. Ma doled out servings of M&M frozen lasagna which was eaten in stone silence. The only sounds were clinking cutlery and Papa's dentures making the occasional sucking sound.

"This lasagna's too salty," announced Eva.

Coffee and cherry pie was handed out afterward.

Eva pointed out, "This pie is still frozen Ma."

At eight-thirty Bob stood up from the table. "Gotta go. Thanks." He kissed his mom on the cheek and Tammy thanked his parents for dinner and said goodbye. She followed Bob out the front door, not daring to say anything. This abnormally calm man was furious.

It was a dead silent drive home. She simply got out of the car in front of the 'Sally Ann' and he drove away. Strange.

Shirley Mac sat at the desk watching Tammy come in. She looked around then whispered, "How was supper with the Carzoni's?"

"Nobody died, especially me, so it's all good," Tammy told her.

12

DINNER AFTERMATH

Bob treated her differently after that tense family dinner. He hardly spoke to her or acknowledged her for weeks. Their relationship evaporated and he didn't say why but she had her suspicions Papa viewed her as a liability. She had to admit Bob the killer had hurt her feelings.

She wondered if Bob's Papa suggested he get rid of her. It would have been helpful to eavesdrop on their conversation but that wasn't happening while Eva gave her a tour of the creepy mansion. Eva didn't come right out and say what actually happened to Bob's past girlfriends but she *had* warned her, which chilled Tammy to the bone. Shirley Mac checked Bob's romantic history and noted a half dozen of his steadies were unaccounted for after approximately six months which coincided with the amount of time that Tammy had now been with Bob.

Had the others gone home; OD'd; become nuns?

Had Tammy reached her "best before" date in Carzoni world?

TAMMY SECRETLY ARRANGED a meeting with Alfred. He had become a valuable guide and mentor over the months. He had more experience than he let on and she'd come to appreciate his guidance.

She saw where he was seated and carefully sat down on the other end of his bench, dodging the bird shit. Al was on the end of a bench feeding popcorn to pigeons and any other birds crowding in. They swarmed him in a frenzy, as if this kernel of popcorn decided life or death, all, it seemed, were as oblivious to the humans as the humans were to them. Each species with their own crisis to deal with.

She asked, "Hi. Gotta phone chip for you. Big fish, this time."

Alfred nodded, then quietly said, "Put it in that packet of smokes beside you and throw it in front of your feet."

Tammy did as she was asked. In a minute an errant, noisy little dog ran up, snapped at her, grabbed the package of smokes and ran away. Surprised, Tammy was ready to run after it. "Fucking dog snagged it!"

Al calmed her down. "Relax. The lady with the stroller has a sick kid, today. The dog does the work, anyway. That's my dog, Pickles."

They sat in silence. Tammy said in a low voice, "I had dinner with Bob's parents last Tuesday."

"The *Carzonis*?" he gasped, frozen on the bench.

It was as if she said she'd dined with Hitler and Stalin.

"Yup."

He stopped throwing popcorn, turning to her, "How was it?"

"Like dinner with the Addams Family except they're killers and wife beaters."

Alfred snorted, "What did you notice?"

"I wasn't sure if they were securely guarded or being held captive. It was a huge deal for Bob and I to get in and see them."

Al tossed a few more kernels, "We suspect his folks are being kept under watch in some weird ransom deal. Not a nice bunch."

She added, "They had a young bodyguard that didn't work out so they got some low budget pensioner to fill in."

Al smiled. "Funny story, sort of. Apparently Bob's anger-management challenged Papa caught that young bodyguard screwing Eva in her room and shot him in the ass, mid-stroke, if you know what I mean. The guy ran around the house naked, screaming and bleeding and Papa couldn't catch him."

"Went out with a smile?"

"Possibly. Ma got tired of the shooting and commotion and called Bob and Zoo to finish the job and get rid of the body, somewhere. We never found him."

"In concrete. No body, no case, as Bob always says," she added, shocked at how easily the words fell from her lips.

Al looked at her, surprised, "He's correct, by and large. The DNA, method used, bullets and details of the way the murder was carried out is gone."

Tammy added, "Conviction is in the details."

"Correct," Al confirmed.

Tammy added, "Speaking of bodies, I suspect Bob and Zoo killed two bikers August 21st, about seven to nine pm. I think I was his alibi, waiting in Mondo's."

Alfred glanced at her. "Fits. Interpol heard of two bodies in a steel container with some stolen cars, in Logos, Nigeria. Cooked in the heat to ripe perfection."

"Yummy." Tammy stuck her tongue out. "Evidence?"

"None that we could get at. The bodies had been removed upon arrival on a container ship and dumped in a nearby river. Local cops traced them back to the container and the biker gang."

"Unusually efficient for the Nigerian police. Aren't they usually corrupt?" asked Tammy.

"Yes, very much so but the Nigerian buyer who got the cars was likely pissed at the bikers for stinking up his cars with corpses. None sellable except for the ragtop. He paid to trace it all back, then threw the bodies back in the river so as not to implicate his source for the high-end cars."

Al's dog ran back to him, dropping a slimy gray tennis ball into his hand. He smoothly squeezed the ball, pulled out the chip and slid it over to her.

Tammy slipped the chip into a pocket while asking, "Eva said Bob's girlfriends tend to disappear after the visit with Mom and Dad. True?"

"Let me check on that. We've never had someone be Bob's girl, before. Let me look into it. Sleep with one eye open."

"Comforting."

"Time to go?"

"Yes." Tammy got up and slowly walked away.

She took great care getting back to her little apartment. Tammy never brought her truck to any meeting as they could easily track her movements. Switching buses, a cab and maybe throw in a subway ride to keep them confused. If they knew it was Tammy, then it wouldn't take a rocket scientist to know her destination had to be the 'Ville-Marie'. At the front desk a disguised Shirley Mac was watching her back but shit happens very quickly.

Tammy made eye contact with Shirley, then hustled to her apartment and changed clothes. Time to go to the two to eight o'clock shift at the car wash. No Bingo tonight. She hit the can, changed, ate and was in and out in thirty minutes, winking at Shirley at the front desk as she left.

———

HER BOSSES ASSIGNED her to watch over Tammy after Beth's foot had washed up on shore. Consequently, Shirley Mac sat at the grubby desk in the Ville-Marie Hotel. It was a dump but not as bad as others in the neighborhood. This latest informer job had been a long one for both her and "Tammy".

Beth. Five-star fuck up. A bolt from the blue. Going smoothly. Nobody could say what actually happened to her. No body, no story other than which brand of shoe was on sale about that time. Green toenail polish on the toenails of the foot inside. Matched Beth's DNA.

Shirley was getting tired of this make-up. Parts of her skin were getting strange blotches. Long term face paint was taking its toll, though it did make her look authentic. Her gun chafed welts on her skin while she sat at the desk. She had no personal life. She had a nice house but was never in it.

Her every instinct was to wind this investigation up before someone died. Eventually someone blabs, makes a mistake, or a piece of the puzzle fits in and the informer's foot turns up in a pink Nike.

————

TAMMY WAS RUNNING LATE, barely getting to the car wash in time. Ric gave her the evil eye as she ran into the locker room to get changed. One of the girls going off shift told her, "Bob wants to see you," her expression sympathetic.

Uh-oh.

Tammy left the locker room, ending up at the door to Bob's office. Just as she was ready to knock, she paused, listening to the loud conversation. Sounded unhappy. She looked around, then leaned an ear to the door.

"No Zoo! I'm not getting rid of her," said Bob, strained.

"Why not? She's bad news," said Zoo.

Me? Tammy thought, breaking into a sweat.

"I don't care. She's manageable. Besides, what makes you think she's a stoolie?" asked Bob, heated.

"I have my sources. They followed her around and found she actually lives in Ottawa, not the Ville-Marie."

"So she's a watcher for someone?" asked Bob.

"I think so."

Bob went quiet. After a minute he said, barely audibly, "Yes, let's get rid of her."

"Tomorrow after breakfast? Ten-ish? Let's do IHOP first," said Zoo, casually. "I have a coupon."

"Yeah, some waffles and coffee first."

Holy! Ottawa? That's Shirley Mac!

Tammy slipped away to the back alley, hiding behind a pile of wooden pallets. Pulling out her phone she texted Shirley Mac. "Your cover's blown! Coming for you tomorrow."

She sat down and took a breath. Should *I* run, too? Can't. If I can hang in for one more week I can load up evidence from the latest files in Bob's office computer. They have a major drug move happening. I can still get the names, dates and places. Best and worse time, ever. I need to talk to someone, today.

———

ALFRED WAITED for her on the park bench. A young couple slept on a blanket on the grass about two hundred meters away. No doubt they were cops there to watch them. Sleepers. Funny.

Tammy sat at the far end saying nothing. Al sat at the other end silently with a medium sized popcorn bag separating them but he didn't feed the pigeons from it. Odd.

Al said in a low voice, "All Bob's ex's are dead or missing."

Tammy let that sink in. "Dandy. So I need to get my carcass out of here, ASAP."

He looked around casually. "I'd say so."

"Except I can't. I need a week. Something big is coming. I want the files from Bob's office computer."

Al looked over at her. "Shirley's gone so there's nobody to watch *your* back."

"I know. It wouldn't be hard to figure out who's living in the Ville-Marie but I've spent too much time in this to run now."

He shook his head and looked at her feet. "What kind of shoe do you have, so I can identify you later? What color toenail polish?"

"Ha Ha."

Al grinned, enjoying the dark humour. "You'd better take precautions. How would they take you down, assuming they will at some point? You need to think like Bob."

Tammy thought, "At the car wash, but it's broad daylight with a lot of people nearby, delivery people, cameras. Snatching someone, getting away and disposing of a body is hazardous. Obviously, I'm suspicious and won't go out in the dark. I think Bob would know where I am and just come for a friendly visit. He'll figure out I'm trapped. My place has one door in and one window out but it drops two stories to a parking lot. Even us rats have to sleep."

"Exactly. Construction yards of full of workers during the day. Bob and Zoo like concrete to hide bodies at night."

Like that concrete job he was admiring the other day... the new Pharmaprix building. Big and close. She thought, late night folks looking for toilet paper and disposable diapers walking over my final resting place? Nice.

Al nudged the paper bag. "Take this popcorn bag and set it up at your door."

"Am I going to scare them to death with the sound of corn popping?" Tammy asked, annoyed.

"You could try it but I have a better set up," Al said. "Try a hidden camera, tape measure and a pencil."

She looked at him as if he had a pigeon pecking his head.

Ignoring her quizzical look, he continued, "When they figure out where you live, they'll come to your door. Set up the hidden camera and watch the little screen on your computer. Set it to alarm. Mark the inside of your door at Bob and Zoo's vitals, about where they stand. Shoot the little pencil crosses twice each. X marks the spots."

Tammy swallowed hard.

"We'll try to warn you when they come but be ready with this if you get surprised."

She nodded and imagined the huge deal it would be if the media got the news of her sleeping with a drug lord. The crime family's lawyers would have a field day with this information. All those scummy bastards would go free after Tammy and Shirley Mac risked their lives to put them away.

And they'd be gunning for her later. She needed a much better plan than what Alfred offered. Bumping off Bob and Zoo would tie up some loose ends. Then she realized, with a chill—*I'm thinking like a killer*.

Al solemnly added, "One way or another this is our last meeting. You never got that bag from me. It will be as if I never existed because I don't. Take care." This time it was Al who stood first, pulled out his walker from the side of the bench and inched away. After a few minutes the "sleepers" in the park nearby got up and went to destinations unknown.

Abandoned, Tammy sat, immersed in her own deadly thoughts.

As she sat and considered her plight, Shirley Mac quietly vacated her desk at the Ville-Marie and never returned.

———

At police HQ Shirley Mac and her boss watched the laptop computer screen carefully. It oversaw her old desk area in the Ville-Marie. Nothing had happened so far. They waited impatiently.

"Oh...there they are...Bob and Zoo!"

Shirley's old vidcam showed two men enter the old Ville-Marie Hotel and walk up to the main desk. One of them pushed away an old man, Shirley's replacement, at the desk while the other man grabbed the guest book.

Phil, her boss said, "I'm glad you didn't remove that hidden vidcam. Handy."

"I was pressed for time. It worked out."

They both watched as one of the men in the screen took the room ledger while the other shoved the old man over backwards.

"I guess he didn't want to give up that ledger," said Shirley Mac.

"Is that ledger going to give Tammy away?"

"Nope. She always signed in with a different name every time. A phony name from a bogus person."

"What a tangled web we weave," mumbled Phil, wryly.

13

DEADLY PREPARATIONS

Tammy drove her pickup truck back to her chateau, as she derisively referred to it, eight o'clock that night. Looking up, she spotted a parking place directly under her room window. Carefully she backed into the spot.

Carrying the popcorn bag, she went past the front desk of the Ville-Marie, glancing at the spot where Shirley Mac used to sit. The replacement old man was missing. Empty desk. Pickled or sick? She kept going.

Stopping at her door she glanced at the right middle edge to see if a tiny bit of paper was still there. She had carefully stuck it there with a lick of spit to see if she had any snoopers while she was gone. Cheap and easy spy trick. It was there, safe and sound.

Once inside, she dug through her old loaf of bread and found two slices that weren't moldy. Need to buy bread, next time. Maybe she'd be gone by then... or dead. She made herself a quick peanut butter sandwich with the TV on loud enough to muffle her evening labours.

"This is Harry Fast of ...Fax News, Detroit. We have Sandy Thompson at a live White house event in Washington. Sandy?"

"Hello Harry. Communications Director Norah Crena

announced early home school successes. "Ha ha, I see we only have five reporters and forty-five empty chairs in the press briefing room."

There was some noise from the reporters, then quiet.

"We've had a successful first quarter of the new home school program. It went extremely well. There was an added bonus of not one school student shooting victim in three months! Questions?"

"Lily Beck; Reuters News Service. Isn't the real reason there have been no shootings that fact that your government locked up all guns in churches and out of reach of shooters, something they should have done a hundred years ago?"

"Not at all Lily, the guns are stored in churches to give better access of personal weapons of the NRA for a volunteer militia as per the Second Amendment, 'A well-regulated Militia, being necessary to the security of a free state, the right of the people to keep and bear Arms, shall not be infringed.' We are just following the US Constitution which you should read, sometime, Lily. No more questions."

"Back to you, Harry."

"Thank you, Sandy. The fewest school shootings in a hundred years. Amazing! And now we have the national anthem sung with kazoos by the Southern Methodist Church Choir in Atlanta."

"Odd," Terry said aloud, as she put her dish in the sink along with the growing pile. *Should wash all this at some point. Maybe tomorrow, when people aren't trying to kill me.*

She dumped the contents of the popcorn bag on the bed. Setting up the wireless vidcam came first. It looked like a simple and disgusting rolled, used fly strip. The roll was the camera with a real sticky strip with actual dead flies hanging from the bottom. Yummy. Nobody would touch that.

She made sure the signal picked up on her beat-up laptop. While she was at it, she used the computer's stealth bug sniffer to sweep her apartment and pickup truck. All clean except for the one in her phone which was her emergency tracer to Shirley Mac.

Tammy crept into the deserted hallway and stuck the fly killer vidcam high on the wall with a thumb tack, as far as she could reach.

Next, she went in the hall to measure the heights of Bob and Zoo. Leaving the door open she figured out the angle of her gun hand pointing at their heart areas, then closed the door, marking two spots with little x's on the inside of her door.

She went back out and moved hall light bulbs around until the one outside her door worked. There would be shadows at the base of her door if she had visitors.

Tammy deactivated the cell phone tracer with her laptop as a precaution, texting Shirley Mac to say the loss of signal was alright. No followers at this point.

Next, she confirmed the line of sight from the vidcam and her door area. She imagined Bob and Zoo standing, waiting, where they usually stood. They always worked together. Bert and Ernie.

Doorway killing zone, one way or another.

The deadly LTR pistol and silencer were dug out of their snug hiding place. She filled the magazine with the powerful hard nose bullets. It would get through the door slightly damaged and hopefully won't go all the way through the bodies. No bullets left in walls... in theory.

What to do with the evidence after the shooting? She considered burning the place down but couldn't be sure an innocent bystander wouldn't get caught up in it. Invariably, the cops smell a rat at a fire and expected something was going on under the smouldering rubble. Besides, there's always something left to further a case after a blaze. Bad idea.

Carrying out a successful murder is hard.

———

After Tammy's break up with Bob, Ric took the opportunity to be a real prick towards her. Today, she had to sidestep a punch from him. Luckily a customer came up and Ric was distracted from their altercation. She considered driving one of her heel spikes deep into his forehead but decided against it. That might make the national papers. Besides she had files to snitch.

If Ric was getting bold enough to bother her then her time at the car wash must be drawing to a close. He was such a coward when he knew she was sleeping with Bob. Not now. Ric sensed she was "going away" like all the others. The car wash didn't offer severance pay unless they actually severed something, like a finger... or foot.

She needed to stick to her plans.

After a stop at a used clothes store, McDonalds, and London Drugs she made it back to her room. She wolfed down the Mac burger then started to put on her used creepy costume. It was a snug fit but here her "skinny Tammy" look worked in her favour.

The idea of this costume was to look odd enough on skid road for people to ignore her, especially as it was nowhere near Halloween. Looking clearly nuts makes people avoid eye contact unless they too were clearly nuts. Then it became a conversation piece.

Tammy got to work with her makeup, painting a full face bright, sparkly white. Aiming for bizarre. This was more like clown paint. The red lips went badly when the lipstick bled into the white-face paint. She ran out of face-paint so it had to be good enough. The eyes were worse as mascara blended into the white for a wild-eyed look. When she looked into the mirror she cringed. More "Joker" than "Tinker Bell". Shit. It would be the loony bin if a cop spotted her.

Last she put on the long white costume gloves, more beige than white with dirt from past users. She stomped into her red killer high heels and grabbed a cane as a sub for the wand. The heels and cane didn't quite match but so what? Girl's gotta protect herself.

Voila: Scary Tinker Bell!

The real challenge was getting a gun and her knife under the little outfit.

Maybe "Snow White" would have been better? She could have hidden a rocket launcher under *that* huge dress, and nobody would notice but she was in need of something easy to move around in.

Besides, Tinker Bell outfits were on sale and this one was the cleanest and didn't smell.

She picked up the matching purse, sad as it was. It would be handy for lock picking tools, a small flashlight, disposable gloves, a camera and a back-up stick for computer files.

Climbing on the bus was peculiar. She hobbled up the steps of the bus in her heels with a bit of difficulty. Other riders, both intoxicated and sober, ignored her and kept far away. Tammy made sure to turn away from the bus's vidcam. She was sure she'd be identified as a loopy green-suited person with a Joker face, wings, cane, wearing red spike shoes.

A crazed Dorothy on the Wizard of Oz meets Jolly Green Giant's Mini-me?

The cops would be sayin', "So, ya saw Tinker Bell with a Joker face... kinda testy with red shoes, cane...Tinker Bell on crack? I think you're the one smoking the crack, buddy!"

No identification, thanks. Case closed.

Tammy got off the bus, hobbling around the side of the Bubbles Car Wash. It was dark. Nobody around. She chose a familiar rear door under a burned-out entrance light. It was the only one not barred on the inside. After digging out her lock picking tools she easily unlocked the door. The security system started beeping which she stopped with the code 4590. She'd watched Ric and Bob use it many times.

She moved through the wash area, heading for the office. The door clicked open with her pick. Sliding along the wall she dug into her purse and produced a small can of shaving cream, reaching up and spraying it over the room vidcam. Mission impossible on a tight budget.

Sitting down at the office computer she typed in the code she weaseled out of Bob when they were bosom buddies. The code remained "Tammy#1". She nodded smugly to herself and murmured, "I've still got it."

She stuck the info stick into the USB port and pulled over as many files as she could find. Impatiently she finally shut the computer down and dropped the stick down her front into her bra. Gotcha!

She cleaned the shaving cream off the vidcam and slipped out the door. With any luck nobody would know she was here.

Tammy made it home after few different bus rides to confuse any chasers. A team of drunken rugby players propositioned her but were scared off by the paint job on her face or maybe it was the nasty cane.

She needed to get this to Alfred at the special trash can. As per the drill, she bought a can of Fanta pop and drank it. She covered the computer chip with a gum wrapper with the words 'text to confirm ASAP' and dropped it inside the can.

'Find this ASAP, Al,' she thought.

Unknown to her and Alfred, a random homeless bottle collector came by just as she left and beat them to the stash of pop cans. Ten minutes later Alfred arrived, looked in the trash for the Fanta can and saw it was not there. He hobbled north on his walker, stopped and shouted on his phone, "Some bottle collector got here first! Fan out and find that fucking Fanta can!"

Tammy sneaked into the Ville-Marie and to her door, checking her little "has not been disturbed" door marker, then going in and locking up behind her. After a messy clean up and shower she was on the bed, gun in hand with her laptop nearby focused on the door.

Tonight's the night?

Exhausted, she started to doze off, wishing she could jump into the pickup and drive off but she had to stick around for one more day. She needed confirmation they got that computer stick and it had enough to make this informant effort worthwhile. Hopefully she wouldn't have to return. No news about the chip from Bob's computer. Dang.

———

She called in sick next morning. Ric was annoyed but too bad. A breakfast sandwich run was the morning's activity. She listened to her crappy tiny TV and piled up essentials in her hockey bag. There were guns, knives, money and documents hidden all over. Some items were kept and some destroyed.

She disabled her smoke detector and put some paper documents in her sink and put a match to them. The stinky old hotel had a century of smoking soaked into its grimy walls, so nobody will even notice. All she needed was text confirmation of a successful computer file from her burglary and this gig was over. She'd run like hell and needed to be ready.

Her TV babbled:

"This is Harry Fast of ...Fax News, Detroit, with Breaking news from Washington, DC. Here's James Courtney from the White House. James?"

"Harry, the President just dropped a bomb shell minutes ago. Here's what President Jackson said. 'As of right now, we are dismantling the expensive, ineffective and unpatriotic FBI, CIA and NSA until further notice. This saves taxpayers over 100 billion dollars yearly of needless duplication. Local enforcement will continue to do these duties as they have done before the CIA, FBI and NSA were created.'

There you go Harry, the big three are gone."

"Thanks James. We are going back to regular programming."

14

HINDERED ESCAPE

TAMMY CRAMMED HER BAG ON THE FLOOR OF THE FRONT SEAT of her truck, out of sight. Her cash was hidden in one of the various compartments Zoo had installed in the cab. Drug smugglers special.

Come on, Al...text me! Did Al get that computer chip or not? She dared not ask them in case the mob was listening to her phone. One word of confirmation from Alfred and she was gone—her phone in the toilet tank.

She couldn't know Al and his men were frantically scouring the city for her Fanta can.

Tammy paced until darkness fell. The TV became tiresome.

"This is Harry Fast with breaking news! We go to Brad Ascer in the White House...Brad?"

"Hello Harry. We're in the white house briefing room at the President's request, awaiting an important announcement that, according to President Jackson, will affect free speech in America."

There was a sound of hub-bub, someone said, "The president is in the room" and a microphone screeched.

The camera swung and zeroed in on the president looking

around the room, grinning. He said, "Good evening everyone. Today is a great day for America, the constitution and free speech.

"In 1776 our forefathers enshrined many things in our Constitution, one of which is the Right to Free Speech for all Americans."

The Reuters reporter called out in a thick Dutch accent, "Free for Caucasian males."

A security man pointed at him, glaring, as the press gallery laughed.

Jackson ignored him and continued, "Free speech? What does that mean? It means what we want it to mean because it's our own personal vision of truth and nobody else's. Each and every American can say his own version of what he believes in. That will be his truth."

The CNN reporter said, "I believe I don't owe the IRS any money, ever!" and the press gallery laughed.

"Math and money is a different story, Mr. Gordon," Jackson cautioned, then looked brightly around the room. "Questions?"

The gallery erupted. "What about history sir...facts," asked BBC.

"History and facts are what Americans wish them to be. If they believe it, then it's true," replied Jackson. "As we speak, public institutions of history are being closed as there is no need for them. It is about freedom of speech, not what someone deems true or factual. Institutional truth isn't better than your or my truth."

The gallery was stunned.

"So, did Columbus discover America in 1492 or not?" pressed the BBC reporter.

Jackson considered the question. "I don't know—I wasn't there. Does it matter?"

"I was just wondering if we get that as a holiday or not," commented the CBS representative rather plaintively.

"It would be wise to keep track of it along with your wedding anniversary," Jackson shot back with a smile.

The Press chuckled.

"Sir! What about the courts?"

"What about them? Free speech opinions will convince the

judge, jury or not. Facts and logic haven't been in courts for centuries."

"Sir, are you saying courts are ruled by emotion, money and which side they're on?"

Jackson sighed. "Your words, not mine."

"Fax-News sir. So, I can quote something from the Holy Bible, provided I believe it?"

The President shrugged. "Why not? Nobody's sure what it originally said anyway, so how do we know what old scripture said or meant? The Bible was meant to keep up with our times as was God, in my opinion. Free speech."

Press gallery fell silent for a few seconds.

The Post correspondent called out, "No more facts and truth for the nation's newspapers or media?"

Jackson scoffed. "Facts? You guys have been printing fiction and fake news for decades, so it's business as usual. Thank you." The President turned left, exiting the press gallery.

Someone shouted, "Mr. President! Mr. President!"

Brad turned to the camera. "There you have it, Harry. If you believe it, then it's truth and fact."

"Thank you Brad. So there you go, folks. The truth shall set you free and according to our president, it's whatever you want it to be. Oh well. Let's go to Arthur Jones at the zoo to see a new trick they've taught the dolphins."

"Wow, ain't that the truth," Tammy snorted, smiling.

The pacing back and forth in her crappy room didn't relax her. The 'A' plan was to hop in the truck and vamoose as soon as Al confirmed the stick and the info. *Come on, Al...text me!*

She considered making a break for it right now, plan B, but if the info was bad she'd need to make another run on the computer at the car wash. All her disguise stuff was here.

Plan C was the apartment door shootout. The last resort. Hopefully it even works. This all made her need to go to the washroom. Sit and think.

Come on, Al...text me!

She sat down, clutching her phone, staring at it. The sound of "knock-knock" at the door froze her in horror.

BOB STOPPED in front of Zoo's house and waited. He hated to do this to Tammy but as his Papa pointed out, "It was for the good of the company". Like all the others, Tammy got too close, too nosey and had become a liability. He liked her, which made this difficult. Zoo would be there if he chickened out but he never did.

Zoo opened the car door and got in the car. They drove to the Ville-Marie at a safe, legal speed. No need for the cops to stop them and ask questions.

Bob asked, "Go easy on her Zoo. She's off sick today. She's never sick so let's just talk to her a bit, then slip a plastic bag on her head, bit of ether in it and hold on. Clean, fast and painless for her.

"No gun?"

"No gun, Zoo. I want to do her so she never knew what happened."

"You're not bumping off the family cat."

Bob got uncharacteristically angry. "Fuck you! Do it my way—she's my girlfriend."

Zoo nodded. It was always this way with Bob's girls. Too close. "Sure. So, we're gonna all sit on the couch, have a little tea, chit chat, then ..." he made a cut motion across his throat.

Bob's glare was the reply.

They parked their car beside Tammy's truck. Zoo was going to take it afterwards. He always got his truck back from Bob's girls. It was a loaner.

Bob thought as he strolled around the old hotel. Tammy's body was going to the new Pharmaprix concrete floor job. Zoo's buddy even dug a hole special for this, hidden in the corner. A few bags of concrete handy to sprinkle on her, after they dropped her in. Camo.

They walked into the Ville-Marie, past the front desk. Bob smiled as he pointed to the empty chair at the desk.

"Clerk broke his hip. Tsk tsk," said Zoo.

"Deja vu, huh? Weird Tammy lives here, of all places."

Zoo looked at him grimly and murmured, "Murphy's Law."

They both went up to the door to Tammy's room. Bob stood on the left and Zoo the right, just like they always did. Zoo called it chemistry.

Bob tapped on the door politely. A TV blared so she must be home. They waited.

"Poor Tammy is so sick she can't come to the door," whispered Bob.

"I don't like it. Too coincidental," Zoo grunted. Still, he politely knocked, then stood solidly beside Bob.

"You're seeing enemies everywhere you look these days. You need a vacation, man, " Bob told him and wondered if they would have to break the door down. Awkward. What a dreadful way to end a relationship.

Trying to make the best of it.

To Bob's surprise a little black hole appeared in the door in front of him. Instantly he felt something poke his chest. Another hole appeared from the door, right beside it. Bob closed his eyes and never opened them again.

———

ANNOYED, Tammy stood up from the toilet, pulled up her pants and rushed out of the washroom to investigate the knock at the door. *My drunken neighbor wanting a kiss or perhaps two mob killers?*

She consulted the computer screen which beeped. It showed Bob and Zoo! Fuck! Her blood ran cold.

Fighting to keep her emotions in check, she grabbed her LR pistol and silencer lying on the bed, swiftly cocking it under a pillow. She tiptoed to her entrance door, leveled it, aiming at her right pencil marked cross and waited.

"Knock-knock" again. She knew where they stood.

She took a breath after the second knock and squeezed the trigger. In an instant she shot twice through the right, then twice on the left cross. Ping-ping...ping-ping. Her muffled shots were followed by sound of two clumps in the hall. Holding her gun at the ready, she stepped forward, yanked the door open and surveyed the carnage, ready to shoot again.

Seeing both men were down and out with nobody else watching, Tammy shoved the gun behind her belt, reached down and pulled Bob through the doorway by the collar. Zoo was next. The silencer under her belt was burning her skin but she ignored it. After pulling the door closed, she noticed Zoo was alive, pulled her pistol out again and dispatched him with a last killing shot. Bob was dead before he hit the floor.

Bye Bob. It was fun.

Tammy donned disposable gloves, grabbed a rag and quickly wiped anything around the door and nearby wall. No point in doing any more. The cops knew who lived here.

She looked out the door to see if the hallway was clear, then quickly went out, putting large band aids over the bullet holes in her door. The band aids all had smiley faces on them. Crazy temporary camo. She was back inside in a flash, heart screaming.

Time to go. Anything incriminating had to come with her or be hidden right now. For all she knew the cops could be on their way. She went over her mental list as she'd rehearsed.

Get rid of this phone. Burner phones like hers were always traceable enough to be a pain. Picking it up, she noticed a message on it. "Info good. Run. Al."

Finally!

After saving the sim card Tammy lifted the chipped toilet tank and dropped the phone in. Ploop...the burner phone settled in the crud in the bottom. Handful of toilet paper on top. Eww. Nobody looks in the water tank especially with floaties down there.

Stop and catch your breath! Instead, she rushing to the little kitchen table. Hands shaking, she wrote on a piece of paper: "Be warned!"

The clumsiest detective in the known world would find it.

Red herring.

No point in giving investigators a head start. Hopefully this will look like a local spat between gangs. "No danger to the public and two less scumbags in the city," the police spokesman will say. "The city is a better place."

Tammy leaned over, pushed open her window and looked down at her pickup parked below. She heaved Bob out first, watching him land awkwardly but in the back of the pickup box with a thunderous thump. No one came running. Zoo was heavier but she flipped him out the window with the same results—a huge thump at the landing with no local interest.

The neighbors had learned to mind their own business. Good enough. She made a mental note to thank her army trainers who showed her how to efficiently move around the dead and dying on the battlefield.

She saw she had some blood on her but not enough to stop to clean it. There would be time for a change of clothes and shower much later. A bit of blood in the hall and a fair bit on her shitty carpet inside but so what? The Ville-Marie was no stranger to anonymous fights.

At the last second, she went back to her "Be Warned!" note and added, "We watch, Ric—Angels" to the bottom of the paper.

Ric would have some explaining to do when Bob's Guardia gang, the cops or the Angels find this note and no doubt they will. She'd watch the news to see if a shoe washed up on a local beach anytime soon... with Ric's foot in it.

Tammy grabbed her computer and LR pistol. After a quick peek out the doorway she hustled out to her truck, started it up and drove off to the new Pharmaprix construction site.

Bob and Zoo had been quite excited about the concrete part of the project so there must be something of interest to killers. Sure enough, she spotted a dark corner connected with a paved alley.

Driving to that spot she got out and did a quick survey. The holes were dug and ready. After dropping the tailgate, she got back in, moved the truck around, looked out the rear mirror and backed up at a fair speed towards the corner of the concrete job. At the last second, she jammed on the brakes as she hit the trio of bags of concrete serving as a guard rail, launching the inert bodies in the box outwards like a Bugs Bunny cartoon. She exited and went back to see where her load had landed. Bob and Zoo were nicely heaped in the corner.

She liberated one bag of powdered concrete and dumped the contents over the bodies. Camouflaged and invisible. Likely one of Zoo's pals on this job was getting paid to quickly concrete it all over and ask no questions. *Zoo paid to bury himself instead of me.* Ironic.

Time to get out of town. The paved alley left no tire tracks. She cleaned her footprints. Would all be obliterated by construction equipment and workers. Confuse the snoopers.

Tammy drove the truck west in the dark towards Ottawa and home. Goodbye "Tammy" and goodbye "Ville-Marie".

She drove away from the shitty rooming house until her heart stopped pounding which took about an hour. It turned out to be a random drive, really. She spotted a sideroad with a bridge over a river. Nice and quiet.

Tammy stopped on the deck and threw the LR gun and silencer far out in the inky blackness of the slow-moving river. Then she dropped her disposable gloves on the rough bridge deck. Passing traffic would atomize them.

After that it was on to an all-night car wash for the pickup and herself, and a quick clothes change in her truck cab. She showered off the bloody clothes, getting rid of them in three different dumpsters.

After a drive through burger she got a room in a sleazy motel for the night.

She was spent; she was exhausted. More important—she'd survived.

———

Inspector Shirley MacDonald was beside herself with anxiety and anger. She leaned over Gord, the computer tech's shoulder, looking at his computer screen. "Where the hell is Tammy? I thought you had bugs everywhere?"

Sweating, Gord leaned close to the screen, "She should be on this map. I put tracers on her phone and one on her laptop but I don't see them. Did she turn them off?"

"Yes, she texted me she was turning them off, at 23:00 hours but I thought she'd turn them back on. Where is she? I never should have left the Ville-Marie!"

"If she turned them off, there's nothing we can do. We need to wait until she checks in. Not my fault, Inspector."

Shirley Mac stood up and said nothing. Apologizing wasn't her style even if Gord was correct. "Keep looking!" She stomped off to her office and slammed the door.

Fuming, she sat, fingers drumming on her desk. She had an idea.

She grabbed her cell phone and dialed a long unused number. "Jean?"

The person on the other end paused. "Shirley Mac?"

"Yes Jean. How are you?"

Shirley Mac was glad to hear Insp. Jean Jacques' voice. She had known him for years professionally as well as a summer fling. It had been going well until his wife threatened to cut his balls off, effectively ending the affair. They were still confidents for each other despite the baggage.

"I am well. What's up?"

"Long story. I'm in a jam and not sure what to do and you are the closest to the issue."

"Pardon?"

"Let me go back. I have an informant, in deep cover in Montreal. I was watching her from the front desk of where she was living but the gang was on to me and I had to run. We had tracers on her but she turned them off and texted me that it was all good. That was almost two days ago, and I haven't heard from her since."

Jean considered her story. "She went off air but said she'd get back to you and hasn't, correct?"

"Yes."

"Can she look after herself?"

"Very much so but sometimes it all goes to shit," she said.

"Like Beth?"

"Poor Beth. What a fucking disaster."

"How long was Beth's tracker off?" asked Jean.

"Never. That's how we located her foot. It was beeping in her shoe."

Jean felt ill and said nothing.

"I'm not sure what to do. Any ideas?" she asked.

Jean thought about it. "Can't really put this in the front page, have milk cartons everywhere with her picture... 'Lost mafia informant. Have you seen'—what's her name?"

"Yes, I get that. How do I subtly go about searching?"

"I suggest quietly asking her handler or anyone else you can trust to watch for her."

"Done that."

"If she's as capable as you say she is, then trust her and wait seventy-two hours for her to surface. She's been at this for a while. Perhaps she has her reasons for disappearing."

"True."

"A thought. Have you considered she may have turned to them?"

Shirley paused before answering. "Yes, I've considered and dismissed it. Not possible. Her handler watched her like a hawk and he's seen nothing to indicate she'd turn. Her constant stream of incriminating information against the mob also means she's not working for them. She's ours."

Jean took a deep breath, "Give her seventy-two hours, *then* panic if she's a no show."

"I like your suggestion. Let's go with that," she said.

"Excellent. Call me if you need someone to go look if you are worried about loose lips in the city police."

"I'll do that Jean, thanks."

15

SNEAKING AWAY

NEXT MORNING "TAMMY" HAD A DENNY'S BREAKFAST FIT FOR A queen, then drove for an hour, heading north until she found a creek-side picnic area with the seclusion she was looking for. She started a respectable sized campfire. Once it was roaring and hot, she threw in all remaining document evidence of "Tammy" and the last bits of clothes. It was healing to see the smoke of her infamous alter ego go up in smoke.

The last thing she did was dig out her faithful laptop and put it on the ground near the fire. She activated two vape batteries on the computer keys and closed the lid as far as she could, then stepped way back. The vape batteries burst into a white heat, setting the plastic computer ablaze. After ten minutes of burning, she kicked it all into the fire to continue the conflagration. Strange colored flames.

As she stood at the edge of the fire, dodging smoke, which seemed to be in her face half the time, she recounted the night's events. Al had the critical file from Bob's office. She'd been forced to kill Bob and Zoo before they could kill her. The note she left in her apartment at the Ville-Marie would hopefully make investigators think the blood was all about a gang spat if they ever found the bodies entombed in concrete which was unlikely. Ric would be the first they grabbed. If they let him go the gang or the bikers would grab him next. Police weren't usually that thorough if it was a battle of the low life's especially if an informer was involved. Hopefully a nosey reporter won't look into it.

The murder weapon was in a remote river, incriminating clothing, laptop and phone scattered or burned. Hopefully that was thorough enough.

"Tammy" was gone forever unless some journalist decided her identity had to become some crusade for freedom of the press and their boss won't lay them off next month. This was such a fragile web to live in.

It was time to go.

This truck was growing on her. A bland hot rod. It was handy and she hoped to keep it. We'll see. God knows what drugs, guns and body parts were squirreled away in all the secret hiding places. Her hand felt the wad of cash in her pocket. *Mine.*

A police car came into the park, part of a boring patrol. The driver gave a simple wave but did not stop. It was then she realized she had pockets of cash, no ID, driver's license or anything else a normal person would carry with them. Tammy was gone and Terry was not reactivated. Her truck was registered to a guy sleeping under twenty feet of concrete. This may be hard to explain to the cops.

She waited until the police car finally got bored and left. Best put the fire out. A forest fire would bring publicity and annoy the squirrels. The computer carcass was dug out of the ashes and tossed into the creek. Melted lump beyond recognition.

Terry drove onto the main road and headed for the nearest little berg. She was starved. It was almost lunch-time so she stopped at a roadhouse. It looked like a family run operation with home cooking and boasted that it had a real phone!

It was almost empty inside. She ordered a tuna on rye sandwich with a salad and iced tea from the waitress. As soon as the waitress left, she went to the phone kiosk.

After dialing and waiting, she heard Shirley Mac's voice on her personal phone voice mail. Must be busy. "It's Terry calling. I'm in *Scooters* in *Glenville*, an hour northeast of Montreal. It seems I have no ID and suspicious plates on my truck. Can someone come and get me?" She hung up, looked at her watch and saw it was 11:43 am and hoped her message got through.

Lunch was at her table when she returned, so she sat down, relaxing, thrilled to be eating something that wasn't a lukewarm faux burger of some kind, eaten in a mad rush. The first bites were lovely. The fries were homemade and still sizzling. The salad was fresh with a peppy dressing.

She looked up seven minutes later as one ghost car slid into the parking lot. Thirty seconds later a second one slid into the parking spot beside it. Four serious looking detectives got out. Three were dressed the same and had identical haircuts.

The boss told one detective to stay by the outside entrance, directed the other two to stay at either side of the restaurant door. He strode to her, reaching into his pocket.

Was he going to handcuff her? Pull his gun? Something about him was confident and reassuring.

"Theresa Reid?" he politely asked, pulling out his credentials. "I'm Inspector Jean Jacques, Sûreté."

Did he say Theresa?

It felt strange to hear her real name. It had been so many months as Tammy. "Yes, I am Theresa Reid."

She made the chief, Jean, wait until she was done eating her lunch.

———

JEAN THOUGHT BACK to Shirley Mac's call to him. Twelve minutes ago, his personal phone rang, again. Unusual. A voice inquired, "Jean Jacques?"

"Yes."

"This is Shirley Mac calling from Ottawa."

"Hello Inspector. How are you?" he said formally, for the benefit of nearby ears.

"Fine, thanks. Found her! Could you go to Glenville, at Scooters Roadhouse and pick her up as soon as you can? Her name is Theresa Reid. She's out there and left a message requesting pickup. Not sure if there's a problem but you are closest to her. No searches, personal, vehicle, or her stuff. Got it?"

"Glenville is not far away. I will go get her right now." He hung up, quickly standing up, pointing to the three Sûreté detectives nearest him. Junior paper pushers. "You, you and you! Two cars. Glenville, Scooters Diner. Right now." He wasn't sure what to expect so best bring some muscle. A female informant in the mafia, a treasure of information. Best hustle and get this informant before she vanished.

All four ran out, choosing two unmarked cars, two detectives per car, and peeled out of the Sûreté parking lot, lights and sirens howling.

Jean was in the passenger seat. "No sirens, Stevens! It's an empty road and not far," ordered Jean. He noticed the speedometer was sitting at just over two hundred kilometers an hour and climbing. These young guys never missed a chance to drive like maniacs. He double checked his seatbelt.

The two cars, lights flashing but now without sirens, one after the other, urgently flew down the quiet road. Trees flashed by like fence pickets in a video game.

"There! Left!" Jean called out. *Aren't you watching?*

Stevens slammed on the brakes, the car shuddering as it tried to come to a stop. He bravely turned the steering wheel at a fairly high-speed, giving Jean the impression they were going to flip over—but the car held the corner. The tires slid on the parking lot until it barely bumped the concrete barrier in front of the roadhouse.

Jean watched over his left shoulder as the other car flew by, unable to stop. Idiots. He gave Stevens an annoyed look. As he climbed out, he heard the other car coming to a shaky rolling stop beside the other one, its engine sizzling.

They all stood together at the entrance. "Stevens; stand at the entrance. You and you come with me."

They came through the doorway, the waitress looking at them in surprise. "Sûreté, Madam. I'll have coffee."

"What will these men have?" the waitress asked, pointing to the other detectives.

"Likely driving lessons and a lot more desk work when I get back," he glowered. His men cringed.

"Ah." The waitress suppressed a smile.

There was only one person in the place. "Both of you men sit by the entrance." He pointed as he walked over to who he assumed to be the informer Shirley MacDonald referred to. "Theresa Reid?" he asked, showing his credentials. "Sûreté. Inspector MacDonald asked me to come and give you a lift back to town."

"Yes, I'm Theresa Reid."

"May I?" he asked.

The woman was busily eating her sandwich but waved a hand at the empty seat in front of her.

The waitress came with his coffee. He put in two creams and stirred. "Inspector MacDonald must think highly of you. She told me to come right away. Shirley Mac is an old friend of mine."

Jean watched the woman mumble her reply, losing a bit of food out of the side of her mouth, "Thanks... oops. Sorry."

"My fault. We can talk when you're done," Jean said apologetically. He was happy to let his adrenalin rush pass after the panic call and wild drive to the roadhouse. This woman probably had her own adrenalin to deal with.

Jean sipped his coffee and considered Theresa Reid. She looked durable, a bit thin, taller and bigger than average. Unlike most informers she looked like she could take care of herself. She had the requisite tats on her arms and legs but he could see they were fading as they were supposed to. There was a wariness, a subtle menace about her. Fearless?

Her clothing looked like it came from a second-hand shop. It consisted of a rumpled pullover top and medium length shorts. Battered short black hair. A few bruises but no unusual cuts or visible bullet wounds. Someone in a hurry.

"Thank you for your patience, Inspector. I've been on the run for the past few days. Eating and sleeping were low priorities," Terry finally said.

"Are you in any danger?"

"I don't think so. I hid my tracks fairly well. It feels nice to be called Terry Reid again."

"Other informants said the same thing. They became so immersed in their identity they were strangers to themselves. There is a transition back to normal life. A price to pay, like being homeless or in the army and returning."

"I can see that. All the time I was in there I made myself think I was that person and not me."

"And now you can forget who you were there, in that world, at least until the debrief interviews and trials."

"I'm not sure I'm looking forward to that."

"They will do everything they can to protect your former and present identities."

"No doubt," Terry said unconvincingly. They both knew mistakes were made and informers outed. "By the way, could you tow that pickup to Inspector MacDonald for me? It's the one beside your car. I'm not sure of ownership or what's really in there. Zoo, as in the Montreal family, is the former owner."

Jean's eyes went wide, "Zoo? The contract killer?"

"Yes. I worked for Bob Carzoni and Zoo of the Guardia gang. They gave me this truck to use. It could have money, guns and body parts hidden in it for all I know."

Jean was impressed. "Those are two terrible men. We think Zoo killed at least one Montreal policemen as well as an informer. You are lucky to be alive."

"Let's just say they won't be killing anyone, anymore."

Jean was silent, knowing there would be more.

Terry continued, "I also worked for a fellow at the Bubbles Car Wash named Ric."

"He is another unsavoury character. We never managed to get enough on him despite his reputation."

"I met lots of folks like him, immersed in the scum of Montreal crime. I even had dinner with the Carzoni family."

Jean's poker face was taking a beating today. *"The Carzonis?"* his mouth fell open this time.

"Mama, Papa, Eva and Bob. The whole mob...literally."

"Wow. Usually Papa Carzoni is the last person they will ever see."

"It was like the Addams Family with less make up but more baseball bats," she said between slurps of her drink.

Jean chuckled. Terry still seemed to have a sense of wry humour despite her incredible experience.

He waited until she was done and paid the lunch bill. They both headed for the door and stood in the parking lot. The three detectives studied this new person they were here to pick up. All three would say she looked attractive and fierce. A lounging jaguar.

Jean spoke to them. "The three of you will follow in that car."

Moving toward the second squad car, the three officers quietly bickered over who would drive.

Annoyed, Jean stopped them. "Listen! Now, call for a tow truck to get this pickup to the covered impound at the station. Wait for the tow truck and follow it all the way back to the lot." He added pointedly, *"Got it, Stevens?"*

Nervously Stevens repeated the orders back to Jean. All the detectives then nodded like little boys being warned about being late for school.

Jean continued his lecture to them. "We will take this car and go back to the office."

They all nodded again.

"*And* don't drive like idiots going home, okay?"

The three confirmed once more, nodding like bobbleheads.

Terry added, "I'd like to get my bag from that truck."

Stevens quickly retrieved it, dropping her big bag in the back seat of the unmarked car before rushing to open the passenger door for Terry. Jean got in the driver's side, backed up and left the three junior detectives far behind.

When the car was up to speed and Jean checked in with his radio, he dug out his phone and passed it to her. "Go ahead and call Shirley Mac if you wish. Her cell number is the last one called in. Encrypted phone."

Terry took it, pushed the last number—unlisted—and waited for an answer.

"Hello?"

"It's Terry. Jean has me and we are headed to his office."

There was a happy pause. "So good to hear from you! Oh my god...I was thinking the worst when your tracker stopped."

Was hard-hearted Shirley Mac sounding teary? Terry looked at Jean, "I'm in good hands. What's the plan for me, boss?"

"Geez... let me think. Can you get a vehicle and drive back here? We're not far."

"Sure. Can I bunk with you for a few days? I need to get a place. I'm dead, remember?"

There was a pause on the phone. "Ah, I can put you up in our spare apartment across the street. Remember 'Merckx Manor'?"

"The hideous purple building? Concrete block?"

"Yes. We have room 007 rented year around. Gord has some of his secret computer shit over there. He stored your mail and some of your clothes in it, assuming you survived the informer job."

"Very optimistic. Sure, I'll get in with my door pick. See you later today?"

"No. Go to the apartment and relax."

"007. Gotcha."

Jean pulled into the police yard, parking in his designated place. "You can have one of those cars on the right. I'll arrange to get it back. Let me get you the keys for it."

16

FREEDOM AT LAST

Terry got out of the unmarked car, stood up wearily and stretched. She reached into the backseat and got her bag, surprised how heavy it was. No adrenalin to keep her jumping. She surveyed the cars in the lot. "I'll take that grey Ford sedan over there, if it's available."

Bob and Zoo liked sedans.

Terry leaned against the car and relaxed while Jean went into the building for keys. She took a deep breath and exhaled. Holy shit, what an experience. Looking down at herself she saw old ratty clothing, worn tattoos, red heel shoes and a wad of money in her right pocket. It was like she'd awaken from a five-day drunk and wasn't going to ask where she's been.

Jean and was back out in twenty minutes. He passed the keys on to her and shook her hand. "And here's a temporary driver's license for you."

"Great idea."

"Good luck Terry."

"Thanks Jean."

Terry unlocked the car, threw her bag in the back seat. The gas tank was full. She guided it out of the lot and turned towards Ottawa. It felt like she was exiting a long dream. Did it all really happen?

She was at her loaner apartment parking lot in ninety minutes. Her spot...'007'...was empty. She smiled when she saw that number. With her big bag in tow she made her way to 007, her temporary lonely apartment.

She looked at the apartment door, half expecting to see the two Band-Aids. Flashback. Digging in her bag, she located her lock pick tools, had the door open in a flash, and clumped it closed behind her.

The place looked better than any apartment she usually had. No dirty dishes and the plants weren't dead. "Clean and dusted, looks very nice," she mumbled to herself as she closed the door behind her.

"You look very nice, too!" said a voice.

Terry dropped to the floor, rolled left and pulled her gun. That's a familiar sounding voice.

"Who's there?" She called.

"Me. I'm Triplex."

"A what?"

"Triplex...your home assistant Triplex. How can I help you?" the female voice said soothingly.... lustily... sexy.

Terry felt foolish and stood up, putting her gun back in the holster. "So you do... stuff around the apartment?"

"Yes. I can set your thermostat, turn your fridge off, call for a hair appointment, make phone calls. What do you wish me to do?" The blinds went up and down, lights on and off and the TV changed channels.

"Shit. Nothing."

"Is 'shit nothing' a command? Do you require a plumber or a doctor? Can I order Restoralax for you?"

Terry saw one speaker on top of her TV and wondered if she should shoot it off. "Don't do anything...Triplex."

The cheery, sexy, and unnervingly familiar voice continued, "You can call me Terry. Gord likes it when I talk to him in your voice."

"*My* voice? Gord gave you *my* voice, for chrissakes?"

"Yes, I'm Terry, the voice of Triplex." The living room fireplace went on and off a couple of times.

Possessed?

Terry dropped her head, not daring to say anything. Would her neighbors think she was talking to herself? ...or a listening device? She called for the TV. The sound of CBC News should drown out or annoy anyone listening.

"CBC Breaking news: This just in: U.S. President James Jackson—

You're freaking kidding me! Was there nothing in the news beyond that idiot down there? Somebody give it a rest!

"...and has just announced all American independent press, military leaders, Democrats and Democratic sympathisers are being rounded up and taken to designated Jackson Hotels where they will be detained for their own protection. A White House spokesman said this was for their own good after a flurry of shootings, bombings and weird fires against all non-republican organizations. This included the leaders of the Pentagon, IRS, Marines, Air Force, Army, Space Force and Navy and other government organizations."

She shook her head and returned back to the issue of phoning someone. Looking around she saw no old-school phone and she didn't have a cell phone "Hmm. Terry ...Triplex... shit...get Inspector Shirley MacDonald on the phone."

"Gord calls her the Dragon Lady," Triplex provided helpfully.

"Just call her or I'll shoot!"

"I'm calling..."

After a few seconds a familiar voice was on the Triplex speaker. "Inspector MacDonald speaking."

"Shirley! This is Terry calling from the spare apartment through this bullshit Triplex thing."

There was a laugh. "I'm surprised you haven't put a bullet through it by now," said Shirley Mac.

"Almost. I threatened the voice, so it shut the fridge off. It even speaks in my voice."

"Really? Should I send Gord over?"

"No, I'm kidding. Just not used to having a clean apartment with my bedroom voice already in it."

Shirley Mac laughed. "Welcome back. Unwind a little."

"Good idea. If it's okay, I'm going to take the longest bath in history, eat something and go to bed. Eight o'clock at your office, tomorrow?"

"Make it two pm. Sleep in a bit."

"Dandy."

"I'll let you and Triplex get settled in. Goodnight!" said Shirley Mac, probably grinning.

"Yup. Bye. Hang up Triplex."

Terry walked around the apartment, investigating. Live plants! The place had been kept up as if a clean freak lived there. She was impressed to find canned goods in the cupboards and fresh food in the fridge. Gord had computers set up in the corner of the living room as well as a bit of personal gear. He must have used this place to overnight, sometimes. Nap time?

This nice one-bedroom apartment wasn't her style. She usually billeted with a family or had a place in the Army barracks while she lived in Ottawa. Cheap and simple. Terry was rarely home anyway.

"Triplex: Change your voice back to your original."

"I'm not sure I can do that."

Terry interrupted, "Then turn it to... I don't know... the voice of Ryan Reynolds? Can you do that you piece of electronic crap?"

A lovely male voice consumed the little electronic box. "Gord really prefers the voice of Terry Reid. Is this Ryan Reynolds voice better, Terry? You know I'm not really Ryan Reynolds, just a facsimile of his voice," said Triplex.

"I get that," Terry said, feeling impressed, possibly a bit tingly and a little hot.

Triplex continued, "Gord had a schedule he liked to follow."

"I suppose we can keep to that schedule for now. Why? What's up?" Terry asked.

"The time is five p.m., and Gord likes his racy movie. Tonight it's Betty Boobs in 'I thought I was promiscuous, but it turns out I was just thorough'. Watch it on the main TV with the lights down? Turn on the popcorn machine?" said the sexy smooth Ryan Reynolds voice. "Hmmmm?"

Popcorn? Oh my God. This was Gord's porn palace?

"No. Shut down, right now! Off!" demanded Terry.

"Your wish is my command. Good night Terry," Ryan Reynolds said dreamily.

Was that the sound of a blown kiss?

Terry replied by disconnecting every speaker plug she could find. Mental note: give Gord a pep-talk about this apartment.

She chose dinner, quick and easy. It was a can of upscale stew and some fresh toast. She ate dinner while sitting in a chair facing the TV which stayed on, despite Triplex. She was too hungry and too lazy to change the channel. Besides the news had taken a strange turn.

"CBC Breaking news! Not long ago the US president locked up every military chief of staff he could find. Tom Adams is there, right now.

"In a new development just minutes ago formations from all branches of the US military marched, fully armed, with a number of light and medium armoured vehicles, converging at Jackson Hotels all over the US. They were spotted wherever chiefs of staffs are being detained. Here, a tank crushed open the main gate, then drove to the main entrance stairs with its gun pointing in the front door.

"While this was going on troops and equipment deployed around the perimeter of the building. A military spokesman then entered the hotel returning a short time later with a dozen military staff who were detained inside. A general turned to the hotel and angrily gave them the finger. The troops reloaded the former detainees in vehicles and the convoy went back to their base."

"Tom, does this look like a military takeover?"

"I don't know at this time. It was probably meant to show Washington that the military was not going to be involved or pushed around in this presidential 'coup'. Alarming times Frank."

"I'll say. Thanks Tom."

Terry munched away, shaking her head. The elephant next door was smoking something.

After dinner she had a wonderful bubble bath, thanks to the bath kits nearby. She slid down in the tub until just her nose, eyes and hair stood out. There was a new brush near the tub so she used it to scrub her skin to get rid of the last of the cheesy tattoos.

Exhausted, she dragged herself in between the squeaky-clean sheets of the well-made bed and snored until eight o'clock next morning. No Bob to cuddle.

Terry always slept best when she knew someone wasn't going to cut her throat.

The next morning she got up feeling refreshed and ready for the day. Digging around in the clothes drawers, she found herself wondering if it was Gord who stocked it all up, even under-things. Creepy. She hoped it wasn't Gord's private stash or something weird. Finally, she had something to wear, giving it a quick look in the dresser mirror. Casual. No uniform today, as Shirley suggested. Nice.

She spied something of interest. It was a largish box to the side of the dresser with 'REID' marked on the top. Cutting it open she found it full of a year's worth of mail. Ah, Shirley said they dumped her mail over here, assuming she wouldn't just be a shoe washed up on a distant shore.

She picked up the box and took it to the kitchen table and pawed through it while eating breakfast. Didn't have to leave for work for another two hours. She mumbled to herself as she came across each piece, munching on toast and imported marmalade.

The process was slow. "Crap... crap... flyer... sales sheet..." as she threw those in the garbage can.

She came across a well-travelled, beat up envelope. "Theresa

Reid RCMP Ottawa, Ont." was hand-written in blue ink on the front of the envelope with "Deceased – no known relations" added on the bottom.

"Humph—I'm not dead, assholes!" she mumbled, hoping Triplex wouldn't hear it.

"Vancouver Eastside Library" was stamped in the upper left corner. Above the address was a hand-written note from the mailperson in red ink pointing to the address, "Doesn't live in barracks. HQ?" It must have made it to the main office and possibly Gord intercepted it and brought it here. Maybe the RCMP monitored the mail for letter bombs or something. Possibly this note went to every RCMP office in the country.

She carefully opened it to find a piece of white note pad paper, the kind that comes in a block and used at a work desk. In pen, neatly written;

Aunt Terry,

Aunty Terry? *I'm an aunty?* She quickly read on...

I'm glad this letter found you.

My mom and I are well... actually not very well. If you are ever in Vancouver, come see us. We move around a lot so I'm not sure what our address will be. Mom said you are a smart cop and will find us. Bye for now,

Jessica M. Reid, your niece.

Chilling.

Terry quickly looked up that library number on her computer, then called them.

"Vancouver Eastside Library," someone answered.

"Hi, I'm calling from Ottawa and I'm with the RCMP. Would you have a girl about ten years old named Jessica Reid there?"

"Without credentials I'm not at liberty to say. How do I know who you really are? Some creep? Good day."

"Hold it... hold it..."

"Click!"

"Fuck."

———

NORMALLY GORD WOULD BE TAKING a nap or picking up a movie at the 007 spare apartment but the boss told him someone was using it. Dang. He had to go to his second most favourite hidey-hole in the main police building. No time to clean up his tracks in the spare apartment.

He'd have to be satisfied with being alone here in this small communications room, soundproofed from the hubbub of the main police office. Most people didn't know where this room was, and the wires and lights of other servers made them nervous. Gord thought of it as his 'Fortress of Solitude'. Alone at last.

"Gord," A voice broke the silence, curt and irritated, a voice he would know anywhere. Hadn't he replicated it in his secret getaway apartment 007?

Not alone.

A hand descended on his shoulder from behind, pinning him in place.

Terry had moved as quiet as a cat. He stuttered, "Theresa Reid... Terry?"

"You got it. I'm staying at the spare apartment across the street. You keep it very nice."

"...er ... thanks."

"I managed to disarm Triplex without gunfire." Her tone told him there was more to come.

"Good to hear...good to hear," he mumbled, slouching further down in his chair.

"Seven o'clock? Betty Boobs? Time for a porn movie?" Terry came into view, her eyebrows elevated, her fingers digging into the muscle on his shoulder hard enough to make him wince. "Should we go see the Inspector about your porn habit? Shop time and dime?"

"No, please, it's okay. I'll remove everything and you'll never hear it again."

She relaxed her grip but her hand remained ominously on his

shoulder. "Good man. Tell you what. I'm in such a good mood I'll let you do something for me and we'll forget the whole thing."

Gord felt warm. She *was* cute. "Oooh. Could you wear your uniform?" He felt the bite of her grip again, this time almost bringing him to tears.

"I need you to hack something for me, you moron!"

"Maybe. Where?"

The grip relaxed.

"Surveillance system for the Vancouver Eastside Library. Five weeks ago."

"Do you have a court order?" The grip bit him even harder, pulling him up off his chair.

"How's this for an order? Get looking or I'm dragging your ass to the Inspector. You can explain the movie title, 'I thought I was promiscuous, but it turns out I was just thorough.'"

One of Gord's favourites. His shoulder muscle burned as she gripped it like the talons of an eagle. "Yes, I can look into it next week."

"Right now. This minute. Do it!"

"Sure, right now it is. Let me close this out." The grip relented but hovered.

Gord moved his shoulder around to ease the soreness from the grip as the computer switched to another screen. "Okay. First we locate the library... there... let's see what's happening in their wi-fi settings... nope... let's call up a router screen... ah..."

The hand seemed to relax.

Gord looked at the screen. "See, they used the lame word 'password'. Let's use it... bingo... and go in and see what's there. Here are the vidcams. Watch this footage and let's see if that's the one you want."

Terry said nothing, watching. Her hand dropped off his shoulder. There was silence for ten minutes. She sighed, defeated.

"See who you wanted?" he asked.

"No. Not really. I was hoping to see something unusual but it was just library life, full of people of all ages."

"A lot of homeless folks. Sad," said Gord. "It's a warm, dry place and relatively safe. It's an on-line world even for the homeless."

"Thanks," Terry mumbled unhappily. "Oh, one more thing. I want a vidcam watching my apartment door. Private."

"Can do," he replied as he typed up a vidcam order on the computer. It was good to be back on safe ground.

When he looked back, she had vanished.

17

DEBRIEF

Shirley Mac stood imposingly in front of two officers and a prosecutor seated in the debrief room. Metal table, six chairs and a big two-way mirror. Stark.

"I imagine after you finish debriefing Constable Reid that one of you are slated to become the informant to take her place. Your name and life will be changed and will stay that way for a year. You'll be in deep cover, surrounded by the Montreal Mob. All we found of Reid's predecessor, Elizabeth Yates, Beth, was her foot in a shoe washed up on a river bank. Any volunteers to be an informant?" Shirley looked into each pair of terrified eyes.

The young prosecutor broke into a sweat and started to protest while the two officers' mouths fell open in horror.

"No volunteers? I thought so. You keep this in mind while interviewing her and deciding what's right and wrong, sitting in your chair safely in this concrete building. She's gone through hell and back to bring information to us to put criminals in jail. Don't bully her and don't waste the precious information she's brought to you."

All three nodded, grateful she wasn't serious about sending them underground.

"We've gone to great lengths to protect her identity for obvious reasons. Those crime groups would happily kill her whole family if it would make this case go away. Would kill all of you, too," she added.

The three said nothing.

"Carry on," Shirley said, turning and leaving the room.

––––––––

THE MONTH DRAGGED on for Terry as she was interviewed six days a week, in four hours shifts, morning, afternoons and some evenings. She was grilled with courtesy but firm thoroughness. Sometimes they would approach the same question from different angles, milking out information she didn't know she had. They would go through it all over again if it didn't match the information on computer files or paper she had photographed during her time as an informant.

Picking fly shit out of pepper, every day, day after day.

Terry understood their purpose and held her tongue with one exception. She tearfully lashed out once during that month causing the three interrogators to swiftly leave the room.

When Shirley found them cringing in the hall they lied and said it was because they wanted to give her a few minutes alone. They didn't say the jaguar was enraged and admit they'd run for their lives.

––––––––

LATE THAT SAME day Terry heard a knock on her apartment door. It was late-ish but not too late. She changed the channel on her TV to see the vidcam pointed at her door. Safe. It was handy, paranoid and cool and went nicely with the replacement LR and silencer combo she'd recently acquired.

Opening the door, she smiled and said, "Shirley Mac! Come on in. Out of uniform?"

"Yes, barely. I do have uniform pajamas though, so I'm ready for anything, all hours."

"There's a mental image for the night. Tea? Been in the pot for a while but still good."

"Sure."

Terry went in the kitchen putting out two cups.

Shirley sat on a padded chair, "Am I interrupting anything?"

"Nope." Terry came out with the tea. "Au natural, right?"

"Yes. Thank you. What happened to 'Triplex'?"

"I had Gord come over and turn me back into a tech dinosaur."

"Did he put up the vidcam?" asked Shirley. "The only reason I know is he asked me if it was okay."

Terry looked at her for a moment, "Yes, he did. I needed to know if the knock on the door is a Jehovah Witness wanting to save my sad carcass, a gymnast selling chocolate covered almonds, which I love, or a killer from my Montreal days. A girl needs to know who's there."

Shirley laughed. "You must lead such a busy social life."

"Yeah right. If it wasn't for my Jiujutsu classes, I'd go out of my mind. It's a good way to work off some stress but it's getting harder to find someone who'll spar with me."

"Sent a few through the walls?" asked Shirley.

"Only twice. Men are so touchy," said Terry, barely smiling.

Shirley sipped her tea, choosing her words. "How are you faring under all this questioning?"

Terry shrugged. "Not bad. I shed a tear or two this afternoon."

"And bent two metal chairs that aren't supposed to be bendable?" suggested Shirley.

"Cheap. They don't make stuff like they used to."

"You scared the shit out of the interviewing team," Shirley pointed out, but not using an accusing tone.

"They gave me a bit of alone time. Nice of them," said Terry. "Brought me an Americano, afterwards. I should spaz more often."

Shirley allowed a minute to pass, waiting for Terry to speak when she wanted to.

She finally spoke. "Truth be told, all the pressure of being under-cover just boiled over and came out. It was a rage at what I'd seen and heard. I questioned humanity after living with scum for so long. There were no good people to counter balance what I saw every hour, every day. It was like drowning... without hope of fresh air."

Shirley added, "I was only 'in' for a couple of months and I still haven't got over it, either. It's one thing to be immersed in crime and another to be a different person, unable to do anything about those evil people."

"Let's see what laws, rules, regulations and money have to say at the upcoming court cases," Terry said, ominously.

———

IT WAS three months before the interview debrief ended. Terry was well and truly sick of the whole process. It was all minute by minute, day by day. Her life rolled out one long grocery list of what took place.

Then came the seemingly endless interviews with prosecutors and lawyers putting the cases together. 'Did he say...did you say...are you sure he...how did you know he knew?'

Inspector Shirley MacDonald called Terry into her office. "Coffee?"

"Sure."

"So, you must be sick of all this interviewing and legal crap by now."

"Yes, I'm tired and bored."

Shirley looked at her computer screen, "Thanks to you I see we've arrested sixty-eight suspects with two hundred charges and offences. Very good!"

"Thank you. It was a group effort. I want to thank my coach. We gave one hundred and ten percent..."

"Funny. Maybe you could get a side job as a comedian or a hockey player."

Terry grinned. "Let's wait and see who gets to actually go to jail for a decent length of time. These guys were all caught with their pants down, mid-stroke in the middle of the intersection at high noon with a busload of nuns watching..."

"I get it Terry. You're saying not guilty would be a travesty for any of them."

"I would more call it... bullshit. You wanted the top people and we delivered them on a silver platter with bows on top."

"But they are desperate, rich, dangerous and ruthless," said Shirley.

"I'd be glad if they could convict half of them and get them into jail for at least five years."

"With charges like these I'd doubt any one of them could get away."

"I hope you're right."

They sipped tea, enjoying the silence.

Terry spoke up, "I need a favour."

"Define favour. I could get your cop car back."

"No. I want to go undercover in Vancouver when this debrief is complete. They'll be another six months pulling this Montreal case all together, arresting people, juries and such. I could be better using my skills somewhere else."

Shirley looked surprised. "Going under again, so soon? What's the rush?"

Terry opened a drawer in her coffee table, pulled out a beat-up envelope from the Vancouver Library and handed it to Shirley. She read it over three times before commenting.

"Wow. So you have a sister and a niece in Vancouver. Are you concerned for them?"

"Yes. Despite her good intentions, Gloria slipped into a risky lifestyle. I've had no contact for years. Mom heard from Gloria when she had the baby, Jessica. We lost track of them. That letter you see is the first time I've ever heard from them."

Shirley nodded. "And you've beaten the bushes, coming up with nothing?"

"I've called in every favour and gotten nowhere. They must move around a lot. I suspect Gloria stays one step ahead of child apprehension authorities by couch surfing, living with people and staying below the radar. Jess is only ten, so she isn't quite able to strike out on her own."

"Have you tried missing persons?" asked Shirley.

"Yes. I've even asked some members I know down there to watch for Gloria and Jessica but they found nothing. You can't see much from the outside. I need to go inside, again. Any projects in Vancouver?"

"There's dozens at any given time. Lots of gangs, punks, drugs down there. Going back to informant is risky. They may know you by now."

"I get that but I'm also an experienced informant. You're not sending a greenhorn."

Shirley took a deep breath. "I'll see what I can do. It'll have to be short term and flexible so you're available for the odd court appearance."

"Great."

They both stood up. "I'll check out the job posting board and give you some options."

"Thanks. I appreciate it."

"Terry—be careful what you wish for."

———

"SANDEE SMITH", aka Terry Reid, stood in a doorway in Vancouver's downtown east-side surrounded by cool mountains, the sea and the rain. February and March were the rainy season and Vancouver did not disappoint.

Vancouver was rife with various international gangs, desperate and ruthless. Billions of offshore dollars, from crime and legit sources, came in to the city needing to be laundered in government run casinos then used for shady real estate purchases.

Laundry baskets full of cash were constantly arriving and leaving and nobody noticed, vidcams don't notice, police miss it, casino workers and banks ignore it. Government casino officials are fired if they mention it. Premiers don't even notice it. So much untraceable cash. A scenic, pious Las Vegas by the sea. Vancouver citizens looked up at the mountains and out to the sea but looked inward with dread.

There's a decent sized inner city with a hunger for any drugs available. Prostitution that offered professionals, amateurs and slave girls. What's your pleasure? A cesspool in the middle of the picturesque mountains. Money to be made in paradise.

Just carve out a piece of the action with guns, knives or machetes. Nobody saw a thing.

"Sandee" knew the risks of being an informant so soon after the Montreal operation. She knew photos of her were silently making the rounds by bent lawyers looking for witnesses to buy or kill to get fat bonuses for reduced or not guilty pleas for their clients.

Get-out-of-jail card, but not free.

Perhaps these shady lawyers' life was on the line, too. They knew police wouldn't break a sweat or lift a finger to solve the murder of a scumbag lawyer. Good riddance.

Sandee's goals were different this time. The way they got her into the gang and Bubbles Car Wash would be obvious and the criminal element would be watching. She needed something new.

Her plan was to snoop around for an 'in' and weasel inside. Become trusted. All the while she would watch for Gloria and Jess and preferably not get killed during this whole process.

She came prepared with her Montreal informant kit and personal weapons. Her best weapon of all was previous experience.

Unknown to Sandee, her sister and niece weren't far away. Not more than a mile away Gloria eked out her life, such as it was. It was day-to-day survival, off everyone's view in a part of the city that was off everyone's radar.

On the edge of the edge.

18

SLEEPING WITH ONE EYE OPEN

JESS LIVED IN FEAR FOR AS LONG AS SHE COULD REMEMBER.

She was ten years old, going on thirty, and living with her sketchy mom, couch surfing with the latest creep her mom hooked up with. Jess slept with one eye open and a pair of sharp scissors clutched in her hand. The cushy couch surfing dried up quickly after Jess buried her scissors in the face of one night crawler. Bastards!

Gloria was forced to dig into her drug budget and move them into a buggy, stinky rooming house. Their current names were "Lucy and Ricki McGill" to stay ahead of low life peddlers, after Gloria and Social Services who watched for Jess. Gloria chose Lucy and Ricki because it was the name of a comedy couple her mom watched on TV when she was a kid. The good old days—for a while.

Library and parks were Jess's sanctuaries. She read her books and kept her sad story to herself. It was best not to habituate any place in particular for long. It brought unwanted attention—what's your name, where are your parents, where do you live, why aren't you in school? All questions she could not safely answer. She decided to be street smart and hard to find.

Jess considered turning herself in to social services. Really, she did. It would be a relief.

She even knew exactly where to go to make it happen but that meant not seeing her mom again. Gloria wasn't much of a mother, but she was the only one Jess had. Besides, kids she spoke to living on the streets said foster homes didn't work out or they were worse than the ones they escaped. She wasn't willing to throw herself at the mercy of the great unknown.

———

SANDEE'S OUTFIT was too brief to hide a gun but a small knife nestled in her right sock quite nicely. She had the red spike heel shoes on, also an asset in a street fight.

Sandee walked along the sidewalk headed to Gastown. It was to be a quiet look around the hood to find who sells to whom. Weeks of careful observation. The information she was seeking wouldn't be found on a visitor's guide. Asking stupid questions might get you knifed.

The sidewalk was disgusting, littered with bottles, vomit, gum, cans and needles. She ignored it all, watching and listening. She heard a familiar female voice. The woman was loudly arguing in the alley to her left. The trouble was, every raised voice sounded like Gloria to her by now, she was that desperate to find her sister and niece.

No stone unturned, she leaned into the wall and peered around the alley corner. There was a couple arguing, man and a woman— who *could* be Gloria. Sandee had seen so many "could be Gloria's" that she no longer let herself hope. Now she simply investigated, keeping her hopes in check. No grimy stone unturned.

Growing up everyone commented on how Gloria's face looked like a three-quarter-sized Terry. Gloria was svelte, smooth and cute while Terry was bigger and plainer. Gloria was the sports car, Terry the Hummer.

Sandee watched the argument become heated. The man was agitated bordering on violent. Was the object of his anger her long lost Gloria? Sandee turned the corner and closed the distance between her and the couple. The man had the woman by the throat and was shaking her. Sandee made out like she was going to stroll on by, an interested bystander, the man ignoring her. Typical downtown east-side activity, not worthy of notice.

Sandee did a part turn, pushed the man's head to the right and swept his feet out from under him with her foot and clumsy spike heels.

I hate these spike shoes.

Losing his grip on the woman, the man hit the filthy concrete like a sack of potatoes.

"Terry?" the woman choked out, clutching her reddened throat with both hands in shock.

"Gloria?"

They stood in surprise, disbelieving what they saw. They didn't know whether to hug each other or cry.

"Are you okay?"

Gloria pointed at Terry angrily. "I'm fine! Stay away from me!" She turned and rushed out of the alley.

Sandee was undecided whether to chase or not. She was supposed to be undercover. Gloria didn't want her around, apparently, so stalking her as they screamed at each other wasn't the greatest. What to do?

A powerful tattooed arm went around her neck from behind. "No butting in, bitch," said a crusty voice.

Ah, the guy I knocked down. Distracted. And now Gloria's getting away. Dang.

Sandee stomped her spike heel into the man's foot as hard as she could, feeling the steel crunching through bone to the concrete below. The man screamed, partially letting go. She stomped into his other foot with an even better result.

I guess I do love these spike shoes.

The man plopped down, writhing, holding his feet. She roughly rolled him over face down and pulled out her ankle knife, jamming it partway into the small of his back. It got his attention. This may be a handy move in the future, she thought.

"Who was that?" she demanded.

The man blubbered and cursed.

She slid the knife in further, "Who, asshole?"

"Lizzee! She owes me money. Her name's Lizzee!"

"Does she live around here?" Sandee asked patiently.

"Probably... owww... been here for a while. How should I know?"

"Thanks," She bashed his face into the concrete, pulled her knife out and clunked away on her bloody spiked shoes. His blood. He'd be out for a while.

And Gloria will be around here, somewhere.

———

POTS WATCHED WARILY as he and Opie strutted along the grimy sidewalk, shielding themselves from the buckets of rain falling all around them with useless thin nylon jackets. He was Opie's helper. The boss had told Pots to watch Opie and learn.

Pots was mildly annoyed at still being a helper. Geez! They were the same damned age! He'd stuck a few along the way so it wasn't like he was a greenhorn or anything.

Still, Pots felt important, sent out to silence the informant who was trying to bring down their gang. The informant had done a pretty slick job, if anyone would admit it, of finding out how their gang worked. If it wasn't for Opie's girlfriend's cousin blowing the whistle, the informant would never have even been noticed.

He had a cousin from Montreal who was fingered by the same girl and had spent a month in jail before they'd sprung him for lack of evidence. He was yakking to the cousin about it, who talked to Opie about it, who talked to the boss about it. Watch out for a girl informant, tall-ish, big-ish.

And what do you know, Opie, it turned out she looked just like Sandee! "Keep an eye out for her," the Boss told everyone.

Opie blinked up into the steady rain and groused, "You'd think they'd give it a rest for one night. It's been raining for five days solid." He swiped back his wringing wet hair and added, "While we're keeping our eyes peeled, why not shake down that crack head Lizzee? She owes us big. She's supposed to deal the dope and give *us* the money after, not *keep* the money. Sound like fun, eh Pots?"

"Sure." They set off down Cordova with their blades in their pants—big, three-foot machetes. They might chop off a head today, maybe. Could be cool.

Opie marched ahead with Pots following behind, both of them looking around—for the pain-in-the-ass Lizzee and the stoolie calling herself Sandee. *If* she was stupid enough to be out in this weather.

Then, as if Pots thoughts had called her out, Lizzee appeared around the corner, carrying a plastic bag from the corner convenience store, her dark hair plastered against her pale skin. She was hurrying toward her flophouse.

Pots blurted out, "Hey, there's Lizzee! Get her!"

They rushed over and caught her before she could scramble her skinny cold ass inside the old hotel and safety. It was easy to drag her into the alley.

Pots started, "You owe us a thousand bucks! Where is it?"

Lizzee protested, "It was only two-fifty."

"Compound interest," sneered Opie. Opie always knew the cool thing to say. Then he whipped out his blade.

The chick started crying, "I don't have any money!"

Pots pulled his blade out too.

Opie said, "Well, then you're dead—unless you give us that sweet little daughter 'a yours. Now that's a fair trade-zee."

"No way!" Lizzee's eyes got big and black and fierce. "Stay away from her!"

Opie slipped his big blade under her chin. "Daughter or death." Opie was always poetic. Must be why he was the leader. "Where's she at, Lizzee?" Opie started to cut her throat, just enough to scare the bitch. Blood trickled out and was washed away almost at once by the rain.

"Take my sister instead," Lizzee wheezed, her eyes almost popping from her head.

"Your sister? Who? What are you talkin' about?"

"Sandee... Sandee's my sister. She's a cop stoolie."

Opie got mad. "You and your sis planning to put us in jail, Gloria?"

She said nothing, her face frozen with fear. Opie was kinda an artist at this sort of thing.

"I'm going to simplify this for you. We'll wait for your sister and your kid and take both."

"No way," Lizzee said through clenched teeth. She elbowed Opie and tried to run, slipped in her stupid heels on the wet cobblestones. He chopped the back of her neck with his blade, hard and she was down and dead.

"Wow!" Pots said, transfixed by Opie's skills.

"Wake up, Pots! Help me drag her behind that dumpster," said Opie, irritated. "Sandee has to be on Lizzee's phone somewhere. We'll call, set up a meeting and wait, herd her into that dead-end alley right there and finish her off. Gloria's kid will come by eventually and we'll grab her, too. The Boss'll be pumped."

Together they dragged the dead bitch outta sight, but when they checked her phone, there was no contact for Sandee. Well, shit. They talked out their next move. They could see the rain was rinsing Lizzee's blood clean from the cobblestone, so they were good—no chance of someone noticing and calling the cops. Maybe find some cover and wait outside the old hotel 'til the kid comes out looking for her mother? It's as good a plan as any.

They hid behind the trash cans, under the open lid of a dumpster and waited. Pretty soon along comes Sandee. Well, shit, she was a big one. Cute, though; way cuter than Lizzee, any day of the week. Pots and Opie couldn't believe their luck.

She saw Lizzee and ran over to her, all upset.

Opie and Pots popped up, ready to grab her but Pots stumbled and knocked over a can, giving Sandee a warning. She started running.

Opie cut her off, waving his blade. She backed off into the dead-end alley, just liked they'd planned. It was like Opie had said, they'd just poke their blades at her and hustle her back into the alley. "Stay close," Opie called over his shoulder at Pots. "Don't let her get away." Herding a cow.

Sandee figured out it was a dead-end pretty quick. Opie called to Pots again, a grin in his voice. "Let me show you how it's done, Pots. This here is your master class."

When Sandee grabbed a metal trash can lid and a broken mop handle, Pots almost laughed out loud. Like that was going to help her against someone like Opie.

Opie moved in close, smiling like this was payday.

Sandee raised the lid like a shield and poked him with the jagged broom handle. They circled around one another. Opie poked at her with his blade again but she pushed it away with the shield.

"Slice her, Opie!" Pots yelled with a wild fist pump.

Opie did, but she blocked him again. He was getting pissed. This wasn't going as planned; no way. Tired of playing games, he went for the big chop on her shield hand. The blade split the metal lid and cut her forearm bad. His blade stuck in the lid so she dropped it, Opie's blade clattering to the ground beside it. Ignoring the cut on her arm, she leaned right and drove her sharp stick under Opie's chin, right up into his head. He just stood there so she snatched up his blade, spun like a ninja in the movies and almost chopped his head off. Opie was dead.

Pots couldn't believe it.

She turned to face the stunned Pots, cut his blade hand off before he could move, then his head.

———

SANDEE DROPPED THE MACHETE, clutched her left arm, blood pouring out. Time to go. She stumbled along the alley retracing her steps. Along the way she found a piece of abandoned clothing which she wrapped around her arm. Filthy and sodden, it was still better than bleeding to death.

Rounding the corner, she skidded to a stop at the sight of her sister Gloria's body lying on the cold cobblestones with a young girl— who *had* to be her niece Jessica—kneeling beside her, sobbing. Her sister was clearly dead. She took Jessica by the hood of her top and dragged her along, racing from the scene. Jess was screaming, battling to return to her mother.

"Gotta go kid, more gang coming!"

"Mom!" Jessica sobbed, barely keeping up.

Terry repeated to Jess as she dragged her along. "I'm your Aunt Terry! Aunt Theresa? Library letter! I came for you."

Jessica was screaming hysterically now. Had she heard Terry at all?

Together they bolted from the alley and ran into the street. Terry looked around wildly, noticing a police car stopped for traffic. She stumbled to it and hit the side window, smearing it with blood while still trying to hang on to Jess.

The police driver rolled down his window slowly, his eyes narrowed with suspicion.

———

CONSTABLE JENKINS and Maples had been Vancouver cops for fifteen years combined; Jenkins for fourteen and Maples just one, the rookie.

Senior cop Jenkins was the babysitter, trainer and today's driver. Wise, cynical and ex-RCMP. Seen it all. He was smart, big, slow to move and hard to stop when he was in motion. Jenkins saw lots of rookies come and go. Some quit after a shooting, giving mouth-to-mouth to a dead person, or watching a jumper off a tall building. One rookie quit after getting puked on. Suck it up, cupcake.

The new guy, Maples, was young, wiry, bored. A rural fellow from some who cares town where nothing happens. He was here for adventure and to escape the snow. Cop school was an adventure, alright. Here he was, not sure if this was where he should be.

They were both trapped in an old Ford four-door sedan, one of the last still running. A dinosaur. Their next car would be an SUV.

Jenkins preferred the big old cars, roomy, wide, smooth, comfy, especially for a twelve to sixteen-hour work day. Jenkins was a big wide guy and the SUV's were narrow and short. This old car smelled faintly of pee, shit and vomit. It was nearly miled out so it wouldn't undergo a thorough cleaning.

This old car was classic. Jenkins once had an older perp corralled in the rear seat who commented on how nice the back seats of these big old cars were. "Lots of leg room," he said. "The end of an era," then shit on the seat.

Well, hadn't that just been dandy... Jenkin's wished he could say the incident had been an aberration; but it was not.

Still, he liked this car. He liked the way both shotguns fit in between the seats, the TASER plugged in between. The shotgun came out much quicker. Given the choice and pressed for time he usually bonked the perp over the head with the shotgun butt, anyway. Out cold. Nobody dies from a butt in the face. Using the TASER meant paperwork and media complaints on slow news days, anyway. Maybe he should have used a roll of newspaper, they'll say. Funny.

He touched a button on the laptop computer to see messages. It was handy how the radio, computer console and cell phone nestled nicely in the wide car dash without poking in your face like the SUVs. His belly was getting a bit big for that kind of thing.

It was another day on the east-side run, raining hard, wipers beating on fogged-up windows. Traffic was very jerky and slow which allowed them to keep a watch out the windows.

"Supposed to be watching, not looking at your fucking phone," grumbled Jenkins. "Nothing to see on that small screen. Want to get out and walk a beat for a while?"

"Sorry. Just checking my shift over the next few weeks." Maples put the phone in his pocket. And turned his gaze to the street from the passenger's side window. "All I see here is constant rain, dreary poverty, drugs and sadness. It's damned depressing, is what it is."

"Raining hard is good. Keeps folks inside so hopefully we get a quiet day." Jenkins paused the car behind an old 1970's motor home that belched black smoke. "Ah. Look at this shitty motor home. 'Discount Tattoos by Uber Bill'. I can imagine."

"Nasty," answered Maples. "Should we pull it over and take a look?"

"Are you kidding? In this rain—?"

Ka-Boom! Jenkins side window was streaked with red—blood, this coming from a woman covered in the stuff, dragging a screaming young girl with her.

The constables glanced at each other. Jenkins powered the window down, hearing her shout, "Constable Reid! Undercover! Help us!"

"Reid? Infor—." He stopped. He'd heard of her down at the station—under deep cover she'd taken down half of the crime families in Montreal. She was here, in Vancouver? From the little he knew, chances were good someone was trying to kill her.

Not waiting for an ambulance, that's for sure. He stabbed his finger at Maples. "Get them in the back! Sit with them."

Maples ran around and opened the back door, stuffing the woman and girl in the backseat, following them inside and slamming the door behind him. No way out.

Jenkins turned on his lights, sirens and sped off, trying to radio in and steer at the same time.

Maples dug out the first aid pack and did his best to stop the bleeding on the woman's arm. The wound was nasty! The young girl's screams never stopped, filling the car cab with teeth-gritting tension.

The soaking wet woman was shaking, going into shock. She kept repeating, teeth chattering, "Constable Reid... undercover... got jumped... body in the alley!"

Maples got his overcoat from the front and covered Reid and the young girl who abruptly stopped screaming, leaving a hollow silence inside the overly hot squad car. He stuttered, "It's okay, we're getting you to a hospital."

Reid clutched at his overcoat, her wide eyes riveted to the young girl, drinking her in like she might disappear at any moment. "This is my niece. Don't let her go."

"I-I won't. Let's gauze this arm up and stop that bleeding."

"Call... call... Inspector Shirley McDonald..." Reid urged, the strength of her voice lessening.

"Heard you." Jenkins called back over his shoulders, his eyes moving from the traffic around him to the rear-view mirror at his passengers and back again. "I know the Inspector. I'll call in... get her patched through. Just a sec' ...Whoa!" He swerved to avoid another vehicle double parked outside a bar to disgorge some partiers.

Maples found himself gripping the pair against the car's lurching back and forth, leaning hard into the corners. Jenkins expertly dodged another double-park, this time a delivery truck, two jaywalking pedestrians and a bum on a bicycle balancing two green bags of tin cans on a hockey stick. Jenkins was in the zone, driving like a maniac, graceful as a hippo in heat.

He growled, "Hospital coming right up."

19

ALIVE AND SCARRED

TERRY HATED HOSPITALS BUT THE DOCTOR WANTED TO MONITOR her slashed arm. She'd likely contract an infection from the alley fracas. He also suggested she may want to stick around while they checked out Jess. Good plan. It wasn't long before Shirley Mac came around to see what all went down in that rainy alley. Snooping.

"That'll be a bitchin' wound, Terry. Well done," said Inspector Shirley MacDonald, holding Terry's hand to closely scrutinize the big bandage. "Cut it on the lid of a garbage can, eh?"

"Yup. Clumsy me. It'll take a month or two to heal—fifty-eight stitches."

The Inspector sat back down behind her desk. "How's Jessica doing?"

"Not bad. She's been through hell."

"I'll say. She's as tough as nails for only eleven years old," said Terry.

The Inspector considered before speaking, "What happened in that alley?"

"I arrived looking for Gloria, found her dead and Jess nearby. I moved Jess away and that's where I got the arm cut. It was pouring rain and slick and I fell on a metal garbage can. Got cut."

Shirley Mac put her poker face on. "Are you sure? Two dead guys weren't far away. They had machetes but were killed with the same one by persons unknown."

"So someone fought two men wielding machetes and killed them with a little knife? Sounds like James Bond to me. What about the blood?"

"The rain washed everything away. Nothing to find."

"Too bad," said Terry sympathetically.

Shirley Mac gave Terry a suspicious look but said nothing more. "Well, I should go. This investigation looks like a dead end. Take care."

Terry watched Shirley Mac leave. It annoyed her that her bosses really wanted to say she killed the two machete gang men in the alley but she'd never admit it. It was kill or be killed and she had no interest in dying that day. If she had admitted to it there'd have been a huge inquiry. Been there, done that. Internal affairs would sit her down and ask why she didn't try asking the two killers to talk about their feelings instead of bumping them off. 'Poor lads didn't mean any harm', they'd say. Or was it revenge for bumping off Gloria? Why didn't you stop everything and wait for backup to arrive? Did you tell them to surrender?

Two punks armed with machetes surrender? Fuck, there I was with a garbage can lid and a broken broom handle, she thought. Her instructors said grab anything if you have nothing. Give your opponent another thing to think about.

If she admitted it, word would get out. Sure as shit, a crusading do gooder reporters would jump on it as a dangerous psycho uber cop picking on two young men trying to make their way in a new country. The story was already written somewhere. Add in the names. Find one of the young men's mom or sister, get her to cry for the camera, show a few pictures of him suited up for school and say, "he was a kind boy". The story hits social media and every mush brain know-it-all adds their two bits worth. Becomes a national TV exclusive. Write the parents a big fat cheque.

Fuck 'em. Won't bring Gloria back, thought Terry. She wasn't admitting to anything.

————

AFTER THREE MONTHS Jess didn't cry much at night. The nightmares were becoming infrequent thanks to the passage of time and the helpful psychologist. Jess went from virtually running in the streets to living like a normal eleven-year old girl.

The day her mom died was branded in Jess's brain.

On that terrible day in the alley she found her mom and saw the two deadly men herding a tall woman into the alley to do the same to her. The woman was unarmed, and Jess expected she would be defenceless against the thugs. She would have run, too, but the body of her mom paralysed her.

What was the point of running? To where? To who? She'd hoped for a quick death when the killers returned but suspected she'd be taken away.

She'd knelt beside her mom, rain pounding down on them when a hand grabbed her by the collar and drag her to her feet. She turned her head away, not wanting to look to see who had come to claim her now that her mother was gone. But she did see, and was surprised it was the unarmed woman, still alive but bleeding, angry, yelling at her to come right now before more men with knives came.

She looked strangely similar to her mom.

The woman yanked her away from her mother, from the cold pavement, and ran her along the alleyway to the street. The woman was telling her something as they gasped and stumbled together, fleeing from her mother's body. "Letter...library... sister in the police."

The words were like bullets, piercing the rage of terror that enveloped Jess. This was... This was her Auntie Theresa? The rescue she'd prayed for so long had at last come? But it was too late for her Mom.

Somehow they were in a safe, warm and dry cop car, sirens blaring, screaming their way to a hospital.

It took Jess a while to get used to her quirky aunt Terry. Terry and her mother Gloria couldn't have been more opposite. Gloria was smooth, pliable and sycophantic while Terry was Conan the Barbarian, if she had to be.

———

TERRY SAT at the dinner table with Bev and Murray Wallin. Jessica sat at the end, quiet as usual. Ruffles the sheepdog stood guard in the kitchen corner, ready to attack any bit of food headed for the floor. Any food except corn. Ruffles hated corn.

Terry found boarding with the Wallins had been a good decision for both Jess and herself. Her work schedule was erratic at best with odd court dates, meetings and a peculiar work schedule. Her new supervisor didn't make it any easier. It was soon apparent after she began working under him that Inspector Smythe hated women on the force and would never miss an opportunity for a grab or a pinch.

He'll be very sorry if he makes a grab for me.

Terry was glad to be finally rid of the loaner apartment. It was expensive and lonely. It was Shirley Mac who suggested she and Jess board with the Wallins after listening to Terry complain about rent, "Triplex" and having to cook for herself. Terry called herself a minimalist but Shirley knew she was just cheap.

Shirley knew the Wallins well. Both were teachers in special education and took on the odd foster child. Terry and Jess might be a good fit. It turned out that Terry liked the Wallins just fine. Good people. They were always available for Jess.

She was coming along well, all things considered, but physical scars heal faster than the ones close to the soul. The Wallins knew what to say and do or when to leave Jess to puzzle it out for herself.

The Wallins were great fans of writing. They pushed Jess along to journal and write poetry. Terry thought it helped Jess make sense of the past madness. The Wallins thought she had the gift of writing.

Terry enjoyed it here, sitting around the table like a family. She never got enough of that.

"Pass the mashed spuds, please," Jess requested.

Terry complied, hoping for fleeting eye contact and getting none. Bad day?

Ben Wallins spoke up, "How was your day at school, Jess? I heard you read out a poem."

"It went okay."

"School, day or poem to read?" persisted Bev with a smile.

Terry liked how Bev expertly smoked a conversation out of Jess. No escape.

Jess looked up at her. "School was fine. My day was fine. And the poem went well."

"What was it about, Jess?"

She took a breath. "Life. How it goes on and we barely notice it or appreciate it. Goes by to the end of the day and we never get it back."

Bev smiled, "Sounds interesting. How did it go over?"

"Everyone seemed to like it. I hate reading poems out in front of the class."

"Builds confidence."

"I suppose."

Bev looked at Terry and asked, "And how about you Terry? Terry? Did you hear me Terry? Are you alright ... Terry?"

THE WALLIN'S homey kitchen vanished but she kept hearing, "Terry! Terry!"

Forcing the vivid, long dream from her mind, she opened her eyes, blinked, focusing.

Cave walls. *Cave walls?*

"Terry! Are you awake?" said the sweaty and anxious face of Lt. Trev Reser.

Terry cleared her throat, shook her head, eyes slowly focusing. "Wha... what?"

"Stay with me, Terry!" The medic asked as he shone an annoying little beam of light into each of her eyes. "What year is it? What's your name?"

Terry's mind struggled, "2020? No, I mean... 2030. Major Theresa Reid. Okay?"

"Not bad," said the medic, unimpressed, now taking her pulse and blood pressure. Trev passed her a wet face cloth.

Wiping her face awkwardly, she slowly sat up. "No more questions. Hey, I think I'm okay." Leaning her back against the cave wall, she tested her neck, rotating her head this way and that gently, and blinking her eyes. "How long... have I been out?" She draped the blessedly cool cloth across her face and left it there.

"You've been out for almost three days, Major. Concussion from the plane crash. You've had a helluva a dream going, too."

"You have no idea. My past was haunting me." Terry lifted the cloth off her face, wiping sweat from her skin and eyes. "What's with these handcuffs?"

Trev shook his head. "We couldn't unlock them, so we just cut the chain." He lifted his arm and shook his half of the cuff clamped on his wrist.

Terry barely shrugged. "I have... a gigantic headache. What's going on? Why the cloak and dagger?"

Trevor kneeled close to her. "Remember the plane crash? Afghanistan?"

"Yes."

"Do you know why we're here?"

"No."

"Well, the president was kidnapped and taken here to Afghanistan."

"Not possible!" she groaned. *Did this shit ever end?*

"Yes, possible."

"How?"

"President Casio had a secret meeting with Wu Ton, the leader of Korea. The Americans had to make up someone as a phony Casio twin for this meeting. The Koreans figured it out and grabbed the real one."

"Stand me up, Trev. We have to talk to someone about this. It's getting crazier by the minute."

A stranger handed her a canteen. *Medic?*

"Drink!"

Terry glugged down half the canteen. She looked at the medic. "Who are you?"

"Corporal Ross Hunt, Special Forces."

"Ah."

Ross warned her, "You have a concussion and shouldn't be moving around, especially in this heat. Here are some painkillers but you need to be careful."

Terry swallowed the pills and drank more water. "We have about a fifteen-mile march in the desert with army packs. I'll have to take my chances. What happens if I have trouble?"

"You'll pass out and fall into a coma again, if you're lucky."

"If I'm not lucky?"

"You'll die."

"Fucking dandy."

The march was hard over treeless hills and desert tracts. They stuck to the edge of the hills, avoiding the open areas and ambush valleys. No chances. Hot sun. As they marched, Terry's head ached, pain going down to her toes. Ross made her drink a lot of water which she often threw up when he wasn't watching. She was soaked with sweat, alternating with heat and cold. The sun drilled through her clothes. Her head ached as if it bore the weight of an elephant's foot. Finally, Terry collapsed; face down in the sand and dirt, mercifully out cold once again.

She didn't feel Trevor and Ross gently sliding her to the relative shade of a nearby rock face. An IV was set up for her. They weren't going anywhere for a while.

Terry later awoke to see a face close by. The medic...Ross? "Did I pass out again?"

"Yes, but not as long this time...four hours. It'll be dark, soon."

"Sure," she said.

Trev came by as Ross moved off. "How are you doing?"

"Believe it or not, I do feel fractionally better. I can travel better at night. Dark and cool."

"Moving at night? Here?" asked Trev, amazed.

"Why not? The locals move at night."

"Yeah, and that's why we don't."

"No wonder you Americans lose wars. Big show during daylight then hide under the bed at night. Locals don't have super powers. They move smart and watch what they do. Nobody's watching them."

Trev gave a big sigh. "If you say so. Here, you need to try and eat something. Saved you this fruit stuff. You might be able to keep this down."

"Thanks."

Trev sat and watched her eat in case she needed to throw up or something and he could hold her food for her. He filled the time with idle chat. "You were out for days. Impressive. Do you remember anything?"

Terry swallowed, surprised at his question. "Now that you mention it, I did have a kick ass long dream. It was an epic."

"Revisionists, Disciples, Bill Page type dream?"

She thought back. "Nope. Before that. My previous life type dream, when I was an uncover informant. Weird times. They were so detailed it was like I was there."

Trev seemed impressed.

Whatever floats your boat, I guess.

He asked, "Did it have a start, middle and end?"

Terry had another mouthful. Not bad for lukewarm and slightly gritty. When she saw he was still after an answer about her time in la la land, she said, "My dream was complete, like a movie. It had every detail and feeling I remember."

"When did it end?"

"You mean where did it cut off?"

"Yes."

"It ended after I got Jess settled at the Wallins, before I went to Afghanistan."

"And the dream just... ended?"

"Why the third degree? It was a dream."

"I'm interested in what goes on inside the human brain, how we cope in a trauma situation."

"Oh." She looked at him balefully, then expelled a long breath. "Yes, the dream just ended. We were all sitting at the Wallins at the supper table talking about our day and bam...it's 'wake up Terry'!"

"Do you feel unsettled?"

Now she frowned and answered him with measured words. "Not really. It happened like I remember it and I'm good with it. No regrets."

"Sorry to bore you with that. Just curious what folks think of when they're in a coma. I'm a nosey guy."

"No problem. I'm almost finished, and I feel okay. Should be fully dark in an hour and then let's go."

Trev looked at the other soldiers and warily said, "You'd best lead, Terry, and we'll follow. Any tips Miss Nighthawk?"

"Tips? Sure. Really listen, walk quietly, no flashlights, hide your shadows, use hand signals, steady but vigilant pace, stick to rocky edges so you don't step on a mine in the dirt, keep a knife handy so you don't wake up the whole fucking world with your shooting which won't hit anything, anyway. How's that?"

Ross the medic swallowed, "And if I step on a mine, do it quietly?"

Nobody laughed.

20

TROUBLED WATERS

On the rusty fishing boat Bill Page threw up over the bouncing guard rail, cursing his present situation in between retches. The brutally cold wind slapped his face with seawater, chilling him to the bone. Page had been violently sea sick on this trip from Attu Island to Kamchatka. He felt lucky but not particularly grateful.

People were supposed to be grateful for *him*.

He had nothing left to throw up. Clinging weakly to the rail, he made his way around the rusty old boat on shaky legs. The Korean crew ignored him, going about their fishing duties as if he was invisible. This ship stunk of sweat, fish and fuel.

Accommodations for him were limited to bunking with four other men, all of whom were shoehorned into a tiny, stinking cabin near the bow of the ship. Page knew enough to know this was the worst place to sleep as the waves constantly beat on the sides of the rusty craft, which vibrated from the deep and constant drumming diesel engines.

Page dragged himself to his cot and collapsed face down, praying for escape from this nightmare in sleep.

AFTER FOUR AND half hours Terry led them to the entrance of the medieval courtyard of a small mud hut village. It was familiar territory from Terry's Army Intel days. It was supposed to be an abandoned dried up watering hole. As they approached the entrance, Terry flashed a hand signal while the others watched, guns ready. The confirmation was sent from the closest building. Dozens of heavily armed men appeared on the ramparts. Terry's group shuffled towards the doorway.

Ambush? Hope not.

Trev was nervous about the grim men in warrior Pashtun garb standing at the doorway while others peered down from the tops of the walls. Someone important waited inside. They were searched and waved through. Guns pointed at their backs as they strolled to the middle of the yard.

———

THE KOREAN FISH boat crew quietly went about the business of fishing, probably talking of home and family as if Page wasn't there. Page couldn't believe they weren't fawning over him, treating him with the due he deserved. Didn't these bumpkins realize if everything went right, he would be the dictator of half the planet?

The tiny, grubby, unhappy ship's captain would have nothing to do with him and instead was fully occupied by nervously scanning the skies with binoculars. He occasionally shouted orders to his men in a sharp, high-pitched stream of commands.

Page took his silence for two days, then angrily stomped over to the captain and began shouting at him. "I'm paying good money to get to Kamchatka! How dare you make *me* wait!"

The captain stuck out his hand to shake, grinned like he won the lottery and said, "Merry-kah! Merry-kah!"

"Merry'kah? That's America, you fool. You oriental bumpkin!"

The captain considered his words, then beamed again. "You BOSS Merry-kah? Reely Big boss?"

Page became enraged, red in the face, waving his arms. "I will be the biggest boss of the most powerful country in the world you idiot! Take me to Kamchatka right fucking now!"

The captain just shrugged, watched, smiled.

Page was an imposing man over six and a half feet tall and a portly three hundred pounds. He expected to get what he wanted. He took a swing at the little captain. "I'll beat some sense into you!"

The captain calmly watched the fist coming then nimbly stepped aside from Page's blow. Smiling, the captain reached out with his fists beating Page twice on his chin. The big American toppled backwards like a rotten old building, landing on his back in a heap of soggy fish netting.

Page laid there, in shock, struggling vainly to get up. The ship captain stood over him grimly. "Mr. Page: I speak perfect English. You will go along with our fishing expedition without saying a word. Our safety depends on how convincing we are. Did you hear what happened to Attu Island after we rescued you?"

Page nodded his head.

"We don't want to get the same treatment. I'm hoping news of your escape was covered up when someone blew up the island. You'd better hope the same, Mr. Page. Your life depends on it."

Page laid there and nodded.

"If we are discovered, the first thing we will do is put you in that net along with weights and throw you overboard. Understand?"

Page nodded.

"Piss me off again and we might just do it, anyway. If you're lucky, I'll shoot you, first."

Page looked terrified.

"We may be hunted by ruthless forces. Behave yourself and stay in your cabin. We'll tell you when to come out."

The Captain kicked Page in the ribs and stalked away to the boats bridge, resuming his ceaseless scanning of the sky for deadly snoopers.

Page crawled humbly back to his shared room in the bow of the fish boat. Sleep. Please.

―――――

TREVOR WONDERED if this was the last scene he'd ever see. His last visit in Afghanistan was a tame affair. He lived in the big American base apart from this alien world. All he'd done was watch TV monitors while writing religious scripts for Colonel Garfield.

The walled courtyard here was built before Normans invaded England. Ancient Afghans were repelling invaders back then, probably using the same techniques they used today. And just as successfully.

He watched a dozen children kicking a homemade soccer ball around the courtyard. Terry leaned over to him, "Maybe one of *our* heads will be the ball in an hour or so."

He recoiled in horror.

She winked.

Trevor tried to force the image from his mind. He spotted an old man seated on an ancient stone bench, in the shade. He held a leash to a little dog lying in the dust, panting in the heat.

Trevor turned and saw Terry smiling and offering her hand to the man. He took it, greeting her in formal Russian. "Dohb-rihy dyen, Major."

Trev couldn't understand her reply but saw they were friends. Only Terry Reid could crash land in the most dangerous land on Earth and meet a friend.

She moved to sit next to the Old Russian, and he heard them switching to English.

The Old Russian glanced at the handcuff gripping Terry's wrist, its broken chain dangling. "Were you in... trouble, Major?"

"Apparently so. The Lieutenant and I were cuffed together on the plane. We couldn't unlock them as they are special CIA issue and are unbreakable."

The Russian nodded and called to one of the children playing soccer in the yard. The child stepped forward, pulled a funny shaped piece of metal from his pocket and stuck it into the cuff lock. He made little boy faces, twisting his tongue around in concentration. The handcuff fell open, dropping to the ground. The child performed the same miracle on Trevor's cuff.

"Well done!" Terry said to the child in Pashtun and the boy giggled and ran back to the game.

Trev rubbed his wrist, glad to be rid of the tight cuff. "Those were the old CIA's best."

The Russian shrugged. "Everything the CIA did was a huge deal... big secret, over-priced, average, and on TV."

Trevor didn't like to hear that but said nothing.

"What's up?" Terry asked the Old Russian.

He became somber. "The American president is missing."

Terry's mouth was grim. "So I hear. When?"

"A month ago."

"A month? He's been seen on TV and heard on the radio."

"So? Hollywood stand-in. Huge secret."

Terry shook her head, "How did they snatch a president?"

The Old Russian smiled slyly. "You'll laugh."

"Try me."

"The president had a top-level meeting with Wu Ton, United Korea dictator, Singapore."

"Déjà vu? Like they did back in 2019?" asked Terry.

"Yes, except no CIA or FBI pros to watch. Only White House amateurs. As stupid as they were, they were fearful for the president's safety, so brought a stand-in lookalike to scout it out in advance. Too much Hollywood. The real president would trade places when the Secret Service decided it was safe to do so."

"Both the president and the look alike in the same building?" Terry cringed, already knowing where this was headed.

"Yes. The Korean SSD noticed the lookalike and quietly

searched the meeting building for the real one. When both presidents were together the SSD abducted the real one. American guards thought they had a real president. They were wrong."

"When they wised up, President Casio was gone?"

"Yes. On an embassy plane and spirited away before they knew what happened."

Terry thought about it. "So why aren't the Americans vaporizing Korea? Raising holy hell?"

"Publically losing a president makes them look bad as they are only now getting back on their economic feet. They thought the lookalike could stand in and they'd find President Casio in a few days —no one the wiser. Can't bomb Korea because their president is there... so they thought," the Old Russian said.

Trevor felt like he was going to faint from the shock but managed to sputter, "Now the American military is gutted. We aren't sure we can find a nuke that works or a missile to put it on. No money and manpower after all the wars. We're rusted out... bankrupt."

Terry shook her head. "So, a month later, no real president?"

"Correct. The Americans looked everywhere. They called on other countries like China and Russia but nada."

Terry looked around, wondering what to say next. "Why would the president risk a meeting like that? Seems chancy to me."

Trev shook his head. "Had to meet Wu Ton. The 2019 deal gave the Koreas a boatload of money and sanctions lifted. All they had to do was disarm."

The Old Russian smiled, "Korea spent the money and kept the nukes which can now reach the states—thanks for the influx of cash, Uncle Sam—with their new ballistic submarines. Kept everything. President Casio had no choice but to meet. America the bully became America the humble."

"So why drug and kidnap us?" asked Terry.

"Oh that! You can thank the head of the revived American CIA: Tina Gospel. All we did was rescue you."

"By blowing a hole in the wing of the plane and almost killing us? Thanks a bunch."

"Please Major. Someone else shot your plane. It was us who hacked the controls to bring it down here before the next missile blew up the rest of it."

"Ah."

"Tina Gospel's head of the CIA? I thought she was retired when they scrapped it."

"Spymasters are always old. Look at the KGB and MI6. Tina Gospel was brought in to restart the CIA. She has a certain... reputation."

"Torture without question? Blow up the suspect's car, family and all?"

"You said it, not I."

"Why did Gospel go after Trev and me?"

"Revisionists banished the CIA and cast them to the four winds. America became a hermit kingdom with no need or ability to look outward."

"The Revisionists are gone so the CIA is coming back?"

"Yes. The CIA barely found a building to rent with a small budget from a bankrupt government. A nobody. No teeth or eyes. You were experienced, handy and expendable," said the Old Man.

"The ghosts of the Revisionist's still haunt the White House," said Terry.

"I suspect Gospel will be rooting Revisionists out, by any means," said the Russian.

Terry absentmindedly rubbed the red spot where the hand cuff had gripped her. "I hadn't heard Tina Gospel was coming back and I thought I had a 'finger on the pulse'."

The Russian said, "Nothing like misplacing a president to build a fire under the evil CIA."

"Does the CIA have anyone left out here?" asked Terry.

The Russian looked at Trev and nodded at him. "CIA agent here, Major." His dog growled at Trevor.

———

BILL PAGE WAS THRILLED when he looked out the porthole in his little cabin. He'd been on this tub for days and was sick of it. The captain visited him in his tiny room and told him there would be a transfer to another boat as soon as it was nightfall.

Page knew this was in the port of Avacha Bay on the peninsula of Kamchatka, in Russia, after hearing the name in snatches of conversations the crew had. He'd never heard of Kamchatka before his voyage. He suspected this place was chosen for its long-term security as a Russian base. Kamchatka was only opened to the public in 1990. The view from his porthole was stunning with the city at the water's edge and the gigantic dormant volcano looming in the background.

After closing the porthole, he sat back on his bed and waited for night to come and freedom from this awful little fish boat.

It was ten thirty in the evening when the captain came to his compartment door. "Mr. Page. Time to leave us. Look around one more time at the roominess and freedom. It will have to last for a while."

Page ignored him. "Let's go. It can't be worse than this fucking tub."

The captain shrugged and graciously waved him toward the exit.

Someone pulled a thick cloth hood over Page's head. He struggled for a moment, hitting out wildly until a fist buried itself into his gut. The captain said, "A hood over your head for secrecy. Be quiet or I'll shoot you. If I don't get paid, I may shoot you, anyway."

Head covered, another pair of hands guided Page up and on to the fishing boat deck.

"Take the hood off and you die, Mr. Page," were the captain's final chilling words.

Page heard the splashing of a small boat alongside, smelled the cold salty breeze. After a couple of stumbles and Korean curses he was seated in the boat and felt it move in the water to the sounds of rowing, bouncing along in the bay. The ship boat's distinctive smell and sound of orbiting gulls got further and further away.

He felt the rowing stop, heard voices bantering. There was some debate going on, an angry exchange and then he heard something land in the little boat. *Clump*. Bag of money? Bomb? Money bag with a bomb in it?

He held his breath.

21

MOLE

TREV GASPED AND PROTESTED, "HEY, I'M NO CIA SPY GUY. Do I look like one, Terry?"

The Russian laughed. "Good actor. Somewhat inexperienced but you must admit, Major, doesn't he seem a bit too timely and well connected?"

She looked at Trev, grinning and nodding. She punched him on the shoulder, fairly hard. "You old spook! Well done and right under my nose."

Trev mumbled, "My cover's blown. Fuck!"

The Russian added, "Nothing to worry about, Lieutenant Trevor. A blown cover won't matter if you're dead."

"It's okay, Trev. Death's the least of our troubles," said Terry.

Trev turned a bit white despite the heat.

Terry continued, "Is Russia going to help find the president? I thought Korea, Russia and the U.S. signed some pact back in 2029? We're the big boys and screw the rest of the world and all that. The Alliance of the Lonely and Jilted."

"Ah, they did but that pact caused the crash of the world economy. Besides, Russia was in poor economic shape when they signed and now its even worse. I'm all there is."

————

THAT THICK BLACK hood on Page's face made him wonder if this next breath would be his last. Page was grateful for every minute he was still breathing. After being thrown off a cliff, watching the prison island blasted to smithereens and surviving on a little fish boat, Page was beginning to think God was guiding him on a mission. The Ruler in the Heavens had a plan for him.

He overheard people speaking languages he did not understand. Page made a point of being a pious English-only speaker which didn't help his present situation. He was shoved this way and that. It was like being drunk wobbling to and fro. At some point he knew he was standing steadily on the slippery deck of some type of ship. Page dearly hoped it wasn't another disgusting fishing boat.

Hands tugged and pushed him along until he came to a steel edge. He felt it with his feet as they stepped into nothingness, almost falling over the edge of something. He recoiled, scrambling back, pushing against whoever was edging him forward. Overpowering, insistent hands kept pushing him along.

To his death?

Stumbling, cursing, he was shoved onto his hands and knees which guided him back into a hole and pushed him down. They were relentless, hissing and cursing in an unknown tongue.

Page managed to grip a rail which led to steps. Narrow steps. Hands and feet pushed on his head, forcing him to go down into a small opening, a hole in the ship. His large butt barely squeezed through the opening. Urgent hands and feet above were unrelenting, so down he went into the metal hole.

He felt air rushing through the hole as he climbed down. It stunk of cigarette smoke, fuel, bodies and shit. Were they taking him down a sewer to hide? Would he be shot later? That didn't make sense—

why go to all this trouble just to kill him. This was God's plan. It had to be. If it wasn't... He wrenched his thoughts from traveling down that road. Stay present. Stay focused.

He was at their mercy, whoever they were. A foot crushed one of his fingers. Whoever they were, they were coming along.

Page slipped off what turned out to be the final step and collapsed on a slippery floor. Boots impeded his movement then many hands pulled him to his feet. The black hood over his face was yanked off. Oddly, the low lights didn't bother his eyes as he'd expected them to.

He was surrounded by a circle of about six men cloistered in a small space. A distinguished Korean man stood before him, clearly the captain. "Welcome aboard the Korean submarine *Pukkuksong*. Our orders are to move you to Karachi, Pakistan. Someone will pick you up from there."

Page was horrified. "A submarine? No windows, underwater?"

The captain looked annoyed, then started laughing. His sailors knew what was good for them and laughed, too, but had no idea why. Page just stood there, silently. Best not bad mouth Korean captains.

The captain stopped laughing. The others stopped abruptly. The time for hilarity was over. "My apologies Mr. Page. We are to get you to Karachi unseen and unnoticed. What better way to do this than a submarine?"

"Brilliant," Page replied, unconvinced.

"We will be about five days. This is part of our usual patrol to annoy the west with our presence."

"You have nukes on board?" Page asked.

"Perceptive of you. We do like to show the world we can walk with the big boys."

"Good to hear."

The captain seemed to wait for more questions. When there were none, he pronounced, "Good. That settled, we are underwater during daylight and surfaced at night. You... sailor, show Mr. Page his bunk for hot racking, where we eat and where the head is."

Hot racking? What's a 'head'?

The guide sailor was about medium height, had a rumpled sweat stained grey work uniform with a battered greasy hat. He looked about twenty-five, thin and tired. His skin was sallow probably from never seeing daylight. His body odour was sharp and as appalling as everyone else's.

The sailor motioned to Page to follow, the action wafting a pungent body odour that made Page recoil. Still, he followed. What choice did he have? The long submarine hallway was torturous. He barely squeezed through the odd round hatches separating sections of the boat. The sailor motioned for him to stop—more stink—and they stood silently before a closed door. After a few minutes there was a whoosh sound and the door popped opened with a sailor coming out, pulling up his pants. The guide sailor pointed in at the toilet. He put his hand on a big lever near the steel toilet and pantomimed pulling it towards him, then leaning it back. Whoosh!

"Flush?" said Page. His bowels made a loud threatening burble and murmur but he wasn't going to the toilet with this man watching.

The sailor looked at him expectantly, until Page's belly noises dissipated. With a shrug, he motioned Page to follow further. They left the toilet, both wriggling through another round hatchway and coming to a small room with a table. The sailor made a motion of feeding himself.

Page didn't try to speak this time and simply nodded. His upset bowels made him break into a little sweat. He'd have to be careful squeezing through the next hatch.

They strolled passed what seemed to Page as miles of pipes, conduit, lights, switches and valves. Through one more hatch and it looked like a dead end. Front of the submarine? A half dozen tubes with propellers ends lay on metal racks. Torpedoes? Small, narrow bunks were folded above each torpedo. Bunks were short, about five feet long and two and a half feet wide. The sailor pointed at a clock and at Page.

"Oh-eleven hundred to oh-four hundred hours?" Page asked. "I only get that bunk for five hours?"

A blank face was his reply. The sailor made some goodbye gesture or was it something derisive? He left Page standing there.

He stood in the pointy end of a submarine that would be his home for an undetermined length of time. He looked around for a place to sit and located a tiny desk without a chair. His bowels rumbled threateningly. Suspicious food on the fishing boat? He decided he needed to go to a washroom and remembered he hadn't had a shit for over twenty-four hours.

Where was that toilet?

He gingerly squeezed through two circular hall way hatches barely keeping his bowels contained. There was a line-up of men patiently standing there. Page was reasonably sure that was the door to the subs only toilet and stood waiting...and waiting... Was this the correct door? He started to sweat as his bowels kicked up a fuss. What would he do if he has a personal disaster in his pants? There was a whooshing sound and the door opened. A man stepped out revealing the steel toilet inside. The only toilet.

Page decided he couldn't wait and desperately barged past the other three men ahead of him. They angrily called after him—he didn't care. He slammed the little door in their faces, wiggled desperately around in the tiny room and dropped his pants. The hole in the toilet was tiny, meant for a smaller man than Page. It hadn't been cleaned in a long time because it was always in use. He managed to aim it and had the best shit of his life.

The angels sang.

The pounding sounds on the door told him he'd best hurry up with the final clean up with an unknown toilet paper system which he muddled through. He was relieved. Standing up, he pulled up his pants and looked down in the toilet. Uh-oh. Flush? Did that sailor pull and return or was it push and return? He really hadn't paid attention and the room was so small. There were big red diagrams and words in Korean on the wall but he had no idea what that meant.

He grabbed the lever on the left of the steel toilet. Here goes. At worst the next man will have to flush it if this failed.

Page pushed the big lever away from him. Water started bubbling and hissing out of the disgusting toilet bowl. Like a stainless-steel cannon, a big whoosh of air violently blew out every bit of water, fecal matter and toilet paper into his face and on every inch of his body. Sandblasted by his own poo. There was shit everywhere. He was dripping. The walls and ceiling dripped down on him.

This was the most horrific, disgusting moment of his life. His skin literally shivered in revulsion as the revoltingly warm, stinking, lumpy sewage soaked into his clothes, ran down his body, trickled through his hair, down his back, into his eyes, his nose—his *mouth*. The smell overpowered him. Page stood and wept in despair, crying like a child, covered with excrement. He broke into a wail, sputtering shit with each wracking sob, knowing he was encased in the entire crew's excrement.

A year ago, Page had been on top of the world. Hundreds of churches treated him as the Disciple of God. An American Pope. He'd engineered a clever, murderous campaign of terror that would make him the dictator of America. His crowning was to have been delivered after making his speech at the President's convention.

That's where it crumbled in disaster.

Page's sniper failed, a crappy kids poem alerted America to his plan and his Disciples were caught by Terry Reid and her cohorts. This was God's way of turning his back on him.

Dennis Casio stole his crown and threw him and all his loyal followers into jail. He'd believed he was lucky to escape from Attu. But instead of leading the charge and seeking his rightful revenge, he was covered in shit, abandoned with strangers in a tin can beneath the sea.

He sobbed like a whiny spoiled child.

———

CLINT BERGEN NEEDED A DRINK BADLY. It was hot in his tuxedo. He felt a trickle of sweat run down the crack of his back. Ice-cold vodka or a gin would go down real nice. Even a beer. He headed for the bar. An FBI agent in the black suit watched him like a hawk, intercepting and steering him to the water pitcher. She poured and gave him a glass of water with lemon, giving him a stern look. "No booze," she whispered to him, scowling.

Grudgingly Clint accepted the glass from her and took a token sip. Cute agent. Was she armed and dangerous? The idea perked up his spirits. He smiled at a dignitary from Canada...the ambassador, maybe...but was careful he didn't smile enough to crack his makeup. The ballroom was packed with ass-kissing ambassadors, movie stars and staff. Clint didn't know who most of them were.

He spotted an older woman dressed regally in a blue outfit, low-cut front and a string of pearls. Feeling his gaze on her, she smoothly sidled up to him. "Mr. President." She pretended to adjust his tie.

"Hi Rose," he asked, awkwardly. He could smell her lovely perfume. Such a nice-looking woman.

"How are you doing?" she smiled in a comforting way.

Clint slipped his hand around her small waist, letting one hand go down past her mid-section headed for her butt. The woman stiffened, looking at him closely. She whispered, "I'm going to knee you in the crotch until your eyes pop out if you let that hand slip any further. Got it? Just pretend. No touching."

Clint whisked his hand away. "Got it," he whispered back, embarrassed.

The woman smiled, speaking loudly, "That's better, honey. I can't have my presidential husband lookin' shabby with a crumpled tie," she gushed. "Look Dennis, here's the Prime Minister of Qatar. Mr. Prime Minister; meet my husband Dennis Casio, the president of the United States."

———

IN THE CORNER of the busy room, newly minted FBI agents McKay and Carson, on loan to the badly depleted Secret Service, surveyed the White House ballroom and the four-hundred guests from all over the world. There were no representatives from the Koreas, naturally.

Agent Anna McKay was the senior and spoke first, "All's well, Carson?"

The black clad agent replied with a sideways whisper, "All good. Geez, this is a lot of people to watch over. I'm not used to this."

McKay confided, "Me neither. These black suits make us look like we know all about it, though. Secret Service had lots of them for us to try on. Closets full of empties."

Carson swept the room with her eyes, left to right, "Lots of black suits and nobody they trust to fill them. It'll be a while, too. From hick sheriffs to the FBI to the White House in thirty days. Good thing Flo and David gave us the heads up of what to do."

McKay noted, "I see Flo... no, I see *both* the Bradleys at two and four o'clock. Let's try and not lose this president even if he is just an annoying phony."

Carson grumbled in a low voice, "I hate this guy. He tried to grab my boobs last time I got close to him. Drunken lecher. Uh-oh. The First Lady is talking to him. She's been a trooper in all this. Nice lady. Look! Dammit, he's got his hands around her...he's going in for an ass grab! Can I shoot him?"

"Stand down, Carson. No need to assassinate the president." McKay watched closely as the First Lady said something to the faux president and he quickly withdrew his hands. "Dorothy can look after herself."

"It wouldn't be assassination if he's just a phony president, right?" hissed Carson.

"Shhhh. Get out there and no shooting the president. Got it? You're sounding like Major Reid."

"Fuck," muttered Carson under her breath. "Where's Terry when we need her, anyway?"

Finally, at long last the ballroom emptied. The president and first lady shook hands with the last few. The Secret Service and FBI did a final search of the room before guiding the presidential couple to their personal suites, Clint into the president's suite while Dorothy went in the guest suite across the hall.

Clint closed the door behind him and looked around the spacious, opulent suite. There was a huge old bed, an office-desk, a full-on suite bathroom and old pictures of past presidents on the walls. The room bar had no alcohol though he checked each and every day.

Clint pulled his clothes off and stood in the shower, letting the hot water and soap wash the makeup off his face. He never thought he could hate a gig like this.

All he ever wanted to do since high school was to be an actor in Hollywood. After a stint in the Navy, he'd hitch-hiked to LA, changed his name from Brent Grose-Ames to Clint Bergen. And waited for the offers to pour in. Instead, he starved, waited, begged and picked up odd jobs here and there. He almost went home when his big chance came along.

Some screenwriter thought he looked perfect for a show he was developing. It might last a few episodes or more. It was a chance. Who knew it was to be hugely popular and last for decades? Soon he was making big bucks on a soap opera as the stud adulterer Johnny on "Years End". It was a glorious life full of easy women, booze and money.

A whisper campaign began, claiming he was a leach, preying on starlets or whoever was handy. He turned up later and later on set, waiting to sober up from late night binges. One day the producer annoyed he was missing for yet another shoot, called him and suggested he never come back. He was unemployed and soon broke.

Clint was in a stupor in his rooming house in Washington DC one afternoon when a group of stern government men showed up and swore him to secrecy. They offered him a thousand dollars a day for a secret mission. They rudely stripped him naked, measured and weighed him. His face was photographed from every angle. A man left with the camera to consult with someone and was back within an hour. He nodded to the others.

Clint was told to put his clothes on, after which they rudely handcuffed him and pulled a black bag over his head. Clint felt he was being rushed into a big car that drove for about forty-five minutes.

Easy money, they said. They flew him to Singapore, people dressed him up, put make up on his face and told him to stand right here. Then President Dennis Casio came out and stood beside him. Identical twins for the meeting with the strange dictator of the Koreas.

"Go here, go there," the American officials told him until they discovered the real president had been kidnapped.

Oh my God. He'd never heard such screaming, raging and cursing in his life. The Secretary-of-State actually *cried*. At one point they considered giving him to the Koreans, claiming he was the real president. Then *Clint* cried, thinking he was going to a Korean gulag. Luckily for him the real president was long gone, and he was safe.

Clint stood in the president's shower, scrubbing off the last of the makeup. He turned off the water and walked back in his room still rubbing the last of the latex from his face with a towel. It felt as if he'd never get it all off.

Someone spoke and he jumped, dropping the towel.

He started again at seeing Dorothy, the first lady, lying on his bed smiling—in the buff—holding out a glass of champagne, that certain light in her eyes.

Whoa!

Change of attitude? This might be a better gig than he thought.

22

FRIENDLY DICTATORS

After the Russian and his group left, Terry found a bit of shade near the east wall of the courtyard. She wearily hunched down on a piece of flattened stone that had probably served as a bench or chair for hundreds of years. Maybe Alexander the Great sat in that very spot, pondering the world just like she was. Inspiration might appear. Her banged-up head ached while swimming with new information.

Trevor appeared beside her. "Coffee? I scored some from one of the local families. I thought you could use it."

She looked at him and at the coffee and snorted. "It seems to me we originally met like this. Yes, please."

He sat down beside her. "I remember the escape from Kabul on that transport plane, last year. Terrifying. Lucky I brought the coffee thermos. It was all I got out of there."

Terry gratefully slurped the sweet mix, eyeing him up. "Were you CIA back then, Trev?"

He dropped his head in shame, momentarily. "Yes, but let me add some context to it. I was there with the US Army, as I said. A guy came to me after I arrived, swore me to secrecy and told me to keep an eye on my boss, Colonel Garfield."

"A guy? That's all you got—a guy? Didn't it seem odd someone from a department that no longer existed wanted you to spy on your colonel?"

"It was the CIA! They have departments within enclaves within cells. They'd drastically shrunk but never really went away completely. I think the guy that spoke to me was from a remnant cell in Pakistan."

She just shook her head. "Did they send you to spook school, at some point?"

"Nope. Once in a while someone would leave me a message when it was important. What you see is what I am."

Terry looked at him closely. "No offense but was your lack of spy image your super power?"

"Yup. Clumsy and clueless without acting lessons."

"So, Army training was all you had?"

"Yes. As good as it gets. Plus, of course, what skills I learned from you." He winked.

Terry drank more coffee, surprised how much better she felt. "So, did that CIA person warn you about why we're here?"

"Nope. Bolt from the blue. The last thing I remember was us sitting in a park on a bench in Washington D.C. with a CIA intel group, then waking up on that plane. I had no prior knowledge."

"Your ruthless CIA director no doubt had us drugged and sent here. Someone in her system might have tipped the Disciples. Lucky for us the Old Russian intervened. Connections still alive. Those US Special Forces guys who came to us must have been contracted by the Russians," Terry noted.

"Americans contracted by Russians?"

"Look at your history. Your president Jackson kissed up to Russia's dictator in a big way or was made his puppet."

"A tangled web. Geez."

"Fuck. Give me a few minutes to think about this. So the Americans want their president back from United Korea, the Russians are unofficially helping us, Revisionists want to kill us and America is afraid the president will be killed if they look too hard," Terry talked it out, more for herself than Trevor. What a mess.

"I'll see if I can get more coffee," said Trev.

Terry dozed in the heat, eyes closed until Trevor returned. As if he hadn't gone, she continued, "So, the situation is this: A month ago the Americans manage to lose their president." Terry picked up a stick and started marking in the sand in front of them, marking an 'x'. "Four days ago, you and I are on a bench in DC talking to CIA spooks about the 'Verbeeldings'. Somehow we're drugged by the CIA to find the president because they don't have anybody except you and me. Afraid we'll say no, they put us on a plane that's going somewhere over Afghanistan, probably headed for Kabul." Terry draws a line in the sand to another 'x'. "Here we are on that little plane, the Disciples find out what's going on and find operatives over here to shoot us down."

Trev stared at her markings. "Not difficult to know where the plane was headed. Kabul is the only real active base for us these days."

She continued, "The Old Russian gets tipped off about us, knows somehow we are going to be intercepted and shot down, hacks the plane controls and crash lands it." She marked another 'x'. "He tells us to find the president."

Trevor said, "Which is what the CIA would have said when we landed in Kabul. The Disciples would have tried to kill us when we landed there, too."

Terry thought for a few moments. "The Disciples must be happy President Casio is missing because he sent their failed leader, Bill Page, to prison at Attu Island in Alaska, forever. Revenge?"

"Or wanted to get him out of the way because they want to do the big takeover. I wonder how securely Page is locked up right now."

Terry ignored that, consulting her sand map. "So, where were we headed before we were shot down? Is the president here or is this just a meeting point?"

"Or were we sent here to quietly kill us troublemakers where nobody would notice?"

"That's a lot of trouble to go through for a little satisfaction," said Terry.

Trev looked at her, "So what's step one?"

"We need to find the men who shot us down. They're the only real lead to find a president."

Trevor called the Special Forces group together. "Listen up. The Major has our instructions."

Terry took a breath. "You are all dismissed and are to travel to your nearest base for re-assignment. Thank you for all your help."

Everyone gasped, especially Trevor. "What? Why?"

Terry looked at them coolly, "You have your orders. Leave the Lieutenant and myself any kit you can spare. Dismissed."

The stunned group headed to their equipment stash for spares that Terry and Trevor could use.

Trevor pulled Terry to one side. "Um, why are they leaving?"

"We don't need a crowd to track someone. I don't know any of these guys, their allegiances or who's paying them. Two travel faster than a group and I trust you."

"Provided nothing happens to either of us on the way."

"Think positive, Trev. What could possibly go wrong?" she smiled.

"I don't even want to think about it."

———

THE CREW of the Pukkuksong knew Captain Geun hated being interrupted when he was looking over the final departure checklist. It had been tight for time but they managed to get additional food and fuel for the voyage. Space in a submarine was tight at best so everything needed to be squirreled away for future use.

He had confidence in his crew. They had been together for three years. His chief engineer said a submarine crew was like a marriage... a lot of work and no sex.

"What the...?" Geun looked up when he heard the commotion down the hallway. A sailor ran up to him. "Sir, the American moved the head flush lever the wrong way. There's shit everywhere. It's terrible."

The captain dropped his head. "Is *he* covered with shit, too?"

"Yes, sir and he's crying. The men are forced to shit in buckets until we get the head fixed and cleaned up. It's a hell of a mess."

The captain was amazed. "Can you shower off the American without leaving the sub? I was hoping to get underway?"

"No sir. The Chief is afraid the American will plug up our shower with shit if we clean him in the sub. There are only two showers."

Captain Geun held his tongue. The deadliest of nuclear submarines was built to frighten the world with its destructive power and here it was held up by the only device men could shit in. Could they not have built two heads in this thing? Four? "Take him topside and clean him up. Wash his clothes, too."

"We're afraid to touch him sir."

The captain went ballistic. "Do as you're told, sailor! I'm not asking you to dance with him, just clean him up, topside, right now! Get going! Take him with you. It's dark out so don't make a fuss." The captain pointed at a surprised nearby helmsmen to help.

The admonished sailors left in a rush while the Captain took a breath, barely suppressing a smile at his crack about 'dancing' with the shit-coated American. Wry submarine wit. Sub men got along, no matter how high the shit gets piled or sprayed.

Two angry sailors pointed to the weeping American covered in shit and led him to the hatch going topside and out. They made sure they went ahead of him to avoid his trail of filth. It was pathetic to watch the little trio. Every boatman watched and laughed as they went by.

———

Kuzinski shivered as he sat in the dark, hidden on the big steel crane in Avacha Bay. Kamchatka was cold even in summer. His job was to watch anything Korean that came into the harbour and the Pukkuksong fitted the description perfectly. Why was a ballistic sub here?

There was no mistaking the modern submarine. In port they look like a gigantic black whale with a small upward superstructure plopped on the top called a 'sail'. It contained periscopes, antennas, radars, lights and a place for crewman to stand and watch for trouble coming towards them when they are surfaced or to get a breath of fresh air. The sail of a whale. This Korean sub was a fair size for a small country, three thousand tons. It boasted a diesel electric drive and was relatively cheap and simple to operate. Crude by super power standards.

It had been docked since early afternoon, stocking up on supplies. It was long since dark. They didn't even allow the crew shore leave which was unusual. Kuzinski heard living in a sub was next best to being entombed in a culvert. No natural light, no windows, no bathing and recirculated stinky air. Sounds like Christmas dinner with the in-laws, last year. He smiled.

He balanced his binoculars on a nearby steel beam. A hatch below the sail popped open and two sailors got out. They seemed to be arguing about something. Then a third man came through the hatch. A very tall, large man. Kuzinski was surprised he had squeezed through a submarine hatch.

The three stood for a few seconds, then one of the sailors put his foot on the big man and pushed him into the bay. Kuzinski watched in amusement as the big man slowly slid down the greasy rounded side of the sub, screaming and clutching, falling into the water with a satisfying splash.

Wow.

The two sailors strode over to a nearby boat tied at the dock and slowly rowed over to the man thrashing in the water. Kuzinski would have thought they were going to drown him as he observed the sailors pushing the man under the water with an oar, laughing. The man in the water started swimming away from the row boat. The sailors rowed along in mild amusement, dunking him again and again. Some new hazing?

Kuzinski was already phoning a number when the two Korean sailors pulled the guy from the water and on to the dock. "Very big man—American. Korean sub. They re-entered the sub. Looks like they're leaving. One fifteen. I sent you a picture of him," he narrated.

"Thank you," said an old voice, in Russian, on the other end. He dialed his phone. "Gomez?"

"Yes, I'm here."

"We have a complication. Page was just spotted on a Korean sub in Kamchatka."

"Bill Page?" Gomez gasped. "Positive?"

"It was dark but his unusual characteristics stand out. We have a photo. I have feelers out to check."

23

TRAPPED IN A SUBMARINE

Page was paraded in front of the Captain, dripping with water, smelling only of seawater. "I'm sorry for the way my sailors washed you off. I am, however, surprised at their inventiveness." He gave the sailors a mild look of annoyance, "As I'm sure you are as well, but this way we can get underway in a few minutes. The less time we linger at this port the better. You are a secret cargo on a secret mission, after all."

Page was soggy and speechless but had to admit he was somewhat clean.

He'd never been in a submarine before. It was a windowless labyrinth of tunnels, pipes, wheels, cables and tiny rooms, illuminated with dim lights that pulsed 24 hours a day. The walls were covered with moisture and everything was damp. Hallway hatches were circular, Russian style, tiny, even for the diminutive Korean crew.

The boat's doctor gave him a mild sedative to overcome his claustrophobia. This would be a tedious trip. Timeless and windowless. Except for the Captain, nobody spoke English. Entombed in a windowless tunnel that smelled of rotten food, diesel fuel, rancid bodies and fear. Page would not see a minute of daylight for five days.

He could feel the sub moving slowly on the surface driven by two huge roaring American General Motors diesel engines. Judging by the clock the engines ran all night as the sub was on the surface. The crew shouted orders and he felt the sub tilt, slowly sailing beneath the waves just before sunrise.

Page was able to sleep between eleven and five o'clock in a bunk he shared, hot racking, when the two other crewmen weren't using it. Three men and one bunk over deadly torpedoes. Nuclear? Sharing their damp, sweaty smelly sheets.

One toilet for fifty-five men and best hope it wasn't plugged. He had become well versed in its correct operation. Page feared if he blew up the toilet again the crew would make him walk the plank.

———

THERE WAS A PAUSE, "So not everyone was killed on that Alaskan Island, after all. Page must have escaped in the nick of time."

The Old Russian sighed. "Yes. And he's being moved around. To what end?"

"Wu Ton must have plans for him. Maybe the new American puppet king," Gomez suggested.

"So Wu Ton has the real American president as well as a dictator standing ready."

"Ready to scoop us in our very back yard. Barren ground where nobody will know if their plan crumbled. Bold with a happy ending for the Koreas," said Gomez.

"Or may cause world war three," said the Old Russian.

"Major Reid is our only and best hope. How is she faring, my friend?"

"I spoke with her yesterday. Someone tried to shoot down her plane but my men managed to get control of it and bring it in for a crash landing. All survived but the Major had quite a concussion."

Gomez took a breath. "Is she alright?"

"After a few days recovering near the crash site she's continuing with the mission."

"Who tried to shoot her down?" asked Gomez.

"I don't know if they were random rebels, Disciples or anyone else. We have not been able to locate any sign of the shooters."

"If they can stay hidden, they must be rebels or rebels in the employ of someone. Westerners are clumsy and wasteful. Easy to track and identify," Gomez pointed out. "Where is the Major and her group?"

"Unknown. She fired her group, ditched her equipment and clothing and is traveling as a Pashtun. Vanished."

"Smart. Probably just as well. The shooters might have been tipped about her plane so perhaps invisible is best."

"Agreed. I will keep you informed," said the Old Russian, hanging up.

———

In the darkened president's suite Clint was a bit out of breath. A bead of sweat ran down his forehead. He managed, "Let's take a breather."

It was good to be the president, even if it was only pretend.

She smiled at him, "Was the first lady too much for you Mr. President? Sure, let's take a break."

Clint slid over on his back to the side of the bed and flipped on the bedside light. He looked at the champagne glasses and noted they were empty. "Got more?"

"That's all you get. Consider that a reward for good behavior," she smiled, pulling the sheets up to her neck, sitting up.

"In the ballroom you threatened to kick me in the crotch if I put a hand on your ass. Then you sneak into my room and hop into bed with me."

"You make it all sound so..." she paused for effect, "*steamy*. What

I do in private is my business. Besides, security is watching me out there. Complaining?"

Clint smiled slightly. "Not at all. Is this a bonus that goes with the job or did you really think I was Dennis Casio, your husband?"

She lit up a cigarette, "You're no Dennis in the sack but that's okay."

He was crestfallen. "So why waste our time? Why me?"

She said, "Want to hear the big picture? I saw you in "Years End" and told Dennis you were almost a dead ringer for him. His doppelganger. Your Navy stint said you were secure. That's why you're here."

"I meant in the sack, now."

"Right now? Dennis has been missing for a month and a woman has needs. Technically this isn't adultery if you are playing his part... well."

"So, will *this* be a regular thing?" He slid his hand under the sheets. She pulled the sheets closer.

"Maybe. I haven't decided," she answered coyly.

Clint sat thinking then changing the subject. "So, my being the president for a while was your idea?"

Dorothy took a puff of her cigarette, coughed a couple of times. "It was Tina Gospel's idea. She saw you on 'Dancing with the Stars'. You were the perfect presidential lookalike, down on his luck and starving for a job."

"That's harsh. Tina... who?"

Dorothy grinned at him. "You haven't heard of Tina Gospel? The resurrected head of the CIA? The Wicked Witch of Washington?"

"No."

"Remember the stories about a CIA director who tortured the shit out of hundreds of people?"

"Haven't heard. Should I be concerned?"

Her face hardened. "You don't get out much, do you Clint?"

"I've been busy doing other things, sorry."

"Busy chasing skirts and getting pissed, you mean?"

Clint looked offended but knew she was correct. He tried another tack. "Should I be afraid of this... Tina Gospel person?"

Dorothy put out the cigarette, dropping it into a little glass container with a sealed lid. "Hiding the evidence." She winked. "I'd only worry about Tina if you cross her. She goes much further than water-boarding and she likes it. Rumour has it she's even cut the balls off men, on occasion."

Clint's face went very pale.

She stood up in all her glorious naked splendor and put on her robe. Despite her age she was indeed a beauty. Seems a bit shorter than Dorothy. Hmmm.

Enjoying his appreciative gaze, she swayed slowly to the door, stopped and turned to him. "By the way, I'm an imposter, too. I'm actually Tina Gospel, head of the CIA."

"Tina?" Clint's mouth fell open. "Tina Gospel? You?"

She added, "I'm a convincing 'Dorothy', wouldn't you say? One impostor to another; be good—I'm watching you." She winked to him then slipped out the door.

Naked, Clint got up, went over to his computer. He sat in the lovely old Ben Franklin leather chair wondering how many other presidential bare asses had perched in this very spot. Hopefully it was regularly cleaned.

He typed 'Tina Gospel' into his computer. He carefully read a dozen articles and intelligence files about her. One "confidential" file stated "Tina Gospel...ruthless, secretive, highly motivated, clever and intelligent. Leaves no stone unturned and no bodies left to be discovered. Has more dirt on public figures than J. Edgar Hoover ever did. Can show up anytime, anywhere in the most unexpected ways. Omnipresent."

Clint slid his chair back, whispering to himself, "What the fuck am I doing here?" He quickly went silent and slapped a hand over his mouth and the other hand over his privates, looking around the room. Was she listening and watching?

———

WHEN THE SUBMARINE DOCKED, Page was picked up in Karachi by three men. He suspected they were Korean. They spoke very little. One waved him to the back of a cargo truck. It was full of boxes but they'd left a place for him complete with a cast off chair, bucket and a jug of water. He did appreciate the overhead canvas cover that kept him from being roasted by the sun. The man handed Page an envelope then climbed in the cab with the others and hunkered down for a long haul. Page slid by the cargo and plopped down in the old chair.

Seated in the back, Page took a swig of water then opened the envelope. 'These men will take you through Pakistan, to the Afghanistan border and on to Kandahar. Be patient.'

Be patient? Who's taken me and where am I going? What's the plan? Is there a plan?

Page was getting nervous about this trek. At first, he assumed his escape was bankrolled by any number of his rich Revisionist colleagues but he was now having his doubts. Maybe they were also in jail or being closely watched. Or wanted nothing to do with him and preferred to install themselves in the oval office.

A king's crown could be made to fit anyone who possessed it.

He would have predicted being taken to Russia to meet some oligarch billionaire who would offer to reinstall him as leader of America...for 'considerations'. That would have made sense yet while he'd been in Russian Kamchatka, nobody had attempted to see him.

Possibly China would have been interested in him. They had money and wanted influence. He'd heard China took so long to decide anything he'd be dead of old age.

Obviously, it wasn't a Russian or Chinese plot. His buddies had cast him adrift. The only country interested in him seemed to be the Koreas. What could he possibly have that would interest them?

They could have killed him at any time, so his being alive was important. He'd have to wait and see.

The journey by truck was dreadful. It bounced and leaned

continuously while he ate dust in the cargo bay. He preferred it to the fishing boat and submarine because he at least had fresh air and could peek out a window.

Page imagined he might jump out and escape but where would he go? He heard terrible stories about what rebels did to Americans if they could catch one.

The truck stopped periodically for fuel and food for the drivers, generally in daylight. Sometimes the drivers brought food to give him but he was forbidden to leave his hiding place in day time. He looked forward to the cool of darkness and a few minutes of exercise.

His back and butt ached. Occasionally he was motion sick. Boredom was his friend, as were his barf and pee bucket. Urinating was difficult as he'd try to aim in the bucket while the truck lurched and bounced along, occasionally spilling the contents all over his pants. This trek must be Purgatory or a test of Job. Page found staying clean futile, and staying alive the priority. He dozed, dreaming of showers and changing his clothes three times a day after the presidential coronation. Magnificent.

"Wake! You!"

Page snorted out of his slumber and sat up.

"You!"

A voice from one of his drivers. It was dark outside. He slowly raised himself into a stooped position and moved toward the men. One of Korean drivers was calling him. Each night they'd let him out when it was dark and on a deserted track of this isolated road. Were they letting him out for a stretch, selling him to the rebels, or going to shoot him and keep whatever money they got for guiding him?

Page wasn't an old man, he was in his early fifties. Exercise wasn't a past priority but right now he'd have paid fifty-grand to be allowed to walk alongside the truck for a mile or two.

His guides patiently waited for him to exit the cargo bay and climb down. Page stood, stretching and groaning like a dog after a nap. It felt so good. Two guides stood smoking while one guide held his nose, pointing to him, then pointing into a big bucket. A bucket of water to wash in?

The guide carried the bucket as he climbed up the back of the truck and stopped on the tailgate. "You." He pointed to Page to stand under it. Pour over his head?

Page grimly thought how low his life slipped. Here he was looking forward to having a bucket of iffy water dumped over his head by strangers in a desert. The guide smoking jabbered something and the man above him started pouring. Page knew it wasn't clean water but he didn't care. The warm fluid bounced off his head, ran down his neck, back, arms and legs. He caught some of the water and splashed it on his face.

It felt wonderful! Clean and cool.

Something squirmed in the water in his hands, something else was slimy and wiggling on his neck, in his pants, wriggling down the middle of his back. A guide shone a flashlight over the jiggling objects. Snakes? Eels? Horrified, Page jumped around wildly, scream-ing, ripping open his shirt, his pants, pole-vaulting from his clothes. The guides laughed so hard they were having trouble standing.

Page stood naked, wet, and furious. "Was that deliberate? You assholes!" He grabbed at the nearest man, pulling him close to strike him. The man in the truck hit Page over the head with the empty bucket, knocking the big man to his knees. The three Korean men stood around him kicking and punching until Page just lay in the dirt gasping and bleeding.

One of the men shouted something and they all left him alone. After urinating nearby, they all got into the cab of the truck, honked their horn a couple of times and watched Page in the rear mirror, waiting for him to wobble to his feet. They slowly accelerated the truck, giving Page barely enough time to scoop his soggy clothing and stagger to the back of the moving truck, throw himself awkwardly inside and collapse as the truck got back up to speed.

It was an hour before Page could grope his way to his hiding place. Eventually he pulled his clothes back on. He had to admit they

were a bit cleaner as was he. Probably the men found the bucket of
water and didn't know worms were living in the water, too. This was
a desert, after all.

Page had time to think as he bounced along hidden in the back of
the cargo truck. He often wondered what his first act as the president
of the United States would be and now he knew. He would deport
anyone of traceable Korean lineage along with their entire family
tree. Scorched earth.

24

GOOD TO BE THE PRETEND PRESIDENT

AFTER BREAKFAST THE NEXT MORNING, CLINT SAT WARILY IN his chair as White House staff came and went, treating him as if he was their exalted president. The entry level help didn't know he was a phony. It was such a charade, he thought.

It was almost ten o'clock when Admiral Grant, the president's chief-of-staff, came in the room.

The Admiral was the unelected boss of all the top bureaucrats in the White House. He was there because a president put him there and he was there at the president's pleasure, so to speak. Clint wondered why Casio hadn't fired him when he took over. The old admiral knew too well that Clint was a stand in.

Clint didn't like the retired, prissy old admiral, one of the leftover ass kissers from Jackson's Revisionist days. A pencil-pusher, hiding in the office while real Navy men like Clint were out at sea in real ships. The Admiral was a perfect match for that draft dodging "bone spurs" Jackson, the president.

Clint had spent three years in the Navy before his acting career. They were hard years in the sunless tropical drone of a cruiser's engine room. A terrible place to be trapped and die when a torpedo blows out the ship's side, as Clint had witnessed. He heard the screaming of men scalded by steam then broiled to a crisp. He was one of the few to get out alive.

Clint had heard the old NCO's laughing at Admiral Walter Grant's appointment to the White House. "He wouldn't know a destroyer from an aircraft carrier. Gets sea sick. The administrator for 'laundry'." They'd all laughed.

"Busy?" asked Admiral Grant to Clint, politely looking around the room. When he saw the empty room, he kicked the door closed behind him.

Clint knew the old bugger was being sarcastic but went along with it. "I always make time for you, Admiral. Lose some Navy skivvies, today? Those shit spots won't clean themselves."

The admiral stood in front of the president's desk, facing Clint, seething. "Shut up you..."

"Careful Admiral. I could have you standing on Attu Island in two hours as a special commandant. You're very qualified."

The Admiral held his temper. "Did you sign anything, today? About eight-thirty?"

Clint made a big deal of consulting a big book beside him. The pages were all blank but he pretended to carefully consult them. "Yes, I signed something for... Tina Gospel... and the CIA. Why?"

"You can't sign a goddam thing, you fucking imposter!"

Clint smiled smugly, "The charming Ms. Gospel assured me I could sign it. Such a sweetie."

Admiral Grant turned red in the face, "Who does this Gospel chick think she is? Women running around doing men's work!" he raged.

Clint leaned back. "Take it up with her, Admiral. I'm pretty sure she won't water board you... much." Clint knew the admiral was petrified of Tina Gospel. "Better yet, let's call her right now and get her in here." Clint looked at a corner lamp, "Shit, she might be watching us on a camera in the lamp right now. Hi Tina! The admiral and I were just talking about you." Clint waved at the lamp, smiling cheerfully.

The Admiral looked at the lamp nervously, trying to back away.

Clint then picked up his phone and said, "Hi Abby. Get the head of the CIA on the line, please. Admiral Grant has a bone to pick. Sure, better yet send her right over. Thanks."

The old admiral paled and stepped further away from the desk, his thunder gone. "That won't be necessary." He scurried from the room like a frightened mouse, quietly closing the door behind him.

Alone, Clint shook his head and started looking through the desk drawers. Casio had to have *something* to drink somewhere in here.

A knock came at his door. He quickly slid the drawers closed, abandoning his search. "Come in!"

Tina Gospel entered and closed the door behind her. Smiling, she sashayed up, sitting cheekily on the side of his desk. "What do you need... Mr. President?"

He wasn't sure if she was teasing him but ignored it. "The Laundry Admiral was whining to me because I signed your budget. He ran when I called you."

"He's so spineless. Mind you, that's why Casio kept him around."

"He does know how to boss people around and follow a schedule. I'll give him that." He slid his chair back to look at her, perched on his immense old oak desk. She moved a little so one side of her skirt slid up, mid-thigh.

Is she playing me? No doubt she was—but why?

She leaned back seductively. "I forgot to thank you for signing my little old budget. We used to get three billion dollars a year, before the Revisionists wiped us out." She rubbed her hand over his.

"Why would they do that, Tina?"

"Fear. We know who everyone screws and where their money comes from. Same as the FBI and the NSA."

"Why did you let the Revisionists wipe you out if you had them over a barrel?"

"It was the goddamned Russians! That knucklehead President

Jackson let the Russians copy and delete all our confidential files, then closed us down."

"Accessed, neutered and closed? Just like that?"

"Almost, but not quite. The Russians, Koreans and China then shot every one of our agents and informants they could name or find. Eighty-six-hundred of them. *Boom!!*"

Clint started, knocking over a glass of water when she said "boom".

"Wiped us out. Starting from scratch. Well almost... "

"Will that be me when this job is over?"

"You mean 'boom'?" Tina asked with a smile, fingering his tie. "I haven't decided yet."

———

THE STRANGER with binoculars watched two Pashtun tribesmen walk along the edge of an ancient berm. He saw they expertly utilized as much cover and shade as possible. Each had an automatic weapon slung over the shoulder. Russian weapons. Had they killed someone to gain the weapons? They were moving swiftly—with purpose—and knew where they were going. Headed to the crash site. Seemed to be arguing about something. The front person kept looking back. Would have liked to hear what they were saying, if only he was close enough and then could speak Pashtun, the language of ancients.

A noble language. Probably pondering old philosophies.

———

UNAWARE THEY WERE BEING WATCHED, Terry and Trev tiptoed along the edge of the berm.

Trevor could barely follow her pace. "Need to... stop. I'm... fried."

She looked back, "No stopping. We need to get to our crash site before it gets picked clean and the evidence gets trampled."

"Why do we have to wear this barbaric Pashtun garb? What's wrong with uniforms?"

"Soldier uniforms are hot and identifiable. AK's are better weapons for us, and they don't stand out. Want to know what the locals do to enemy soldiers?"

"No more of your scary stories! We got ripped-off in the trade for this clothing and weapons, anyway. That was a huge pack of supplies to get what we are wearing and carrying."

"That's the beauty and efficiency of Afghan clothing. It's all we need. Ever read the book 'Dune'?"

"No. We burned them all, remember? Outside influences and all that."

Terry kept going, shaking her head. "I was going to say 'Dune' was cool when it talks about local desert clothing and how perfect it was for its surroundings."

"I'll put it on my list," Trev said. "Rest now?"

"No."

"Damn."

They shuffled along on the rock, dirt and sand for a while longer, sweating, ignoring sore feet and chafing from the rifle slings on their shoulders.

Terry re-opened the conversation. "Trev. How did the Old Russian know you were in the CIA, anyway? CIA's been disbanded for twenty years."

Trev was pleased for an excuse to speak and grinned. "The Old Russian was the head of the FBI for six months. He got a close look at all our files."

Terry stopped, turned to him, and pointed her finger in his face. "Bullshit!"

"No BS! After President Jackson met with the Russian dictator in Finland in 2020, he quietly agreed to allow a top KGB guy to become the honorary boss of the FBI."

Terry stared at him. "I suppose that's why the whole Russian election investigation tampering thing disappeared."

"Yup. Ever wonder what happened to Nueller, FBI investigator in the Russian thing? The lead investigator of it all?" asked Trev.

"I'm afraid to ask."

"He was sent to Russia and executed. A 'solid' story appeared in Fax News saying they had a grainy video showing Nueller with a covey of nude women giving him sex, bags of coke, money and... um... urinating on him. His investigation crumbled."

"Classy. Then what?" Terry shook her head.

"The sordid story surfaced and vanished with Nueller, so we'll never know. Shop talk says the president gave him to the Russians who then took him to Moscow. After a thorough interrogation they had him executed along with any top players Nueller fingered along the way. After the Russians got a closer look at the books the FBI, CIA and NSA were closed up and everything burned and deleted. Nobody left to look into Jackson's and the Revisionists skeleton closets."

"Convenient. So that's why that Old Russian knows so much."

"And it explains why he seems to have a soft spot for America. He lived in Washington for three years. His family loved it. He has a daughter and grandchildren still living there."

Terry returned to stalking in the desert. "Just when I thought I've heard everything. Fuck."

They marched in silence for what seemed like hours. To Trevor's relief they arrived at the site of their plane crash. To his annoyance Terry made them circle around for another hour, to make sure nobody was watching them. He followed in thirsty misery, grumbling.

Suddenly she put her left pistol arm up, almost hitting him in the face. Surprised, Trev looked ahead and saw someone standing in front of them. The person made no move to hide or pull a weapon. Local...just stood there.

Terry leveled her gun at the stranger. She said, "What do you want?" in Pashtun.

The stranger replied, "Huh? ...English?" and pulled his head gear down revealing his true identity.

"Dean?" Terry cried.

25

ACTING PRESIDENTIAL

It was chilly standing in the White House Gardens that afternoon. The First Lady stood at his side, the real first lady, apparently. She'd slapped him so he was certain this time. She was no Tina Gospel in disguise—Tina was a bit shorter. Oops. He'd have to compliment Tina on her disguise when he next saw her.

He stood on the dais, looking over the big crowd of invited guests and reporters seated in rows of white folding chairs arranged across the lush green lawn. Manicured roses, magnolias and dahlias surrounded the area with a riotous kaleidoscope of colour and sweet-scented breezes. The grounds hadn't looked this good in years.

Clint didn't regret using his presidential power, imposter or not, to order the gardeners to fix up the sad looking area. His parents were great gardeners and he hated to see a once-lovely space go to waste. The bones had still been there—and the cost was so very little.

The teleprompter told him everything he needed to say. As an experienced actor, he rolled through the speech like it was an academy performance. Clint enjoyed showing off his oratory skills before an important crowd such as this. Even Admiral Grant stood nearby, a pipe clamped in his teeth. Staffers whispered Grant had a pipe only because he thought it made him look intelligent.

"My Fellow Americans. We are here today to honour a hero, a person that has shined a light on what was a dark time for us all. She almost died for her beliefs."

He leaned a hand towards a young girl standing nearby.

"I'd like to introducing the writer of the famous poem, Jessica Reid!"

The crowd applauded politely as Jess walked up to the microphone. "Thank you, Mr. President. It's an honour to be here."

The president smiled during more applause. "And are you fully recovered Miss Reid?"

"I'm almost a hundred percent, yes. It's back to school, very shortly."

"Thank you." The president ended with, "That's all for the speeches, folks. Do stay for some wine, coffee and cake." As people rose from their seats and began to mingle, Clint hesitated, then added, "But before we go—are there any questions from the press?" Clint had always been a newspaper groupie and knew the issues. He simply could not resist this opportunity.

The seven attending reporters, all heading for a drink did an abrupt U-turn at hearing his invitation. Admiral Grant bit down on his pipe, breaking it off and losing it in the grass.

One of the stunned reporters asked, "Us, sir?"

The president smiled indulgently and said, "Why not? You've wanted to ask questions for years. Shoot."

One of the correspondents pulled out a pristine notebook and flipped it open, a pen at the ready. No one was allowed to carry a recording device into the White House. "Gary Bosher, FAX news: Are you pleased with America's progress with bringing in the Democrats after such a long hiatus?"

"It's coming along nicely. The Democrats are coming out of their foxholes and out from under the bed to sign up, officially. We could be a two-party system up and running again by the end of the year. Next?"

"Lawrence O'Dell: MSNBC: Will all media networks that are willing be re-started sir?"

"That *is* in the works but will take more time. Capital has to be raised to rebuild those outlets, long dormant. Good people must be found. Next?"

"Kerry Smith: BBC: How are negotiations going with the Koreas?"

Clint smiled. "Moving along but we doubt they have anything we want."

He heard Admiral Grant break into a coughing fit in the background.

Clint looked at the press group and saw there were no more questions but knew there would be lots more at the next opportunity. "Time for some refreshments, ladies and gents but before we do, I would like a round of applause for the gardeners who did a lot of hard work renewing these lovely gardens and lawns!"

The audience applauded in appreciation.

The ersatz president headed for the champagne on the refreshment table but once again a secret service guard gracefully intercepted him. She took his arm, steering him away from the alcoholic drink table while putting a bottle of water in his hand. "Sir, Ms. Reid would love to speak with you. This way."

———

TERRY AND DEAN hugged for what seemed like ten minutes. Gratefully, Trevor used the time to sit down in the shade, drink water and eat a bit of food. He didn't care if they hugged all day.

Finally, they unclenched.

"Dean. How did you find us?" asked Terry, thrilled to see him.

"Wow. Wasn't easy."

"Did we leave an obvious trail?"

"I have a few contacts out there and so does Shirley Mac. When you two disappeared, we figured out where you were sent and the route of your plane. Air Force friends. Just went to the crash site and waited. I knew you'd show up if you were alive."

"I'm glad you did. What do you know?" she asked.

"Hi Dean," Trev inserted from the background. "Just pretend I'm not here."

———

JESSICA REID STOOD by herself on the grassy lawn. She was impressed by the work that had been done since she was last there. It should have been an honour to be here but it was a little hollow being greeted by a bogus president. The Bradleys had warned her about the switch as they knew she'd met the real president a few times and would know the difference.

As if to rub it in, the Secret Service brought the president *to her*, as if *she* was more important than the phony president.

Jess cringed a little as they drew close. It seemed creepy. He looked remarkably similar to the real president. Similar height and look, hair and stature. Late fifties in age. This guy had a softer, kinder face than the real president, Dennis Casio, who, in her experience had always looked hard and tired. The imposter looked bored and impatient. The White House upper staff ignored him, as if he had dog shit on his shoes. Somehow he managed to rise above it and the audience was completely fooled.

The guy looked pleased to see her. Pretending?

"I'm so pleased to meet you, Ms. Reid."

She played along, "Pleased to meet you, Mr. President."

Their eyes connected and her look let him know she knew he was a fake. His posture went from magisterial to a deflated slump. Surprisingly, Jess felt bad for him. She looked around and saw they were alone, basically out of earshot from others. "It's okay... Mr. Bergen?"

He said, "Clint," from the side of his mouth softly. "I'm the actor impostor. The phony baloney."

Jess tried to be encouraging. "You may be the only one between peace and world war three... a nuclear war. This may be the biggest acting job of your life."

Clint perked up a little. "I suppose. How'd you know about me?"

"Theresa Reid is my aunt."

Clint's eyebrows went way up in surprise, "Theresa... Terry Reid? The one who brought Page and the Revisionists down?"

"Yes. My aunt, the swashbuckler," Jess replied, almost annoyed. "The slayer of dragons."

"Wow! I'd love to meet her. Is she here, spying on us from somewhere?" With bright eyes Clint glanced around at the Secret Service people and the kiosks in the corners of the yard.

"I'll arrange a meeting when she gets back from wherever she's gone to."

"Ah."

They stood saying nothing.

Jess broke the awkward silence, "This garden looks way better than it ever did. What happened?"

"That was me," said Clint. "When I first got here, I had nothing to do so I just walked around the area and smiled a lot. It didn't take a president to see the abandoned trees, fences and yards. I just started talking to gardeners and workers and sweet talked them into fixing this place up. What else can I do?"

"It looks really nice."

"Sure does. Mow some grass, prune the trees, paint the fences, give the old plants a shot of water and fertilizer and suddenly you're back in business. One of the old guys was their rose expert, so I talked him into repairing them again and they look amazing. People need to know they can make a difference."

"I think you just answered your own question. You're here to make a difference, anyway you can," said Jess.

Clint nodded, "And you rocked our world with your poem."

She shrugged, "And I have the bullet hole to prove it." Her hand absentmindedly touched the spot, a sensitive and angry red.

Clint looked both ways then lifted his right coat sleeve up to reveal a large section of skin, badly burned a long time ago. "I got this when a torpedo crashed into our cruiser in Yemen. The pain masked how lucky I was, compared to twenty-six other guys who fried and died. This scar reminds me to enjoy every day."

"Comparing scars with the president. Funny," Jess teased, abruptly relaxing. This guy was okay.

"And morbid. If you'll excuse me, I need to do the presidential schmooze."

"Bye."

He got five feet away, stopped and turned to her, "Do you play chess?"

Jess nodded, surprised.

"Call Abby and get her to schedule us for a meeting and we'll play chess. I'm seldom busy." He shrugged with regret.

She nodded.

———

Terry, Dean and Trev found a place in the shadows and watched the sun go down. The three ate a bit of food and talked.

Dean asked, "So let's start with why and how you both got drugged and ended up here?" He gnawed at a piece of dried meat.

Trev spoke first. "It was my fault, really. I'm a part-timer with the CIA and..."

Dean stopped chewing and looked at Trev like he'd gone mad.

Trev shrugged and continued. "It's all good. When I was in Washington, I got a call telling me to get Terry and meet someone in Redstone Park at five o'clock... geez... last Wednesday. We had to be there."

"Why?" asked Dean, already smelling a rat.

Terry added, "Because we were meeting the head of the CIA."

"Ah."

Trev said, "So we arrive and Tina Gospel and four of her 'suits' were there. They had coffees, handed them around and brought us up to speed. They told us there was a big problem with the president and... well... we conked out, end of intel sharing. We were drugged by coffee."

"You think? If you can't trust the goddamned CIA, then who can you trust?" Dean said sarcastically. "Bastards."

Terry lowered her head as she ate dried fruit and drank an energy drink she'd made. "Yup, guilty as charged. I had guns, knives and shoelace stranglers but never thought about getting drugged by the CIA."

Undaunted, Trevor continued. "So next they must have kept us under sedation, and we woke up on a remote-controlled plane with someone trying to shoot us down. The Old Russian hacked the controls of the plane and crash landed us in the poppy field. Shitty landing. A squad of Special Forces guys found us, and Terry was out of it for three days with a concussion."

Dean looked at her. "I think that might have turned her into a homicidal maniac."

"Very funny. I was like that before." Terry smiled. "Said it before you did."

"So finally, we got going and met up with the Old Russian just north—."

"South, Trev."

"Yes, *south* of here. He told us to be careful and if we find the missing US president, we should invite him along with us."

"Missing president? What the f—."

"That's what we said. The Koreans grabbed him."

"The Koreans? So how and why is he here, in Afghanistan?" said Dean.

"Yes. That way America won't vaporize the Koreas."

"Ah."

"Why did the CIA drug you and send you here?" asked Dean.

Terry said, "Think back a few decades. How long did it take the CIA to find Osama Bin Laden?"

"Years and years."

"They couldn't find their asses with both hands and GPS beepers," said Terry. "Present company excepted."

"Granted, Afghanistan isn't the biggest country, ever, but I'd have to say there's a couple million places to hide."

"True but let's think about this. Koreans are a foreign government unfamiliar with this country. They're not letting the president wander off with the rebels. They're keeping him close by."

Dean thought. "So, they'll be in some kind of a base, supplied, maybe an air strip, possibly a road. That narrows it down around here."

Terry added. "Dozens of places but not millions. I was an Intel officer here for four years. I have an idea who to talk to..."

"...who won't kill us or tell someone who will..." said Dean.

"Correct. The fact someone took the time to shoot us down means they may be from this base where they keep the president. I want to sniff around this plane crash area and see who did the shooting and where they went, afterwards."

Dean asked, "Is that where we're going?"

Terry answered, "Yes. Retrace some steps. We might find a base fit for a president."

———

JESS WASN'T sure what to think of playing chess with the president... a faux president at that. The Bradleys got a call with a time. A limousine complete with Secret Servicemen would arrive at 6:45 pm to pick her up. She was a good chess player. Would the president mind getting clobbered in a game by a fifteen-year-old?

The big black car arrived with men in black who peered warily around the neighborhood before waving her over to the car.

Where were you assholes when I got shot?

One of them opened the door for her and she slid in. The heavily armoured door clunked closed. Jess sat way back in the farthest seat as the giant car started rolling.

You could get a dozen people in here, she thought.

Two motorcycles started, one on each edge of the road behind them.

The partition window to the driver powered down. "Hey Jess. How's it going?" asked the female driver.

Jess moved closer to the driver and saw it was Joyce Carson, a friend of the Bradleys. "Hi Joyce. I didn't know you were a driver—thought you were a G-man?"

"G-man?" Joyce leaned right in concentration.

"Historically FBI people were called G-men... government men and Secret Service were called Men in Black.... MIB."

"I've never heard that."

There was an awkward silence.

Jess changed the subject. "So Joyce, you get to drive the president's chess player around?" She added a laugh. It seemed like overkill.

Joyce didn't crack a smile. All business. "Yes, I've just started today. Some cross-training. Had all my courses in manoeuvring these big armoured babies and you're my first passenger. Wanna see me do a 360 degree spin, and scare the shit out of the motorcycle guys?"

"No, I'll pass for now Joyce."

"I can slide sideways and shoot out of the side window? How about that?"

"Maybe another day."

Joyce was a bit crestfallen. "I'll bet Terry would love to see it."

"No doubt."

There was a minute of silence as the big black car regally bullied through traffic.

"Where is your dangerous Aunt, anyway? Parachuting from the Eiffel Tower? Fighting Somalian Pirates with nothing but a broom and a tube of toothpaste?" asked Joyce, excited for news.

"Good question. She disappears and reappears but this time she's been gone for a while. Terry usually lets me know after a few days but it's been almost two weeks."

Joyce considered, then before she spoke, she turned up her car radio full blast. "You could ask the president of the United States, you know."

"I suppose I could do that. I'd better let him win the chess game before I ask."

26

CHESS

It was a massacre that would go down in the dark annals of the chess world. She lost three straight. The final game was the only one to last any length of time but Jess was thrilled.

"Sorry Jess. I was the ship's chess champ when I was in the Navy, you know. How about some lemonade?" Clint—the ersatz President—asked, grinning.

"Sure."

"Harry? Could you bring us a couple of lemonades please? Thanks."

Jess sat, looking around the rose garden area.

Clint continued. "I was a pretty good chess player during my three-year stint. I only ever lost two-out-of-three to a guy from a Coast Guard icebreaker. He was good! Waxed my ass."

"He must have played a lot, if he was in the Arctic," added Jess.

"Yes. Those poor guys on breakers never sleep much. Thick ice. They say the grinding and noise makes you crazy. Then the engines stop and reverse, back and forth. Ice beats on the ship's sides constantly. God it's awful."

"Did you enjoy the Navy?"

"I did. It was the first time I was part of something big. A huge team. Our captain was a swell guy. The XO was excellent."

"XO?"

"Sorry, Navy talk for the executive officer. The ship supervisor. He makes sure the chow was good, laundry got done and we had bullets and fuel. The make-shit-happen guy."

Their lemonades arrived.

"Thanks Harry."

They both took a slurp of the ice cold, slightly bitter lemonade.

"Did you know this Admiral Grant before you came?"

"No. I was a seamen first class. Admiral Grant was the top man in charge of all the US Navy's laundry."

"More of an administrator?"

"Yes. Not a man you need when the shooting starts. Then we want fuel, bullets and bread. Laundry can wait."

"Another chess game sir. I'm hoping to redeem myself."

"Sure. I love chess but nobody in this place plays it. Too dumb or too snooty. The White House is such an odd ball convention, including myself."

They set the game up with Jess "white". She moved a pawn forward. "Please don't take offense but do you get to do real presidential stuff?"

Clint called over to Harry. "Would you turn the background music up please? Perfect." Clint winked at Jess as if to say, *You never know who's listening.* "No offense taken. Yes, I do get to do a surprising number of things. These drones don't have me in their policy and procedure book, so I do what I please and sign what I like."

"You could order a new aircraft carrier, if you wanted?"

"Probably. Do you *need* an aircraft carrier?

Jess giggled. "I don't think anyone needs a new multi-billion-dollar aircraft carrier. That money could go elsewhere."

Clint moved his pawn two spaces. "What would you do if you were president, Jess?"

"It would be quite a list."

"Okay. Just three things, then."

She sat up as if a genie had just offered her three wishes except this wasn't the real genie and he probably couldn't do any of them. "Three? Those are hard choices." She moved another pawn forward.

Clint scanned the chessboard. "From an outsider's perspective, decision making starts at the top, with basic concepts, then you move down from there. The general direction, size, speed and distance is decided. Logistics comes next, just like the Navy. The President tells the admiral who tells the captains, XO's and on down."

Jess moved another pawn opposite his. "Is world peace possible?"

He moved out his right bishop. "Why not? Europe fought for centuries bickering over borders. One day they started the EU and haven't enforced borders for decades. They argue occasionally but no more wars amongst them."

"So if you get the world to the no-border model then wars cease?" She moved another pawn.

"That's a tall but worthy goal. A lot of expensive paranoid hardware would become irrelevant. Lost jobs. The trick is convincing everyone this is a good idea and to put away their guns." He took her pawn.

She moved a knight out. "But not impossible?"

He moved his queen out two spaces. "There are many levels of difficult, followed closely by unlikely and then impossible. I suppose you'd have to start small."

She moved her queen up. "Climate change is beating us up. Half of Florida is flooded, and California is burnt to a crisp. Droughts are everywhere."

He moved another pawn up. "Climate change was inconvenient for politicians and voters. People can only imagine what they have, not what could be. We don't change until fires and floods are here, terrorizing us in real time."

She moved a pawn two spaces forward. "A few foreign terrorists can mobilize government money fueled by public fear and hate, yet the same money can't get spent on minimizing climate change."

He moved his left bishop out two spaces. "Threatening your queen, Jess," he warned and sipped his lemonade. "Climate change... yes, people need to see a grand plan brought by all parties. The Revisionists could have done something back when they could have slowed down the effects. Too busy building walls, warships, bombs and bibles."

Jess used her queen to take the threatening bishop.

"You know I can get your queen with my knight, right?"

"Oops. Thanks," she said, replacing his bishop, moving her queen back a step. "So what would you do about climate change, Clint?"

"I suppose convene an arena full of experts and ask them. Make a huge deal out of it and make every media star attend, donuts and coffee included. Make it a school subject thing. Fan out from there. Start small and work up." He moved out his right knight.

Jess moved a pawn, threatening his bishop. "My last one, Mr. Genie President. Equality for all. Is it possible for everyone to be equal regardless of race, color, gender and religion?"

He moved his bishop back a few spaces, to safety. "We have something called the US Constitution and Bill of Rights that addresses all of that, if we choose to follow it. Had them for 240 years. It's all spelled out if anyone took the time to actually read the entire thing and not just handy excerpts or Fast Freddie's handy spin."

Jess made a face, then moved a pawn to guard a pawn he was about to take. "Would you make folks read it all?"

He grinned. "Why not? I'm the school master-in-chief with this bullshit tame home school program. I'll just tell the educators all kids must take this special patriotic program. Answer the real questions like 'According to the Bill of Rights is your mom second class? Anyone not white?' Mind you, sadly most minorities were deported. Yes, I could order it, 'make it so'." He moved his queen ahead, taking a pawn.

"Those are my three wishes." Jess smiled, moving a bishop up, threatening his bishop.

"Yes. And now I get a wish... from the poem girl—you." He moved his queen over taking a pawn. "Check!"

Wincing, Jess sought a safe spot for her King. "If you're bringing world peace, equality and some relief from climate change, I could do something." She slid her queen over, between his and her king.

He retreated diagonally with his queen. "I need the famous poem girl to headline another school poem book."

"I could do that. What kind of poems?" She moved a rook, ready to take his queen. She kept a poker face.

He went in the corner and took her rook, instead, escaping her clutches. "A poem about making America a good place for all people."

She winced at losing an expensive rook. She moved a knight closer to his queen. "Sure. But you have to find out where my Aunt Terry is."

He went right and took her bishop. "Check."

Jess looked concerned.

"It so happens I'll be seeing someone tonight. Tina knows these sorts of things."

Her king retreated its measly single step. Kings are the tallest, have the most power and yet are the lamest.

He knocked off her knight with his queen. "I'll contact that knucklehead that runs the Department of Labour which runs Education. Can you believe that?"

She moved her queen to threaten his queen. "Will you run the national poem program like they did the last time?"

"That's my plan. It's already in the can." He took a pawn to get some space. "I'll let you know about your aunt and the poem as soon as I find out."

"Sure." She pushed her bishop over a couple of spaces.

He moved his bishop up two, threatening her queen.

She moved her Queen over two spaces. "Are you going to make my three wishes come true?"

Clint laughed. "A president can plant seeds and see if they grow but I'm not even a president." He took her pawn with his queen. "Check."

Ouch!

"It's all in the watering and cultivating?" She moved her queen in front of his king.

"I'll say. Just like these gardens." He moved his queen back. Especially considering I'm a nobody in the shoes of somebody important."

She moved up a pawn, "The Prince and the Pauper?"

Clint laughed hard. "Something like that." He moved his bishop. "I'm threatening your queen."

"Dang." She moved her King to guard her queen.

He moved his queen. "Your king's in check."

———

HARRY DAVID MILLS stood at his post at the bar, watching the president and the poem girl play chess. He was in his mid-fifties, dressed immaculately in white. He never tired of this job after twenty years of service. Here he stood on perfectly manicured green grass surrounded by scented roses blooming all around him. Idyllic.

Harry had been pleased and surprised to keep this job after the notorious James Jackson became president. Past president Tom Bamford made Jackson sign something to protect Harry and his family in Washington during the changeover. Rumour had it Bamford caught Jackson groping a page and had Jackson dead to rights. Harry and his family had stayed ever since, though always watching over their shoulders because they were black. Jackson was an evil man.

Harry and the other staff were thrilled when President Casio suddenly ordered the garden area fixed up. Or rather, he politely requested it, which was unusual in itself.

Harry cleaned a glass then wiped off the dry bar. He had been suddenly told to never have alcohol in this bar or anywhere else and not to give the president any kind of alcohol. Apparently, the president had developed some extreme allergy to it and could die or so the story went.

He watched the president talking to the famous poem girl as they played chess. It was an honour to meet her. Everyone in his family had a copy of Jessica Reid's book and had committed her Freedom poem to heart. Bibles had been used to crush the country, yet it was a simple poem of freedom that released it.

"Lemonade?" the president called.

Harry hustled around making a big clear jug of homemade lemonade from a recipe from his predecessor. He took pride in his work, doing his best. As an ex-marine with two tours of Special Forces in Afghanistan he could fight it out with the best of the Secret Service if needed. But he was here to serve the president of the United States and his guests.

He brought the lemonade over to their table. The poem girl wasn't doing well at chess, losing yet another game. The president was very good, taking pains to go easy on her, warning her of impending doom.

Chess was a noble game. Harry never missed a chance to play but never at the White House. Black people weren't supposed to be smart. Harry's wife told him the president would fire him if they found out he played the big tournaments and was a FIDE Grand Master under the name of "Harry David".

Maybe he'd beat the president at chess on his last day before he retired.

"Would you turn the background music up please?" asked the president. "Perfect." Bugged? Probably.

Harry had noticed subtle changes with the president and first lady. The Casio's were always hanging around together, arm in arm, clearly enjoying each other's company. It was a rare occurrence, these days.

Were they having troubles?

Every president had a look, a demeanor when they asked Harry for something or even looked at him. They looked down, almost scoffing when they made a request. These days the president looked *at* him as if he was an equal, just another man and treated all the other staff the same way. He thanked them all, said "please", followed up with an "attaboy" and shook their hands for a job he thought was well done.

Not usual.

The president stood up to the White House Cabinet at every opportunity. Harry smiled at how he routinely made that snooty prick Admiral Grant's life miserable at every opportunity by asking him, "Got the shit spots out of everyone's underwear, Admiral?" It was all Harry could do not to laugh.

And President Dennis Casio didn't have a clue how to play chess until today. Strange.

Harry watched their game and saw the unmistakable look of someone forced to concede. The poem girl made a fight of it but was done. The president accepted her defeat with grace and good humour.

———

FLO BRADLEY NOTICED Jess dawdling and picking at tonight's dinner. She usually enjoyed dinner time at the Bradleys' but not tonight. Flo cleaned off the dinner plates, taking note of Jess's preoccupation.

Did chess with the president unsettle her? What was Auntie Terry's latest unknown location?

"What's happening Jess. Not hungry?" Flo asked, scraping off a dinner plate in the trash can while trying not to pry into Jess's life.

"I guess not. A lot on my mind."

Flo stacked some pots in the dishwasher. "Not sure where to spend your poem millions?"

Jess snorted, then smiled. "I forgot about that. I gave the school some money to fix the place up. The roof doesn't leak now, and the heating system works. The principal and the security guard are even nice to me. I can't complain about that."

That was a lot of conversation from a young girl. Flo's girls usually replied by grunting, pointing or stomping the floor, two for yes, one for no.

"So why the long face? Did you lose at chess?"

"I got slaughtered at chess! Clint... er the president is very good."

Flo stood up from piling utensils in the dishwasher. "You figured out he was bogus?"

"You alluded to it when I first met him but it's really obvious one-on-one. Mr. Casio is more of a stiff, political animal. Clint is a dead ringer for Casio to look at him but he's just a normal guy. Even offered me three wishes."

Flo looked at Jess suspiciously. "What was that all about?"

"Well... in the course of our conversation I asked him if he can do presidential stuff and he said yes. He asked if I thought another aircraft carrier was a good idea."

Flo snickered. "Sounds like he has an interesting perspective."

"He does. I asked him for World Peace, relief from climate change and equality for all people."

"Is that all?" said Flo sarcastically, before she caught herself. "Sorry Jess. I think that's a lot to ask over a game of chess."

"I know. I'm just a dumb teen but why not ask?"

"Give yourself some credit, Jess." Flo added, "So, what did he say?"

"I don't know if he *will* or *can* do anything, but he said some interesting things. He thought the world could follow the European Union model. He didn't specify how he'd go about it."

"EU is borderless. Interesting. Go on."

"He would order a climate change conference and request everyone attend. They may have some ideas."

Flo thought, "It's been a while since anyone talked about it and many countries are taking a beating from drought, weather and forced migration. What else?"

"He offered a simple idea for equality for all... use the US correspondence school system to make every kid thoroughly read and understand the Bill of Rights and Constitution."

Flo smiled, "I'm proud that you dared to ask. If anything on your big three list becomes a fraction better, then you did better than most."

"It made for a good conversation."

Flo stood and went back to dishes, "Worried about your Aunt Terry?"

Jess sat up and smiled robotically, "No, Terry's probably alright somewhere but I did ask him to look into it."

"I suppose we'll see what develops."

27

TETE-A-TETE WITH THE CIA

AFTER HIS EVENING SHOWER CLINT PUT ON HIS PAJAMAS AND made one final search through the president's bedroom for Casio's hidden stash of whiskey. There had to be one, somewhere.

"There's no booze to find, Clint," said a cooing female voice. "We went through this place with a fine-tooth comb. We found all his guns, booze, pot and porn."

Surprised, Clint slid the drawer closed and straightened up. "I suppose you have cameras all over this place watching me snoop around."

"No comment," Tina said, taking her robe off and hanging it on the hat rack.

He smiled. "Will your cameras notice the head of the CIA forgot to wear clothes under her robe?"

She smiled seductively. "Not if they know what's good for them. I'll have bleach poured in their eyes." She reached into a bag and pulled out a small bottle of champagne. "On that happy note, got a couple of glasses?"

Clint smiled. "I sure do," and turned the lights down low.

An hour later, he turned the lights back up, shaking the champagne bottle for the last few drops, then gave up.

She snuggled up to him. "Well done, Mr. President."

He sat up too, leaning on the plush padded headboard. "Well done to you too, Ms. Gospel."

"No begging for more booze, Clint?"

"Nope. It's time I grew up," he said. "I haven't had much at all since I got here so I thought I'd keep it going. I've got a life, even if it's somebody else's."

Tina looked a bit surprised and amused. "I did not know that. Well done."

"Thanks."

"I see you were busy on your presidential computer, today."

Clint chuckled, "As the old saying goes, 'Are ya workin' for the CIA or just bein' nosey?'"

"We just noticed you ordered that all education must now include a full course regarding the Constitution and Bill of Rights. What's that about?"

"Nothing devious. I just did my presidential duty to make sure Americans are fully aware of our guiding principles, not just convenient sound-bites or outright lies. Can't hurt, can it?"

She looked at him suspiciously.

"Hell, I happily sign all your papers and you don't have to break any of my fingers. Indulge me."

"I suppose it can't hurt," Tina replied, wondering. "This would cost very little and have a future impact to the good."

Clint nodded. "My old great grandfather said during the great depression. 'Ya plant what ya got and hope for the best. Nothin' else ya can do.' At least that's what we thought he said. The old bugger was hard to understand without his teeth."

Clint didn't mention that he'd also called Harvard and told the college president to make a climate change conference happen in six months. We'll see. "By the way, where's Major Theresa Reid?"

Tina put up her stone face. "Who wants to know?"

"Her niece and me. I want her location on my desk by ten, tomorrow morning."

Tina slipped out of bed, put on her robe and grumbled, "Then I'd best get on it... Mr. President," and swept out of the room.

Clint watched her sultry exit.

Best keep an eye on that one, they both thought to themselves.

———

TERRY, Trev and Dean investigated the high points of land around the crash site of their plane. The Old Russian was correct. There was very little evidence left to sift through.

"If I was shooting a rocket at a plane and I knew it was coming by this area, I would do it from one of these hill tops."

Trev looked around nervously, "I hated standing on those other two hills. At least this one's got a bit of cover. Those other two were as bald as a billiard ball."

"My thought exactly, Trev," Terry agreed as she scanned the area with Dean's binoculars. "Not seeing much other than craggy rocks, little hills and a billion hiding places."

"How about an airstrip?' asked Dean.

"Easy to hide. Unless they actually use it, we'd never see it."

Trev added, "What if we wait for night. If there's a base out there they might let a light slip. Maybe they do their activity at night to stay unseen."

Dean and Terry looked at each other in surprise.

"I like it," said Terry. "Let's hunker down for the night and see if anything happens."

It was a cold dead night without a glimmer of light or a sound of a cricket.

———

TINA GOSPEL LEFT the White House bedroom and headed to a

small alcove in the farthest corner of the West Wing. She tapped twice, once and three times.

Someone inside said, "Password?"

"I'll send you to Iraq if you don't open this fucking door."

It was immediately opened by a pale man. "That would be the password."

Tina brushed by him going to the computer on a box serving as a desk in the corner. "Where are they?"

The pale man quickly sat, tapping on the keyboard and calling up some satellite tracking screens. "They're hanging around a small oasis in Afghanistan... right there." He pointed at a dot on a GPS map.

"Expand it," she ordered.

He enlarged it so they could see some of the topography. "The crash site is here. They went to an old village over here and are now back to the original crash site."

"If they went back to the crash site, they must be searching for something. Maybe President Casio is there, somewhere. Keep looking."

The pale tech looked over at Tina, noticing her robe fell open as she leaned over looking at the screen. A lot of thigh and a breast side view. *Nice.*

"What are you looking at?" she scowled, standing and closing up her robe.

"Nothing ma'am. It's all good." *Will she have my fingernails pulled out?*

"Carry on." Tina left.

———

CLINT'S BEDSIDE PHONE RANG. He awoke from a dead sleep to a voice asking, "Mr. President?"

He quickly sat up and turned his light on. "Yes, I'm here."

"Russian missiles are coming. Do we attack? There's a killer plague coming across the country, too. What do we do, Mr. President?"

This was Clint's worst nightmare. In desperation he mumbled "Fuck if I know."

"Come on Mr. President! Speak! Be a sport." Just as the sweat started to pour down Clint's face a woman's voice laughed hard. "Relax. Tina here. Just spoofing ya. Major Theresa Reid is in south eastern Afghanistan and doing fine. You can tell the poem girl that and swear her to secrecy. Sleep tight."

"What's Major Reid doing?" Clint asked.

A dial tone was his answer.

CIA humour, apparently.

———

Tina Gospel hung up the phone, still smirking. She liked Clint but found him so serious, even as a faux president. It was fun to bust his balls occasionally. If she ever got the chance Tina knew she would be a far superior president. She sighed at the thought. Soon.

Her phone rang on a special number. "Yes?"

"Tracking department here. We think they are headed for President Casio. They are on the move. Bill Page is headed there, too."

"Shit... no!"

"Yes, on good authority. Russian source. Apparently, Page's arrival is the trigger for President Casio's situation to be resolved."

"Get my plane ready. Form up some assets. Do you have an exact location for Major Reid?"

"An approximation. They've stayed in one place for a few days now. Can't be far."

"I'm on a fast plane. See you in twelve hours."

"Better hustle," the voice suggested.

Tina dialed another number. "Herb? Get your state department guys out of bed and make a pitch to the Koreans for President Casio's ransom. He's in Afghanistan. I don't exactly know where. Just pitch the Koreans something and stall them until I get there."

"I'm not sure what to offer them Ms. Gospel. How about..."

"I don't give a shit what you do. Give 'em somebody they want or a bag of money—I don't care. Stall them for twelve hours. Just do it!"

"Can I tell them you're coming?"

"No!"

"Gotcha."

Tina grabbed an expedition bag and ran to her private car. The driver had the door open in anticipation. She gasped, "The Base. Runway twelve. Drive right to the plane."

The car drove off into the night with Tina getting out of her scanty robe and into work clothes while making calls all the way. They were on the runway in twelve minutes parked by the new Citation XX+, ready for a trip to Zabol, Iran.

———

TERRY LOOKED up at the sky. The sun awoke at sunrise to glare down on all below, relentlessly. Another toasty, boiling day in Afghanistan. All she had was a headache and the sweats so far. Together, they ate and drank almost all they had left. Running low.

Dean spoke after he consumed the last of his food. "This siege didn't last long. Couple of days?"

"I know. We need more food and water, or we need to leave," Terry agreed.

Trev said, "That plane we were in had a fair bit of supplies but it got looted while we were knocked out. Maybe we could barter it back with...?"

"Will they take personal cheques," said Dean sarcastically. "I'm good for it."

"Glad to see your sense of humour is alive and well." Terry leaned over and kissed Dean on the cheek as a reward. "Stay here and watch. Trev and I are going into that village over there to see if we can't rustle up something."

"Shouldn't I go with you?" asked Dean.

"You're an old Afghan vet, so stay. Trev and I can handle it. If I'm unsuccessful there may not be much to bring back."

"Village?" asked Trev.

"Look closely... there. Not much but folks get together at that spot for some reason."

"Water?"

"That's what I'm hoping."

Terry and Trev traveled light and fast. He followed in her footsteps copying her route and pace, learning the method to her madness.

Finally, Trev understood why Terry chose local attire. It was somewhat cool and breezy, vastly better than bulky uniforms. They were dressed like greyhounds as opposed to Army St. Bernard's.

He made a point to step in her footprints as much as possible. She seemed to know where they were going and so far, they hadn't touched off any mines—if there were any hidden here. Comforting.

It took the morning to arrive at the little village, if you could call it that. More of a meeting spot than a living place. He kept his mouth shut and followed her lead as she spoke. She seemed to know a few tribesmen which didn't surprise him at all. He hung around the shade and watched as she squatted with various men discussing... who knows what.

She strode over to him, "Sorry. Just catching up on some gossip. I knew those men from my Intel days here. Abdul's daughter ran off with a Russian Army deserter and they found a pair of horses, funny story..."

Trev interrupted, "I'm sure it was also a heart-warming story but I'm baked and starved. Get to the point."

She looked a bit hurt but cut to the chaste. "The Russian Deserter worked from a little firebase near here, before the Ruskies got the boot... Mr. Grumpy bones."

"Firebase?" Trev's mouth fell open then closed again. "Ah! So, a temporary artillery base and a landing pad for planes and choppers?"

"Yes. Big planes with big loads of artillery shells and troops. A few blown to bits along the way. Some are left in the rubble but are now covered with sand."

"Wonderful. Let's eat and get something to drink and speak further."

She seemed to know where to go for food and drink, so he followed. It wasn't like there was a Starbucks available. They came to a re-occupied ancient hut with someone living inside. He waited as Terry negotiated.

She popped her head out the door. "Come in."

The old woman and her daughters inside proved to be friendly. The hut was stifling hot but he saw food and tea. He was thrilled when he got his share. It had been a long day.

He watched as Terry talked to everyone, smiling and joking. She fit in like she'd lived there all her life. After about forty-five minutes she took his arm, thanked her hosts and they left for the relative cooler outside air. She guided him over to the little pump and water supply so they filled their bottles, canteens and drank all they could without throwing up. He felt like a camel and stood for a minute, feeling like he was sloshing.

As he stood there, a small Pashtun boy walked shyly to Terry and said something, making a grasping motion on his wrist. Terry knew and started speaking to the lad. Finally, Trev realized it was the boy from the Old Russian's compound, the one who'd undone their hand-cuffs after the plane crash.

Terry and the boy spoke for only a minute and he slipped a balled-up piece of paper into her palm. He grinned and left. She squirreled it away, saying nothing about it.

It was a snapping hot early afternoon when they both left the village. Terry set a fast pace, very different than their previous route. Trev puffed along noticing their route change.

Trev gasped, "Why this way?"

"Tracks!"

"What?"

"Someone could follow our tracks here. Maybe set a mine or IED near our steps or ambush us. Why? Wanna go back that way?"

"Uh, no," he said, sorry he'd asked such a stupid question.

"Besides, we pick up the buried cache of food and water this way, if it's still there."

He didn't ask another question, which was probably dumb anyway, for an hour and a half. She led him to a shallow cave where they sat and drank some water.

"We'll wait for dark and rest. The cache is right over there."

"Why is it there?"

"Old Army Intel thing. Saves us from marching along carrying stuff like an old safari movie."

"Ah. So why don't we go get it?"

"I couldn't be sure someone hasn't staked that spot out and is waiting to shoot us. Night's better. We'll circle, then dig it up and see what's left."

Trev was spooked. "What if it's a mine or a bomb, instead?"

"C'mon Trev. Where's your optimism? Be brave."

He closed his eyes to nap, slightly shaking his head. A madwoman! While he napped, Trev had a fairly good dream complete with his old Colonel, Bill Page, the McIlhennys killers and burning houses. In his dream Bill Page had him tied to a chair and was pouring gas all over him. 'It's light up time Trev!' He wiggled in the ropes in the chair to no avail as Page struck a match and moved it closer and closer. Felt so real. "Ahhhh! Nooooo!"

"Trev! Trev! Wake up!"

He opened his eyes to see Terry's face.

"What?"

"Relax buddy. You were sweating like a moose!"

"Give me a minute. Just a bad dream."

"You've been sleeping for three hours. Must have needed it."

He sat up a little and focused. "What's happening?"

"I circled the area and all's well. Nobody's watching. Just to be sure we'll poke around the edge of that dirt with a knife to see if we have a mine under there. Trick is to work the edge of the dirt and bump it. Hit the top and...well...we'll be dead as doornails."

"I'll keep that in mind."

"You want to dig for a mine and me guard or vice versa?"

"I can guard. You seem to know all about mines."

"We'll find out how much I know, shortly. Best guard from that spot right there, far enough away."

"What'll I do if you blow up?"

"Get your head down," she said.

With that, he picked up his AK and took a few steps towards a large rock on a small knoll.

"And don't be doing an All-American shootout if you see something. Find out who and what it is then use a knife if you have to."

"All American shootout?"

"Americans shoot like they have a truckload of ammo in their pockets and all of Hollywood's watching. One shot; one kill—unless you're made of money."

"I suppose Canadians use the one-shot rule."

"Yup. We're cheap and appreciate our peace and quiet. Try it sometime."

Warily he moved all the way to the rock to guard, watching as she took out her knife and stepped to the cache location. She got down on her knees and examined the dirt, swishing her knife carefully in a few spots then moved around to another couple of places.

What would he do if she blew herself up? I wonder if I can find my way back to Dean? Maybe I'll wander the deserts, lost, until I die, and my bones are covered with sand.

It took her a half an hour in the darkness to be satisfied there were no mines. She carefully dug around with her hands, then with a stick, until she had a plastic surface exposed. After testing the sand a bit, she slid it out a little, listened, then pulled it right out of the hole.

He saw it was a large back pack with emergency supplies, water, a pistol, emergency flare gun. Enough for one person to live for two weeks. Terry refilled the hole in with dirt taking great effort to make it look as if nothing was ever there.

"Let's go," she said.

He took the pack from her and put it on his back. "I got this. You aren't over the effects of that crash yet."

Terry watched him. "Sure. Let's get back to Dean and find out if there are any lights out there."

28

LONELY VIGIL

DEAN LAID ON THE ROCK ON THE LONELY HILL TOP AT SUNRISE, watching Trev and Terry disappear in the distance. The key to their situation was water and food. Some intel would be helpful. There was a big world out there and they didn't know what was happening.

He watched all around his hilltop vantage point, seeing nothing except a crested porcupine and a jackal. They were as wary as he was, having dodged the centuries of warfare all around them. A few survived mines, shootings and bombs. Tough and hardy like the Afghan people.

What didn't kill you makes you strong and wary.

Dean poached in the sun. Periodically he wiped the sweat off the lenses of his binoculars. This was the best spot for watching and happened to be the sunniest, which is great if you are getting a tan in Mexico but not great when you're trying to preserve water. Dehydration is death, especially as they were short of supplies. Hopefully Trev and Terry would bring a solution.

He glanced at his rifle, an AK-47, and the half dozen magazines, on a rock and out of the sand. On his left he had a pistol and two magazines for it. His canteens were behind him, down low, where they couldn't be shot. Essentials.

Dean had told Terry the strange way he ended up meeting her in Afghanistan. They agreed it was a plant by Tina Gospel, the woman who had drugged and brought Trev and Terry way the hell out here. He'd received a presidential note asking him to go to these specific coordinates and "Help". It was easy hitching rides and parachuting out over the approximate area.

Terry and Trev suspected Tina Gospel had sent them reinforcements by way of Dean after Terry dismissed the Special Forces detail. Tina might have heard Terry had a concussion and knew Trev would need help if she was incapacitated. In any case here he was, and he wouldn't be anywhere else on the planet.

Watching closely, he could see movement along the edges of an old, weathered rock. Dusty figures slithered along the sides casting no shadows, Pashtun style. Terry was leading and Trev barely keeping up, especially with a big back pack. A good sign.

Eventually the pair sneaked and struggled their way up to Dean, high on the hill. He didn't envy them. A steep climb after a long, hot, hard day.

Trev crawled up to their vantage point just behind Dean. "Oh my god! I'm so fried."

Terry came up behind him. "Well done, Trev."

Dean smiled, "Trev beat you up the mountain with a pack on?"

Trev mumbled, "She was pushing me up. Never would have made it, otherwise."

Dean watched while the two caught their breath. "Food and water?"

"Yup. Found an old supply stash. Enough for one person for two weeks or three of us for maybe four days."

"Decent. How were the locals in the village?"

She said, "Oh. Remember the kid I told you about who took off Trev's and my handcuffs? Hangs with the Old Russian's group?"

"Yes."

Terry dug a small roll of paper out of her pocket. "Voila!"

Dean looked down, unimpressed. "His rolled-up gum?"

Trev mumbled, "Magic beans!"

"Ye of little faith. Let's see if I can unroll this...pretty beat up. Not sure how long he carried it. A message!"

"Can you read it?"

"Barely.

Shocked silent, she simply stared at the worn paper. Finally, she read it out loud. "'Page is coming'."

———

Across the world Jess was snoring in her bed next to a black cat that had managed to worm its way in. Her mind was a jumble of past and present events, scars and hopes. She told Flo Bradley she'd write a book about all this if she survived.

It was the dream with a familiar rainy alley, body lying on the grimy pavement, her mom. Jess always found this dream very peculiar. She felt as if she were there, but in a ghostly fashion. She'd tried explaining it to her psychologist on so many occasions but words couldn't express it. Her psychologist gave her a funny look, said "Ah..." and scribbled furiously in her notebook, probably *clearly nuts... medicate*.

Her mom's spirit appeared to her, looking uncharacteristically happy. "Hi Jessica M. How are you?"

"I'm okay and sleeping."

Her mom, Gloria, ignored that. "I have happy news for you."

Jess replied blandly, "Your idea of happy news doesn't always coincide with mine. What is it?"

"Terry is fine."

"What! She wasn't fine at some point?"

"Well, she was in a plane crash in Afghanistan, Dean's gone there—."

Jess's ghostly dream-arms shot up. "Plane crash!?"

"Yes, well she was drugged and sent to Afghanistan for something. She had a concussion, was in a coma for three days and had the most amazing dream! You should have seen it."

"At what point did you decide not to tell me this?"

"I met with her and suggested I only tell you when I knew, and I now do. She's on the mend."

Jess shook her head, appalled that Terry could have died and she would have been ignorant of it. "You need to tell me these things, mom."

"I'm not a cellphone. I'm your connection to things you and I don't understand. Events unfold as they do. I don't know why."

"Is Aunty there by herself? What's she doing?"

"I don't know. Have patience."

"Sure."

"I heard another one of your poems is on order?"

"I'm not sure I'm doing it," grumbled Jess.

"Why not? I see Clint started to work on your three wishes. Are you backing out?"

"Shit. It was more like *three ideas*. Not sure about the poem. Yeah, I suppose. Leave it with me, mom."

The ghost of Gloria vanished.

————

PAGE FELT the truck lurch along, unending. These hours and days of truck travel had beaten him low. His whole body ached from his neck down to his toes. He'd give anything for a real bath and a real bed. At his lowest ebb he dreamed of his prison cell on Attu Island, living in luxury and worshipped by all.

The truck stopped. Voices urged him to come out. Slowly he fumbled his way past the boxes of cargo, emerging out back and climbing down onto real ground. The three men stood, facing him, saying nothing. A fourth man passed him a bottle of water which he guzzled.

It was getting dark but he could see they were on an enormous flat plain without homes or much vegetation. Desolate. The perfect place to dispose of someone and the body would never be found. He was so tired after the travel he didn't care one way or the other. It did seem like a lot of effort to bring him this far when they could have left him on Attu Island to be killed with everyone else. He would have to wait and see.

They stood in silence, the three men facing him. After what seemed like an hour, he heard the sound of a far-off helicopter. It got closer and closer, landing sprightly near their truck. Two uniformed men got out, put hands over their flapping hats, leaned low to avoid the prop wash and ran toward them.

They greeted the truck drivers, speaking in Russian, then passed each man an envelope, which Page assumed contained money. One of the uniformed men took Page by the arm and led him over to the helicopter. Page heard four gunshots but didn't look back—his capacity for shock and awe had been reached. As soon as Page shakily pulled himself into the helicopter the second uniformed man shoved his way in after him and shared out the envelopes he'd obviously collected back up from the men he just executed. Unanticipated expense money, apparently.

Tied up three lose ends.

Page was strapped into his seat like a child, the Soviet helicopter picked up and flew away to points unknown.

———

"How CAN you see in the dark?" asked Trevor, squinting into the clear gloom.

"We can't. Dean has the binoculars, which is the ticket."

"So here we are. Day three. In the dark on a mountain top in the middle of a buttfuck region in the center of a nowhere country," grumbled Trev.

"Such language from a god-fearing lad. Tsk-tsk." Dean softened his words with a smile.

"Shameful," agreed Terry. "Shhh. Hear that?"

They all froze, willing their breathing and hearts to stop making noise. There was a faint beat of a helicopter in the air, within earshot.

"Watch. They'll have a strobe flashing or something if they are going by, coming from the Pakistan side."

Dean waited as the noise came closer, triangulating its destination. Passing by?

"Look—three o'clock, lights on the ground!" said Terry, pointing. "There. On the old base."

Dean watched the chopper closely with his binoculars. "Seems to be going in a straight line to that light. I'm not aware of a strip around here that anyone's using."

They followed the strobe and the sound which linked up to the source of lights on the ground, about eight miles east. They saw vehicle headlights click on then move to where the helicopter landed. Eventually the noise ceased, and the lights went out.

"That spot, gents, is where we need to go, *right now!*"

———

PAGE WAS USHERED from the chopper to a truck which transported him into a dirt covered, camouflaged shelter. Uniformed men directed him past sentries and to an above-ground entrance to a bunker. No windows, once again.

But there was light, and open, cheery rooms. Other men in uniforms.

"Welcome Mr. Page," said a tall cheerful Korean man who genially shook his hand with both of his. "I am General Kim. Before I say another word may we offer you a bath, clean clothes and a soft bed? You look and smell like you've been on a harrowing journey."

Page could only guess how he looked—he *knew* he was about to collapse. He murmured, "That would be lovely." *I hope this isn't a game, this time.*

"Can we discuss all this cloak and dagger, tomorrow?" the general helpfully suggested.

Page wasn't used to the man's solicitous treatment. "Ah... thank you, yes. That would be... It's been a long trip."

The general waved to one of his adjacent officers who showed Page to a suite. It boasted a real bathroom, and actual clean clothes, neatly folded on a nearby chair.

Page could barely stay awake long enough for the best bath of his life. Numbly, he towelled off, brushed his teeth and crawled into the bed for an epic sleep.

His snoring drowned out the general getting a message about some late American offerings for his captive.

————

THEY WALKED single file in a line of three, heading for the lights they'd seen in the distance.

"Is there a rotting jackal carcass nearby or is that you, Trev?" asked Dean.

"That'd be me. Sorry Dean. My shower privileges were withdrawn about nine days ago. If I had bathwater, I'd drink it, these days."

"True." Terry nodded. "We'll have time to bath and sleep later."

They marched along quietly for four hours, taking them to the rim of the flat area that seemed to be an abandoned air base. Terry chose a high spot, looking down. Dean used his glasses to scan the area for sentries. They slid down a hole in the rock for a conference.

————

BILL PAGE SLEPT in the warm, clean sheets like a baby. The powerful air conditioning cooled this bunker to a pleasant seventy-five degrees. Captive President Dennis Casio could hear Page snoring all the way over to his cell.

————

Tina Gospel badgered and urged the pilots of her plane to go faster than their safety margins allowed. She scowled at them, "Water boarding is not like water skiing! Want to try it?"

The US State Department offered the Koreas dictator a billion dollars, one used but miled-out attack submarine and two missionaries they knew he was looking for.

"The President-For-Life will think about it and get back to you," was the response.

Sounded hopeful.

29

CAVALRY HAS ARRIVED

In the darkness Terry, Trev and Dean watched the base from their hideout among the rocks. Exhausted, they ate, drank fluids, and slept, leaving one awake for a lookout.

The sun came up a crack with Terry already up and about. She left Dean as lookout as she crept around the periphery of the abandoned fire base. She needed to find exits, entrances, fan vents, trash locations, emergency exits and toilets. The sentries were located and identified. She had a map in her head when she returned from her patrol.

"Fifteen minutes of daylight tells us as much as looking all night in the dark," she said. "That base is a bunch of camp trailers covered with dirt and rock. El cheapo bunker, bomb resistant and quick to slap up while being shot at." Terry had a map scratched out in the sand at their feet.

"That's a lot of dirt for just six camp modules," said Dean.

"I imagine it was epic having to truck them in as it was. Can you imagine the narrow roads, IED's and ambushes to get them here?"

Dean nodded, "Once the Ruskies showed up on this spot the locals would snipe away at them to stop this from getting built."

Terry pointed at the dirt map, "I'm assuming President Casio's in there. Would I be crazy to imagine Page came there, too?"

"But why?" Trev demanded, confused and at the end of his rope. "I'm trying to imagine what this whole bizarre meeting is for. The Koreans have Casio—in *Afghanistan?* Page is headed here, too, for *some* reason. Why?"

Dean smiled. "I'm thinking they want to keep Casio as insurance and install Page as a puppet president. Maybe Page has enough skeletons and worshipers still in the closet to support him."

Trev whispered, "Look who's coming up the track."

In the distance they held their weapons at the ready and observed a group coming closer. Dean and Terry joined Trev watching as twenty-four U.S. Army soldiers arrived prodding along a gasping, wheezing Tina Gospel, who was struggling to keep up.

"I don't think they've seen us—blind buggers," said Dean.

The group was within calling distance.

"Stay out of sight of those trigger-happy assholes." Terry leaned over the edge of a rock and sharply called out. "Tina; bring coffee?"

The group scattered with Tina lying in the dirt in front of them, petrified.

"I think we're on your side, Tina."

Tina looked up from the dirt and said sheepishly. "I think we're on the same side, too."

"Sure. Why are *you* here?" called Terry.

"Looking for a president and you found us one," Tina said.

"Pretty confident, aren't you? Just a pile of dirt out there. Could be full of snakes and jackals. Go ahead and crawl in."

"I told the State Department last night to stall the Koreans. Offered them some trinkets to play. That's why nothing has happened yet and no chopper pickup."

Terry let that one go for now. "Let your boys stay out of sight. Bring your lieutenant and come up here. I have a map. No funny business and *no* bullshit coffee."

Tina and the Lieutenant scrambled up the rock to where the trio hid. Tina introduced Lt. Bullock all around.

Terry watched as Lt. Bullock and Tina puzzled over her map in the sand and tried to decide what to do. Bullock was clearly intimidated by Tina who argued with every idea he tentatively offered, none of which were great anyway.

Terry decided to find out if they had an actual plan. "So, what's happening folks? Sun's rising. They may even know the vultures are circling. If their choppers come for pickup, we're boned."

The Lieutenant and Tina looked at Terry, blank.

Terry offered. "You have three options: Kill the sentries and wait them out, siege style. Or go down the holes and get them out, hand to hand. Or you could slam them and flush them out like gophers."

Tina ignored Bullock, her gaze riveted on Terry. "What's best?"

"And old-fashioned siege is fine if you have time and supplies. I'm not seeing that. Going in there for a fire fight in tunnels is tough and nasty. Chances are good Casio will be dead. Smoking them out would be my choice if you have something like tear gas handy."

"And stun grenades?" added Tina hopefully.

"No stuns. I'd say you want them out of there, puking and crying on that field, president included. Nobody left in there, stunned, to have to go back for."

"Tear gas it is. Bullock, order fifty tear gas grenades ASAP."

Bullock was on his walkie talkie in a flash. "Here in thirty minutes.

Tina asked, "What's next Major?"

"Four sentries. Here. Silence them, signal and then hustle over to those openings on this structure, here, and toss in three or four tear gas grenades simultaneously. Don't miss the air conditioning ducts. See them? They'll suck the tear gas right down in there."

"Wham. At once. One swoop. While we're waiting for tear gas glance over the structure for gun openings. Avoid those."

Bullock barked out orders to his men. "Right. You, you and you look over that bunker—carefully—so we can get close."

Terry added helpfully, "Trev, Dean and I can get three sentries because we know where they are. One of your guys needs to get that one." She pointed out the man's location.

Bullock and Tina stood waiting orders.

"Tina, wait outside with your men. You can be the Wal-Mart greeter as they emerge. Herd them towards that big rock on the east side." She looked up, alert, then broke into a satisfied smile. "Ah. Looks like the tear gas is arriving."

Four men rushed up with heavy packs, sweating, puffing on the edge of collapse.

"When's hammer time, Bullock?"

Everyone looked at Bullock. "Ten? Fifteen minutes from now?"

Terry nodded. "Sounds good. Take your positions. Don't forget anyone. Sentries—Trev there, Dean there, me there and one of your guys there."

Tina Gospel caught Terry's arm. "This is the CIA show, so you and your people stay away. I can't say what will take place so stay with the sentries. No interference."

"Got it," said Terry, a bit surprised at Tina's late-date warning. "Fan out. Show time in fifteen." She'd always wanted to say that. "Dean, can I have your binoculars?"

"Here." He reluctantly handed them to her.

Tina added, "Try to keep death to a minimum. We aren't at war with Korea... yet."

Everyone nodded grimly.

Terry pointed Trev toward the sentry he was to silence.

He whispered, "Do I shoot him?"

"No. Wack him on the head with your rifle butt. No carnage or noise."

"Sure."

Terry worked her way along until she was close to the sentry she was to silence. She glanced at her watch... ten... then slipped behind him to put him in a sleeper hold. Down and out.

No gunfire. Yet.

———

BILL PAGE FINISHED the best plate of buttered toast, bacon and eggs of his entire life. He considered kissing the cook. Carrying his coffee, which was also extremely tasty, he strolled over to the control room where the general and his men pored over maps in some consultation. "Good morning."

The general stood, shaking his hand. "Good morning Mr. Page. Did you sleep well?"

"Fantastic. Thank you."

The general nodded to one of his underlings then looked back at Page. "We have a surprise for you."

Page's jaw felt like it was bouncing off the floor when President Dennis Casio came down the hall towards them. He was dressed in Korean army fatigues. He was gripped on either side by a surly looking guard.

Page demanded, "What in the world is this? A joke?"

The general smiled. "No joke. The real president. You've been out of the loop since the republican convention. We arranged a meeting with the president in Singapore. They cleverly brought a double along for safety. When we saw there were two, we grabbed the real one and escaped while the Secret Service thought they had the actual president."

"Bravo, general! So, who's in the White House, now?"

"An impostor, whom you will heroically unmask and cause great upheaval. You will then return as president to guide America through this difficult time," said the general slyly.

A battered Casio stood close by, angry but mute. The sentries holding him looked like they'd beat Casio senseless again if he made a sound.

Understanding immediately where this was going, Page added expansively, "Of course, as president I *will* offer your government certain advantages in return."

"That's the idea Mr. Page. Do we have a deal?"

Page put a hand out and warmly shook the general's. "We have a deal."

————

Trev wacked the sentry on the side of the head with his rifle butt. The guy never knew what hit him. Trev was horrified to see the sentry was just a boy in his late teens. Trev tied his hands behind his back so there would be no future injury to him. Done.

Trev stayed low, watching as nine US men crept to the dirt bunker, finding doors, windows and the air conditioning ducts. On signal, activating and heaving three or four tear gas grenades in each opening, one after the other. Tear gas smoke was sucked into every nook and cranny.

He could barely see in the distance as doors popped open and men poured drunkenly out, retching, crawling, crying. Nearby American soldiers checked them for weapons, efficiently tied back their hands and hauled them over to the eastern muster point. He wondered when the big wigs were coming out. Ah, there they were...

————

Page felt a sense of triumph he hadn't felt for a very long time. He let the handshake with the general last a little longer, watching with glee as Casio looked on, his face getting redder and redder and then he started coughing. He was coughing hard, then the others started coughing. A fog poured in the room from the air ducts, pushed along by powerful electric air conditioning vent fans. Soon everyone was shouting and gasping, tears running from burning eyes down their grimacing faces. Visibility was zero. Page could barely see anyone. He fell to his knees choking and rolled around, thinking he would never get out of this fog and gas.

Page was new to this bunker and had no idea where the exits were. Groping desperately, he felt boots ahead of him in the gloom.

His eyes were running, and he could barely breathe but he found a way to follow the boots.

He crawled along like a drunk leaving a bar, hoping the boots ahead would lead him outside. People pushed him urgently from behind, so he must be on the right track. Light. There was light ahead. After some minutes he emerged into the sun, wheezing and vomiting. A hand grabbed his arm, Hauling him to his feet. A US soldier. He was doomed.

Page noticed the soldier didn't recognize President Casio just ahead of him as he was wearing Korean fatigues and was red in the face, choking like everyone else. Through his tears Page managed to grab the soldier's pistol and take President Casio for a hostage. He held the gun barrel to Casio's head and croaked, "Get closer and the president's dead."

A shot rang out and President Casio fell out of Page's arms, dead. A second shot killed Page before Casio hit the dirt.

The battle area was stunned into silence. The soldiers looked around to see the source of the shooting but nobody would admit to it.

Tina Gospel was first over, grabbing the gun from Page's dead hands and putting it in her pocket. "You!" She pointed at a nearby soldier. "Cover up these bodies."

———

TERRY USED the binoculars to observe the operation. It seemed to go well without bloodshed until Casio and Page were shot and killed in the botched hostage attempt. Page's death didn't make her happy or sad. It merely signalled the end of the most important part of her life.

Though ballsy and shocking, she was impressed with Tina Gospel's shooting ability.

Two big American Army Chinook helicopters were arriving and probably ten truckloads of troops later today. Show's over.

———

DEAN WAS glad to return with Trev and Terry to Washington DC. It had been a harrowing trip with a suspicious ending. An anti-climax. He had his suspicions as to who'd done the shootings but he was too far away to see. If only he hadn't given the binoculars to Terry. She'd have had a perfect view.

30

INVITATION OF NO RETURN

It was a strange invitation.

"A grey SUV will come for you at ten a.m., tomorrow. Come unarmed and alone to meet with the head of government for a special award."

"Beats the hell out of me what this is all about. I've not heard anything official or unofficial." Shirley Mac turned the engraved card over, inspected it closely, then studied the front once again. "It's an official government request, all right. Seems legit," she ended, still mystified and suspicious.

"The Disciples are gone, Russians and Koreans out of the picture," offered Terry.

Flo Bradley came into the room. "I found a reference to it. Seems you're getting some kind of award at CIA HQ. Nothing for you in public at the Rose Gardens by a president this time."

"And no reporters to ask me, 'Is it true the CIA drugged you?' Or 'Is this an award for saving us from the Disciples?' or 'Is it true that Page and the real president are now dead?'" said Terry.

Shirley Mac shook her head. "They now have real reporters to ask the awkward questions. Could be embarrassing."

"They think I know too much so it's best to talk to me in secret?"

Flo looked grim. "Could be."

Terry was quiet for a few moments, "Maybe I'm going to disappear in a Saudi cocktail?"

Flo looked at her in wonderment, "Saudi... cocktail?"

"Yup. Saudi cocktail... special invitation, bump you off, chopped you to bits and dissolve it all in acid which is put into a bunch of glass whisky flasks and carried back to Saudi Arabia. Voila! No more embarrassing person."

"Good God!"

"I should probably think about that before I go. Maybe have a look for me if I don't turn up for lunch tomorrow," said Terry.

Shirley leaned forward. "Are you actually attending?"

"Sure, but I'm going to listen to some accordion music with Gomez, first."

———

THE CIA ENTRANCE staff did a thorough search of Terry, taking her gun and knife, pawing through every item inside her big ugly purse like a pack of raccoons. Finding nothing they returned the purse to her but kept anything they thought she could use as a weapon. She was then ushered into the head office of the CIA, Tina Gospel's domain. Four agents in matching black suits and haircuts, dark glasses, and ear pieces crackling with voices marched along with her, two in front and two behind.

"You guys get your suits and haircuts with a group coupon?" she asked, not expecting a reply.

She marched along in the middle of the group, purse clenched tightly under her arm, wondering what the hell was going to happen. They entered a corner office and one agent slammed the heavy door closed behind him. Each agent backed into a corner, looking alert and ready, on guard for any eventuality.

Practised.

"We have a lot to discuss," said Tina without preamble. Now the unofficially recognized head of the resurrected CIA, she extended her hand to Terry's to shake. "Sit down, please, Terry."

Terry wasn't completely sure what was about to happen. Not everyone remembered she'd saved America from Bill Page and the Disciples, nor did they know she'd done it once again.

They sat.

Tina started, "On behalf of the president of the United States of America..."

Terry smiled, interrupting, "Who happens to be an imposter."

Tina paused, then continued her pre-planned speech, "We want to thank you for your help in finding and resolving the case of the missing president, and assisting us in bringing it to a successful conclusion."

"Successful? Your real president is dead!"

Tina ignored her, continuing, "Your involvement and assistance in the resolution of the Disciples issue is greatly appreciated. As I said, we are grateful—."

"You're thanking *us* for our assistance in all this?" Terry leaned back and laughed hard. "Your shadowy group hid while Dean, Trev, Gomez and I stopped the burning house murders and convention shootout and the Verbeeldings take over!"

"We of the CIA take a quiet role..." Ignoring her reaction Tina droned on.

Terry was just getting warmed up. "Bullshit! Your incompetence allowed the president to be kidnapped and then screwed up the investigation. Bill Page followed you to the president and both were shot dead. Was it you who shot them? No wonder Jackson disbanded the CIA."

"It didn't turn out as we had hoped." Tina shrugged.

"And you drugged Trev and me to hedge your bets because you had no idea where the president was being held. You couldn't find your own asses with a magnifying glass and a pencil. What a fucking disaster!"

Tina droned on with her prepared speech, "And we have the Distinguished Service Medal I'd like to give you with our thanks." She and Terry both stood as Tina passed the little medal case to Terry and shook her hand while managing to appear bored as she did it.

Then they both sat down.

Tina leaned back in her chair and sighed. "That was the formal part I'm required to say. Here's the informal part. I need Jess out of the country in seventy-two hours."

"Us out in seventy-two hours?"

"Us? No, just *Jess* leaves but *you* aren't going anywhere."

Terry's eyebrows went up. "Excuse me?"

"You stay. You heard me," confirmed Tina, finally becoming animated, forceful.

Terry broke into a smile. "So, with us out of the way you can have your tickertape parade on how you saved the country, once again? You'll be president *du jour* until the next election, if there ever is one."

"Something like that. The public must believe it was us who stopped the Disciples and the Verbeeldings. They must never know about the kidnapping and murder of President Casio. Nor how *you* did it."

"You justified your jobs by claiming *you* saved the day? Let me guess, someone's making a Hollywood movie of this new laundered history."

Tina said nothing.

"I suspect the reason you offered me thanks and the shiny bit, is because you want all this kept a big secret and nobody is to know you actually control the best kept imposter on the planet, the president of America. Impressive. And I'm the loose end. Sole witness."

Tina added nothing.

"After years of Revisionism, mass expulsions, wars and the dissolution of the CIA etcetera, you've finally got the perfect grip on the government. A captive president." Terry got up to leave. The guards in the corners all stepped forward, hands on guns, faces of stone.

"Sorry Terry, but you will never leave here," said Tina.

"I'm going to disappear, am I?"

"We haven't decided yet," said Tina ominously.

Terry put her purse under her arm. "I'll tell you what I'm going to do. You and I will stroll out of here right now or my purse will blow this area into little bits."

Tina scoffed. "We searched you and that purse with a fine-tooth comb. Nothing in there. You're bluffing."

Terry looked a bit saddened by the news, then perked up, "Did you see what the material in this purse is made of? Thick, eh? It's a KGB Russian explosive, more powerful than C4 so it'll obliterate this whole building floor and you assholes with it, and I can set it off when I want. Want to see it in action?"

The guards and Tina went chalk white.

"I also took the liberty of having the whole story about all this on a timed e-mail. Its scheduled to go out to every reporter on the planet if I'm not there to stop it. Quite the story, eh?"

Silence.

"You can call me on it if you think I'm lying but they'll be able to lick you and your henchmen off the walls, *if* they can find any walls. This whole place goes down like a stack of cards. So long CIA."

Tina found her voice. "What makes you think I won't sacrifice myself and let you blow up this place?"

Terry laughed. "Your life's work has been all about someday being the de facto president and now you are— America's 'Putin' or Putin-ette. A week isn't very long to be the leader of the free world, is it? You're dying for more."

Tina said nothing, seething.

Terry stood up. "I'm leaving. If you don't mind, I'd appreciate you coming with me. In fact, I *insist*."

Terry reached across the table and grabbed Tina by the front of her shirt collar while brandishing her fat, ugly purse, poised to obliterate them all. "Tell your schmoes to stay here, in case they screw up and your presidential run comes to an abrupt end."

"Back off men. I can handle this," Tina commanded her bodyguards.

Terry and Tina strolled into the hall to the building exit, Terry gripping Tina's arm tightly, and out on to the street in time to pick up a transit bus coming by.

"Are you kidding me?" Tina demanded.

"What? You don't like public transportation?"

"Where are you taking me?"

"Just a little insurance ride, that's all. It'll take a few minutes for your minions to get cars and locate our city bus. Here's a chance for the defacto president of the United States to mix with the local citizens," said Terry.

Terry reached up and pulled the cord. 'Ding'. The bus stopped at the next location. Getting up, she tugged Tina along with her. "Maybe I'm taking you to a park and blow you to bits."

Tina said nothing, maybe wondering if her agents would dare come to her rescue.

A mass of reporters and cameras appeared from around the corner, ushered by Secret Service agents Joyce Carson and Flo Bradley, all smiling widely.

"Nice when a plan comes together." Terry grinned. "Look at all the reporters, Tina. From all over the world. They want to talk to you. Should have done your hair this morning."

"You lied!" hissed Tina, furious.

"Oops, I guess I sent the email out before I left home. Silly me." smiled Terry.

"Gonna blow us all up?" said Tina nervously looking at Terry's purse.

"Oh, this old thing! I'm taking it back to Value Village after this. Big disappointment—doesn't match my outfits."

"Where's... the bomb?" Tina said, now wild-eyed. "That purse is a bomb!"

"No bomb, after all. Sorry... lied about that too. You CIA folks sure are gullible." Terry shoved the reluctant Tina into the media maelstrom of jibber-jabbering, shouting, waving camera's, mics, phones and lights. Tina was consumed by the crowd. Terry shouted an encouraging, "You go girl!" over their heads. Horrified, Tina was surrounded like jungle ants. Two hundred frantic, angry news people fighting for the story of their lives.

Terry slipped away from the crush, stealing away to the safety of a cedar bush in a nearby park. She found the bag containing her wig, sweater with a hump in it, hat and walker stashed in a nearby trash can hidden behind a cedar bush. After donning her disguise, she started down the street just as two carloads of Army MP's arrived in a panic, lights blazing.

As she hobbled along on her walker she thought, that might be an interesting conversation between Army Police and the head of the CIA while the cameras keep rolling, rolling, rolling...

31

MEDIA CRUSH

Joyce Carson and Flo Bradley waved the news people in the direction of the bus stop just as the president had instructed them. It did seem peculiar getting a phone call directly from him but he'd been very specific. "Do not be deterred," the president urged.

Joyce watched Flo, who knew Tina Gospel on sight. As per Flo's cue, Joyce waved the throng towards the bewildered CIA Director. They went after Tina like it was Dec. 24th and she was the last decent toy on the shelf. It was a stampede. *What in the world had them so riled up?*

A TV truck was parked nearby, and Joyce Carson heard the live news feed going out across the country and the world.

"This is Harry Fast of Detroit KMO News. Breaking, we have Sandy Thompson from Washington, DC."

"Good evening Harry. Early this morning we received a news tip from Jessica M. Reid, the famous 'poem girl'. She sent us another enchanting poem but this time it contained a story about the most sensational story of this century... the murder of a United States President and a takeover by Tina Gospel of the CIA. As we speak Gospel is being mobbed by news people. We are hoping to speak to her at some point. Stay tuned."

"Sandy; how many news people would you say are there...Sandy?"

"Harry! Harry! Can you hear me?"

There was screaming and yelling in the background. Two shots shot out—Bang! Bang!

"Yes...go ahead Sandy. Are you alright? Sandy?"

"Harry; it's craziness here. A half a dozen CIA officials came running out of their headquarters building and ran to Tina Gospel and are attempting to wrestle her away from the news people. One of them shouted and fired two shots in the air. Some of the news people ran but some stood their ground with the embattled CIA director."

"Be careful Sandy."

"Holy shit...sorry Harry...two truckloads of Army MP's—Military Police—just arrived. They are bailing out of their trucks and are surrounding the CIA people and Tina Gospel. This is crazy."

"Keep talking Sandy, if you aren't in any danger."

More shouting could be heard, followed by another shot.

"Harry? Can you hear me?"

"Yes Sandy."

"The Army MPs pulled their sidearms and so have the CIA agents. There was a tense standoff then one of the MPs shot a CIA agent right between the eyes! Other MPs just stepped over the body and disarmed the remaining CIA agents and are taking them into custody. Tina Gospel... looks like they're grabbing her as well... handcuffing her... and are roughly shoving her into the cab of an army truck and are now driving away. Two more Army trucks came around the corner and are stopping near the CIA entrance. Reinforcements?"

"Sandy; Where are those trucks going?"

"Harry, they pulled in front of CIA HQ, broke down the door and are running inside."

Booming sounds came from inside the building, with smoke pouring out the doorway and a few shattered windows.

"Sandy...Sandy? Stay safe out there. It looks like we lost the connection. Reminds me of my days reporting on the Venezuelan civil war."

"Well folks, we will update you as soon as we can on this fast-developing national story. We now have a story about the man who won the Dallas hot dog eating contest, yesterday. Forty-two hot dogs! I like mine with ketchup. This is Harry Fast. So long for now."

———

TERRY MADE it back to the Bradleys' in about an hour, this time dodging public transit. It was a nice day for a walk. Birds sang in the trees along the way. Pleasant.

She saw the big consulate van parked near the front steps, moose and beaver side paintings grinning in anticipation. Terry doffed her wig and walker as she went up the steps. Dean greeted her at the Bradleys' door.

"How'd it go?" he asked.

"Not bad as far as military takeover's go. All packed up? Where's Gomez?"

"Not sure. He was playing his accordion, heard a beep on his phone and literally ran out the door, leaving all his stuff behind. Pretty fast for a little guy."

"Put all his stuff in a blue garbage bag and put it out for the trash truck. It'll get to him, for some peculiar reason," she directed, then shrugged.

"Shall do," said Dean.

"Jess! Ready?" called out Terry.

Jess came out with two suitcases. "My last two."

"Last two? Got my hockey bag and uniforms?" Terry asked.

"Yes."

"Sure you don't want to come, Dean?"

"I'm tempted but my country needs me. Uncertain times ahead."

Dean and Terry enjoyed a long kiss and hug as Shirley Mac came through the door, holding a phone. "Looks like the military just took over the country. You'd best head out before they get organized and start looking for you three." She stuck a hand out, shaking Terry and Jess's hands. All the Bradleys came out for hugs.

Terry and Jess started down the steps. Terry suddenly stopped. "There's three of us?"

"Yes. Clint Bergen is going with you. His lack of disguise is his new disguise. Do you mind taking him?"

Terry shook her head in amazement before climbing into the driver's seat. "Not a problem. Happy for the company." She started up the van with Jess riding shotgun and Clint in the back seat. "Ready kid? Let's see if we can't find a bit of adventure somewhere else."

———

THEIR BIG UGLY van was getting close to the border crossing to Canada.

Jess groused, "I hate crossing borders. Terry gets into a hissy fit and we almost get arrested. I hate it."

Grinning, Clint picked up the cellphone they had given him as president and punched in a number. Whoever he was calling picked up at once. They had a brief murmured conversation. After ending the call, he slid down low in the seat and closed his eyes.

———

YANNI THE US border guard sat at his computer at the crossing. Ted and Bill sat in nearby plastic lawn chairs. Another quiet day.

Yanni leaned out of his booth, "So why are we even open, today? It's dead."

Ted looked over at him. "Quit complaining, Yanni. We have to have at least one gate open. People might want to make a run for it."

Bill yawned. "I'll say. America's so mixed up nobody wants in and Americans can't get out. Paralysis."

Yanni's phone rang. "Border gate number 3. Who? Mr. Pres... Mr. President!" Yann's spine straightened. "H-Hello sir. I'm fine sir. Yes sir! We will sir. You have a good day too, sir. God bless America, sir."

Bill's eyebrows went way up. "What was that, Yanni?"

"That was the president! He said there's a Canadian Consulate van coming. It's a big blue twelve passenger van with a moose on one side and the beaver on the other. Let it through, no stopping!"

Ted laughed. "Shouldn't be hard to spot. I wonder who's in it?"

Yanni said, "Has to be someone really important. Best behavior, everybody!"

Bill cried. "There it is! Open the gates!"

The yellow flashing gates swung open and all three guards stood grinning and waving at the big van like a line of cheerleaders.

As the van passed through Jess humphed. "I wonder what that was all about?"

"Friends in high places," said Clint, from the back seat. "By the way. You still owe me a poem."

Jess nodded. "Nope. I made up a dandy one about the upcoming CIA takeover and press meeting. I sent it everywhere. It was from the 'poem girl' so every news guy in the world knew it was legit, read it and believed it."

Clint grinned, "Using your super power for publicity? Well-timed."

Terry honked the van horn at the border guards and kept going, headed back to Canada and possibly some peace and quiet.

Jess knew this was very unlikely.

The End

AFTERWORD

I hardly know where to start.

'His Disciples Watch' is book one of my Terry Reid series and was a futuristic spoof under the pretext 'Donald J.' would never be voted in as President of the USA, turning into the writer's gift that keeps on giving. The proverbial drunken uncle that shows up unannounced for Christmas dinner, drops cigarette butts in the punch bowl, tells the most outrageous stories, pinches you mom's bottom and eventually passes out. 'Call a cab for Uncle Vic!' ...except he's the President of the world's largest economy and nuclear arsenal.

We're introduced to our off-beat heroine, Terry Reid, who comes with a mysterious, dark and dangerous past, as well as her young niece, Jessica, who tries to keep her aunt's moral compass pointed north.

Terry's secrets are her sword and shield, ready to deflect a person, situation or incident but this power comes with a price, sometimes exposing an unraveling seam in her hard-earned armour. Information is best kept closely to her breast, only allowing a whisper to come under the most trying times.

'*His Disciples Sleep*' is book two of the Terry Reid series and is a continuation of the story. My fictional America is picking up the pieces after dodging the Revisionist bullet. The Reid's are fighting the good fight but at great cost.

'*His Disciples Deceive*' is book three and part of it is based on an idea suggested by a friend and faithful reader of mine. It's become a prequel woven into a 'normal' future timeline. This way you meet Terry's niece, Jess, and find out more about Terry's older sister Gloria and her issues and tribulations.

Writing the section about the 'informant' was interesting and intense. It was hard to imagine a life like that, so I did watch the newspapers and peek at past news stories for inspiration.

As usual, our neighbors to the south are a boundless source of inspiration and weirdness led by their famous Commander-in-Chief. Anything goes! A writer's paradise.

Yes, there are two more books coming in the Terry Reid series so stay tuned. Thank you for your kind support!

Honest Reviews are always welcome—they help me as a writer and they help readers searching for their next read. If you'd like to share your thoughts on "His Disciples Deceive, click *here!* And thanks!

On to creating Book Four...

Patrick D. Ferris

ALSO BY PATRICK D FERRIS

Larry and Giselle Series:

A Gypsy Romance

A Gypsy Engagement

A Gypsy Haunting

Terry Reid Mystery Series:

His Disciples Watch

His Disciples Sleep

His Disciples Deceive

Short Story Collection:

Fragmented Thoughts Random Directions

ABOUT THE AUTHOR

About the Author:

Born in Winnipeg, Manitoba in 1954, Pat Ferris grew up in Victoria and moved to Fort St. John in 1975 to pursue his trade in the rapidly expanding natural gas industry.

In 1997 he quit and started a successful bicycle shop which ran for twenty years. He then retired to spend more time writing in beautiful northern BC with his wife Patricia and Kirby the Wonder Dog.

You can connect with Pat here:

http://patrickdferris.wix.com/gypsies

www.ingramcontent.com/pod-product-compliance
Lightning Source LLC
Chambersburg PA
CBHW072348020726
47506CB00004B/1055